My Silent Daughter

BOOKS BY EMMA ROBINSON

The Undercover Mother
Happily Never After
One Way Ticket to Paris

Emma Robinson

My Silent Daughter

bookouture

Published by Bookouture in 2019

An imprint of StoryFire Ltd.

Carmelite House
50 Victoria Embankment
London EC4Y 0DZ

www.bookouture.com

ISBN: 978-1-83888-237-2
eBook ISBN: 978-1-83888-017-0

Previously published as *Where I Found You* (978-1-83888-018-7)

For Scarlett
The girl of a thousand faces

'It's only when we look with eyes of love that we see as the painter sees.'

To Paint is to Love Again, Henry Miller

PROLOGUE

Do you know that I dreamed of you before you were born? How you might look and sound, and how much I would love you? Even so, when you came, I was knocked sideways. You were so tiny, so beautiful, so precious. How could we have made something so perfect?

Birth is noisy and frantic, but when they placed you on my chest it was as if time stood still. Bending my face to yours, breathing the warmth of you, my heart was full with pride and love and an overwhelming desire to hold you tight and never let go. That night, when the ward was quiet, I leaned into your cot, placed a hand onto your tiny chest, watched the rise and fall.

'Your mummy loves you, little girl,' I whispered. 'I will keep you safe.'

But I didn't, did I? And how can I ever forgive myself for that?

CHAPTER ONE

Moving house is a good time to declutter. Sara sat on her haunches with a *History of Art* A-Level textbook in one hand and a purple Thigh Master in the other, trying to decide if she would ever have need for either of them again, when Ruby started to cry. Mike, laid out on the sofa, lips moving as he memorised his lines, didn't even look up. He'd finished 'his' packing half an hour ago and was now lost in Tennessee Williams' Mississippi – with selective hearing, apparently.

Sara crawled over to Ruby. 'What's the matter, Ruby? Can Mummy help?'

The floor of the small lounge was covered in piles of their belongings, bags filled with their clothes and toys and phone chargers. Ruby was pulling at one of the cardboard boxes, angry tears dripping from her hot, red cheeks.

A quick rummage around in the box and, from underneath the DVDs, mugs and coat hangers, a tiny orange and black fin poked out. Pulling it free, Sara waved the toy fish at Mike before delivering it into Ruby's eager hands. 'You packed Nemo, Mike. Schoolboy error.'

'Hmm?' Mike pulled his eyes away from the script and looked over. 'Oh. Sorry, Ruby love. I didn't realise.' He shuffled himself onto his side, yawned and turned the page.

Last night had been a bad one in the sleep department and overtiredness was fuelling Ruby's temper. It wasn't doing a great deal for Sara's patience, either. If she could have a clear run at getting this packing done, she could give Ruby her full attention. 'Mikey, any chance you could come and play with her for a bit? After I've packed the kitchen stuff, I'll take her for a walk in the buggy, see if she'll have a nap.' Now that Ruby was three she should be dropping her daytime sleep, but after a disturbed night it made all the difference. For all of them.

Mike swung his legs down from the arm of the sofa, stretched his arms above his head and yawned again. 'I can't let you do that, my darling. You've already packed so much. Let me go and do the kitchen. You stay there with Ruby.' He winked and patted her shoulder as he passed and Sara made a swipe for his legs. Packing saucepans was definitely the easier option.

'Coward.'

What must it be like if you had to pack up a complete house? All they had was a lounge, a bedroom, a tiny kitchen and bathroom and it was still taking forever. Mind you, it must be easier if you were excited to be moving. Sara had hated this flat the whole time they'd lived there. The shabby furniture, the peeling doors, the damp. But now she was reluctant to leave. The prospect of moving in with your mother-in-law could do that to a person.

When Mike had first touted the idea, she'd laughed. Surely he wasn't serious? They'd been together for four years and she'd seen Barbara fewer than ten times, even though she only lived about fifty miles away. They weren't particularly close. Even after Ruby was born three years ago, they hadn't seen much of her. Any hopes that Barbara would turn into a doting grandmother were dashed on the few occasions they had met up. She'd barely held Ruby.

But the more he'd talked about it, the more Sara had been sold on the sense of it. They were never going to be able to save up the deposit for a house while they were paying rent here. Barbara had been very kind to offer to let them stay there and it would only be a short-term thing. Once they had their deposit and first month's rent, they could finally get a little house of their own.

Mike's voice called out from the tiny kitchenette. 'We don't need the kettle and saucepans anyway, do we? Mum's got all that stuff.'

Sara shook her head in exasperation. 'What about when we move out of your mum's? We don't want to have to buy everything from scratch again. Can't we put it all in her garage or loft or somewhere?'

Ruby still wasn't settling down. The pulling on the ear lobes had started, which didn't bode well. *Taming your Toddler* – the book from the library – had warned about the 'terrible twos', but it hadn't prepared them for the unpredictable strength of Ruby's tantrums. Sometimes the world would end over a piece of toast that was cut. Or not cut. Or cut into triangles rather than squares. It must be nice to have the kind of mother you could call and ask about these things. Maybe Barbara would have some ideas?

Lying down beside her daughter, Sara made her voice as calm and soothing as possible. 'Ruby. Ruby-Roo. It's okay, poppet. Mummy's here. It's all okay.' Stroking Ruby's back like this sometimes did the trick, but today there was no settling her. Maybe a treat would cheer her up? Biscuits. 'Are there any custard creams still in the cupboard, Mike? Can you bring them out?'

She heard a cupboard bang open and closed and then Mike appeared waving half a packet of rich tea. 'Will these do?'

It was worth a try. 'Yeah, can you chuck them over?'

Mike leaned forwards and swung his arm over his shoulder as if he was going to bowl them to her, cricket style. Then he stopped, grinned and tossed them underarm. She had to give it to him; he kept himself looking good. At thirty-one, he could easily pass for twenty-five with his boyish grin and clean-shaven face. Even in a white T-shirt and long, baggy shorts – in *March* – he looked stylish. He winked at her again, his dark brown eyes the image of his daughter's, and disappeared back into the kitchen, whistling to himself.

When Sara untwisted the packet of rich tea, the first biscuit was broken. Wasn't worth trying to fob Ruby off with that. She stuck it in her own mouth and pulled out a whole one. 'Biccie, Rubes?'

Ruby held out a chubby hand for the biscuit. Before she'd even finished it, and still hiccupping from the effects of her grief, she reached out for another.

Thank God. The biscuits seemed to be working their magic. How long before she could get up and carry on with the packing? Moving too soon increased the risk of the crying starting all over again. It was worth waiting awhile. Lying on the floor, she rested her head and watched her little girl.

When you're pregnant, you're not supposed to care what sex your baby is. At least, you're not supposed to admit it. But, from the minute Sara found out she was pregnant she'd wanted a girl. A daughter.

Actually, that wasn't quite true. The first minute after taking the pregnancy test, the only thought in her head was, *Oh God.* Pretty much on a loop. *Oh God. Oh God. Oh God.*

Once she'd got used to the idea, though – once she'd told Mike and he'd been okay with it, once they'd decided that, yes, they wanted this baby – *then* she had instantly pictured a daughter. In fact, it was a very good thing that Ruby had been a girl because she was so sure of it throughout her pregnancy that, had they handed her a boy at the end of her exhausting labour, she probably would have questioned whether he was actually hers. A daughter. A best friend. Dresses and hairstyles and boyfriend chats and a million other precious moments.

Ten more minutes and Ruby was humming to herself and rocking rhythmically; the worst was over.

Very carefully, Sara edged away and then began to stand. 'Mummy is just going to finish tidying.'

Picking up an empty box, she pulled open the bottom drawer of the sideboard. Beneath the spare nappies and wet wipes were her sketchbook and a tin of watercolours. Sara ran a finger over the ridges of the tin. Was there any point bringing these with her? Opening the sketchbook, her heart squeezed at the sketches of a sleeping infant Ruby: her full lips, wispy hair, long eyelashes. How had she thought that those newborn days were difficult? They were nothing compared to now.

There were far fewer sketches of the toddler Ruby. In the last six months, Sara had barely picked up a pencil. It was too difficult to find the time. Ruby still didn't sleep well and, even if she did, between looking after her and the evening shift at the hotel, Sara was just too tired. Not that she had a job any more. She'd have to look for a new one as soon as they got settled at Barbara's.

Sara stuffed the sketchbook and paints into a box.

Twenty-five minutes later, Mike came out of the kitchen, staggering beneath the weight of a box of plates, mugs and glasses, which he dumped near the front door. 'Kitchen is done. How's everything in here?'

'Getting there.' Sara wrestled with the top of the box she'd just filled, trying to interweave the four flaps to close it. She was getting hot and sticky and needed to find a hair band to get her hair off her face.

Mike, script in hand, sidled up and pecked her on the cheek. 'So, can you take her out for that walk then? I really need to get these lines learned.'

Maybe it would be a good idea to take Ruby out in the buggy now rather than later; it would be nice to cool off a bit. And if she did have a nap, it would be a lot easier to get the last bits done. 'I'll take her out for some fresh air. You've got an hour to yourself, but when we come back, I need some help.'

Mike gave her a mock salute and flipped back onto the sofa, head on one of the arms, feet crossed on the other.

*

There was a chill in the early evening East London air, but Ruby was wrapped up and Sara welcomed the breeze. Soon, she'd left behind their tatty street fully of student lets and was in the smarter part of the area. Large Victorian houses fronted with black metal railings looked like something from a Mary Poppins film. Ruby was quiet now, happy with her fifth rich tea biscuit. It would probably spoil her dinner, but there were no guarantees she would eat dinner anyway. That was a battle for later in the day, if Sara had the energy.

It must be lovely to live in one of these houses. The large windows radiated warmth and light. The solid front doors promised security and safety. What must it be like to come home to that front room every day? To sit on that sofa with a hot drink whilst the children play and your husband enquires about your day before telling you about something funny that happened to him at the office? Maybe you flip a coin to see whose turn it is to cook dinner before deciding to do it together, a glass of wine in hand. The fridge would be full of healthy food and decadent treats.

A woman around Sara's age came to the window to shut the curtains and caught her looking in. Sara picked up the pace. Why was she torturing herself? The residents here probably worked in banks or law firms. They weren't actors and wannabe artists working temporary jobs.

A glance downwards confirmed that Ruby's eyes were closed. Sara kneeled beside the pushchair and gently lowered the seat back so that Ruby was almost horizontal. Ruby sighed and fidgeted into a more comfortable position. Was she going to wake up? No. Fast asleep. Sara extricated the disintegrating biscuit from Ruby's clammy fingers, before bringing her daughter's small chubby hand up to her lips. 'One day we will live in a proper house of our own, little girl. And you will have everything you need. Including a mummy and a daddy who love you very much. I promise.'

They just needed to stay with Barbara long enough to get back on their feet. Sara's fears about Mike picking up his acting again had been unfounded. He'd got this part in *Cat on a Hot Tin Roof* pretty quickly and it would be at a proper West End theatre. It was a shame that the commute from Barbara's small town in Essex was well over an hour, but Sara would look for a job straight away too and they could save that deposit for a proper home of their own. Once they had their own place, Ruby would settle down, she and Mike would be okay and life would be better. It was all going to work out. She threw the biscuit into the gutter for the birds and turned the buggy to walk back to the flat. Tomorrow was going to be the first step towards the life she'd always imagined.

CHAPTER TWO

When Sara was nine, Jessica Friedman had told everyone that Sara had nits and no one spoke to her for fifteen long days. It was as if she didn't exist; the other girls would turn away when she passed. Other than the odd sideways glance or whisper, Sara was invisible. And that was kind of how it felt when she first arrived at Barbara's house.

The lawn was manicured within an inch of its life and red azaleas stood to attention along the path. Mike released Ruby from her car seat. She was finally quiet after the first hour of the journey when she had screamed non-stop and writhed in her baby seat as if it was electrified. No amount of singing or soothing had done any good. In the end, Mike had just turned up the radio and Sara had lain back with her eyes closed, waiting for the storm to pass.

As soon as they got to the front door, Barbara threw it open as if the prodigal son had returned. Her neat dark hair was threaded with grey and, though she was well put together in a dark navy woollen dress, Sara was struck again by how much older Barbara looked than her own mother. According to Mike she had been almost forty when she had him, which would make her late-sixties, at least fifteen years older than Sara's mum. Barbara threw her arms around Mike, patted Ruby as if she might break, nodded at Sara. 'I'm so happy that you're finally here!'

Mike grinned. 'Good to be here, Mum. Is that roast beef I can smell?'

Barbara beamed. 'Of course. Your favourite. And there's homemade Yorkshire pudding. Come in! Come in! I've cleaned out your room. It's all ready for you.'

'Sounds brilliant.' Mike leaned in to kiss his mother's cheek then strode towards the lounge with Ruby.

Barbara held the door open and Sara edged into the hallway with the box she was carrying. She caught her foot under the doormat and, not able to see over the top of the box, scraped her leg on the telephone table and dropped it. 'Shit!'

Barbara raised an eyebrow and coughed. 'Why don't you take that upstairs straight away? I don't like to leave things lying around. Your room is the first door on the left.'

Sara rubbed at her leg. 'Actually, could we get everything in from the car first? It looks like it might start to rain. Mike, can you give me a hand?' She called after him for support.

Mike appeared in the doorway from the lounge. 'Give us a minute, Sarz. We just got here. I haven't even said hello to my mum properly.' He disappeared again and she reluctantly followed.

The lounge was comfortable, coordinated and very, very tidy. A blue sofa and chairs with fully plumped cushions at one end and a mahogany dining table and six chairs with blue velvet seats at the other. Across the mantelpiece and the bookshelves were photographs of Mike the chubby-cheeked toddler, Mike the gap-toothed eight-year-old, Mike the teenager, Mike the student, Mike the perm years. Between the frames were sports cups and certificates and a rather large shield for drama. This wasn't a lounge; it was a Hall of Fame.

Sara nudged Mike and pointed to a picture in which he looked around eighteen. 'Nice hair.'

Mike laughed. 'Yeah. And I wondered why I couldn't get a girlfriend.'

Barbara bustled in with a tray of biscuits. 'I don't know if you're watching your weight, Sara, but I know Michael never turns down a biscuit. The kettle's on. What would you like to drink?'

Barbara was clearly doing everything she could to make them feel welcome and Sara didn't want to seem ungrateful, but if they sat down now, the car would still need unpacking at midnight. She widened her eyes at Mike and jerked her head in the direction of the door.

Thankfully he took the hint. Sort of. 'Sara just wants to get our stuff in, Mum. Then we'll sit down and have a catch-up.' He bent to put Ruby down on the rug, but she wouldn't let him, keeping her legs wrapped around his waist and holding on for dear life. Standing up again, he shrugged. 'I think she just needs a minute or two before I put her down. I'll follow you out and see what I can do with one hand.'

From the depths of the car boot, where she was trying to disentangle the lead to Mike's electric guitar, Sara heard a metal clang. Turning, she saw a woman around her own age – dark shiny hair, full make-up, expensive clothes – collecting mail from an old-fashioned postbox at the end of her drive. Did anyone actually use those anymore? The woman glanced in Sara's direction and nodded hello, before turning back up the path until Barbara appeared at the front door and caught her.

'Lisa! Perfect timing. Mike you obviously know, but you haven't met my granddaughter. This is Ruby.'

Sara watched as Barbara nudged Mike forwards. *How would the neighbour already know him? He'd never mentioned his mother's neighbour before. Were they old friends?* Sara took a deep breath. *Stop it. You're being ridiculous.*

Lisa nodded and smiled. Her dark hair swung forwards and back again. 'Hi, Mike. Nice to see you again. Hello, Ruby. That's a pretty dress.' Lisa tapped the envelopes against her hand and looked from Mike then back up the path to Sara. Was she wondering how the hell a good-looking guy like Mike had ended up shackled to the hot, sweaty mess struggling up the path with a huge pile of a crap?

Sara's heart thumped like it always did at the prospect of meeting new people. But this last year, she had started to think that it would be really good to have a friend. Especially a friend with kids. *Just take a deep breath and say hello.* She put the box down next to Mike, straightened her top – as if that was going to make her look any better – and held up a hand. 'Hi. I'm Sara.'

Lisa nodded again and the perfect hair swung forwards and back.

Barbara looked at her with barely disguised admiration. 'Lisa has two *beautiful* children. How old are they now, Lisa?'

'Five and three.' Lisa looked from Barbara to Sara, glanced at Mike and blushed. 'A boy and a girl.'

Of course she had one of each. They probably had a chocolate brown Labrador and a cat called Fluffy.

'Gosh, it only seems like five minutes ago you were bringing Olivia home from the hospital. Such a beautiful baby. Doesn't time fly! Ruby is three too, isn't she Mike?' Barbara reached for Ruby's hand. 'Say hello, Ruby.'

Sara's stomach tightened. Ruby was really shy around strangers. It wasn't as if she *couldn't* say hello, they had hours of video of her repeating it over and over, but lately she ignored them every time they asked her to say it to someone else. Now Ruby pulled her hand back from Barbara and looked away.

'Come on, Ruby,' Mike jigged her up and down in his arms. 'You can say hello.'

Sara's fingers itched to reclaim her daughter. Surely she didn't have to say hello to a stranger if she didn't want to? She needed some time to adjust to a new place. After an hour in the car with a screaming toddler, Sara needed it too. Her face began to heat up at the sight of the three of them staring at Ruby. *Just say hello and they'll leave you alone.*

Barbara shook her head and sighed. 'Lisa's youngest is such a little chatterbox, isn't she Lisa?'

Lisa laughed. 'She certainly is. Grant says she takes all the oxygen from the room. Actually, I'd better get back inside to the children. I don't like to leave them alone too long.'

As if on cue, a mini version of Lisa appeared at door. 'Mummy!'

Barbara put her hand on the fence and leaned over. 'Hello, Olivia! Come and meet Ruby. She's gone all shy. Come and talk to her. Show her how it's done.'

Sara dug her fingernails into her palms as Lisa picked up her daughter so that she could see over the fence. 'This is Ruby, Olivia.'

Barbara was all smiles. Somehow, she'd taken ownership of the granddaughter she barely knew. And she wasn't giving up on the performing monkey routine. 'Say hello to Olivia, Ruby.'

Ruby didn't respond, but this didn't put Olivia off. She must have been a good few months older than Ruby. Her faced was animated and friendly as she chattered away like a little old woman. 'Hello, Ruby. Come play? Come play with Livvy?'

Ruby responded by putting her hands over her ears.

Olivia gave up on Ruby and turned to Sara. 'It's my birthday. I had a party. I'm free.' She held up three fingers.

Lisa lowered her daughter's arm. 'She means she's three. Last week. She's very excited because she is hoping to catch her brother up.'

Just turned three? That meant she was a couple of months *younger* than Ruby. Yet, the difference between their speech was huge. Maybe having an older brother helped? 'She's a bright one for three.'

'She is, isn't she?' Barbara gushed. 'You're always doing things with them though, aren't you Lisa? Always off to some baby group or other?'

Another hit to the guilt button. Sara had tried to take Ruby to some baby groups, but the few times she had, they'd sat on their own because she had no idea how to spark up a conversation with complete strangers. That was probably why Ruby was a little behind in her talking. She should try to make friends with this woman and her little girl for Ruby's sake. 'Maybe you could let me know which groups there are locally.'

Lisa nodded. 'I'll write some down for you. And there's a nice park around the corner. We could go together if you like? Well, I'd better get Livvy back in. It looks like it might rain.'

'Of course, of course. You get back in. Must be nearly their lunchtime. I know how important routines are with little ones. Maybe Ruby will be more talkative next time.' Barbara waved at Olivia over Lisa's retreating shoulder.

They had barely shut their front door when Barbara started to extol Lisa's virtues as she walked back up her own path. 'Lisa is *such* a good mother. Her children only ever have home-cooked food. All organic. They even eat olives of all things! And she dresses them so beautifully. Mind you, her Grant earns a bob or two. They have a huge flashy car. You'll see it parked on their drive later on.'

Mike rolled his eyes at Sara and turned after his mother. Sara picked up the box she had left beside the fence and carried it inside. A large drop of rain fell directly on the top of her head, followed by another.

CHAPTER THREE

It was surprising how many adjectives you could think up to describe roast potatoes if you really tried. Sara had been so enthusiastic about dinner, you would've thought she was the one with the acting career. It was important to convey to Barbara how grateful she was. She'd tried to make Mike insist that Barbara accept rent, but it had been waved away as an insult. It was a godsend and would really help them out.

'This apple pie is amazing, Barbara. Did you make this pastry yourself?'

Barbara sat up straight and frowned. 'Of course. I've never used shop-bought pastry in my life.'

Sara was relieved they'd eaten up their freezer stock of Iceland's finest rather than bring anything that might soil Barbara's kitchen. 'And the apples taste so… well… appley.' *And the Overacting of the Year Award goes to…*

'Well, that's because they were picked fresh, cooked and frozen immediately. They come from Lisa's garden. She's so green-fingered. I helped her to pick them one weekend when Grant was away and she gave me a huge bucket full.'

It wasn't an attractive quality to be jealous of another woman, especially one she'd barely met. 'Lisa seems nice. Maybe we can get the children together some time.'

Barbara beamed. 'That's a marvellous idea. Her two are so bright, I'm sure they would help to bring Ruby out of herself.

And if you and Michael wanted some time to yourselves, I could take her next door for you.'

Actually, Sara was hoping to get to know Lisa for herself and she wasn't ready to hand Ruby over yet. 'I think Mike's going to be busy for the next little while with rehearsals, aren't you?'

This was a genius tactic. Getting Mike on the subject of his big break was guaranteed to turn the spotlight away from her and onto him. He could regale his adoring mother with tales from the stage and she could finish her apple pie in peace. Ruby was playing happily at the other end of the room after her dinner of one potato and a carrot – according to Barbara, Lisa's kids ate a full plate of vegetables with a knife and fork – so this was a good time to excuse herself to finish the unpacking upstairs.

Their bedroom was small with oppressive floral wallpaper and an eighties fitted bedroom suite, which meant you had to shuffle around the small double bed. Barbara had emptied the gilt-edged chest of drawers and wardrobe for them and had laid out two sets of towels of ever-decreasing size on the bed: blue for Mike and yellow for Sara.

In the 'box room', Barbara had even set up Mike's old cot bed for Ruby. At least, Sara hoped that she'd set it up recently and that it hadn't been sitting there like a shrine for the last twenty-five years. The bed was old but perfectly serviceable and it had pink bedding, which Barbara must have bought especially for Ruby. Sara had to admit that was thoughtful.

Mike poked his head around the door. 'Want some help, gorgeous?'

Sara flopped down on the bed. 'I've done most of it. I don't know where you want to keep your guitar.'

Mike picked the guitar up like a baby and lay back on the bed with it across his lap, plucking at the tinny strings. All he needed was a Bon Jovi poster behind his head and the picture would be complete. He patted the bed for her to sit down.

Sara shuffled up next to him. 'What's Ruby doing?

'She's still on the rug. Mum is talking to her. I thought I'd let them *bond*.' He winked and continued to pick out a melody on the guitar strings.

Sara laughed. Clearly this was a euphemism for his goldfish-like attention span for watching their little girl, but it was nice to have a break. Actually, she was glad she had him on his own because she wanted to ask him something. 'Do you think we need to worry about Ruby's speech?'

Mike turned his eyes to his left fingertips as he tried a more complex chord. 'Hmm? I don't know, Sarz. She's still little, isn't she?'

That's what Sara had been trying to tell herself. But after seeing the little girl from next door, she wasn't so sure she could keep believing it. 'But she *was* talking, wasn't she? She even started to say some of her colours.'

Mike shrugged. 'Well then, she'll be fine. She just doesn't want to do it at the moment. She's got her father's instinct for timing,' He placed his hand flat across the strings and winked at her again.

He was a veritable stand-up comedian this evening. It was nice to see him smiling. The last couple of months had been much better between them. Since he'd got that part, it really felt like they were on the way up.

Maybe she was overreacting. It wasn't as if children *forgot* how to speak, was it? If Ruby was going to have a problem with her speech, she wouldn't have said the things she'd already been saying. And she had. There was video evidence on Sara's mobile. Clip after clip of 'Dada' and 'Mama' and 'Nemo'. Lots of 'Nemo'. It was all going to be fine.

On that note, it was time to get on with the next item on her mental To Do list. 'Does your mum have Wi-Fi? I'm going to go online in a bit, see if there are any local jobs going. I only need something temporary for now. There's no point getting a permanent job until we know where we'll be living. Unless something amazing pops up, obviously.' She leaned in towards Mike and put her head on his shoulder. 'With both of us bringing in money and your mum kindly putting us up, it shouldn't be too long before we can get our own place.'

'My mum have Wi-Fi?' He laughed. 'Have you met her? No, but you don't need to rush into getting work. Why don't you have a rest for once? Mum doesn't mind feeding us for a bit.'

Sara was grateful, but she wasn't about to take advantage of Barbara's generosity. 'Your mum's great, but I am going to need to get a job.'

Mike went back to plucking the guitar strings. 'Well, give yourself a week off at least. Help Ruby to get settled.'

That wasn't a bad idea. It would give her a chance to familiarise herself with all that Ashbridge had to offer. Barbara had mentioned the High Street, which was only a short walk away, and also a park for Ruby. The small Essex town seemed very quiet after the noise of East London and it would be nice to take Ruby out in the buggy and get her bearings.

'Okay, I'll chill my beans until next week, but I'd like to start looking, just to see what's out there.'

Mike picked out 'Blackbird' on his guitar. It was one of Sara's favourites. 'We'll be all right here for a bit anyway, won't we? Mum said we can stay as long as we like – and we've got a room for us and a separate one for Ruby. Plus, Mum can help with the childcare and stuff.'

Help with the childcare? That was the first time he'd mentioned that. 'Actually, I was going to find a nursery for her. Or maybe even a preschool.'

The more Sara had thought about a preschool, the more it felt a really good idea. They would be experts. They would know whether she was worrying about nothing with Ruby's speech and, if Ruby was a little behind, they would know what to do to get her back on track. Sara herself hadn't been the brightest student at school. Her exercise books had been littered with doodles and her school reports with words like 'daydreamer'. Maybe if she'd paid attention more then, she'd have more of an idea how to help her daughter now.

Mike laid his guitar carefully across the pillows. 'You can still do the preschool thing. I was thinking more about childcare in the evenings. We could go out a bit more if Mum is around to babysit. Have a social life again. Do you remember what that was like?' Shuffling towards her on the bed, he put an arm around her lower back and kissed the top of her shoulder.

Did she remember? It seemed so long ago. They did used to have a good time. Out at the pub, watching bands, hanging out with Mike's actor friends. It hadn't mattered that they lived in a shoebox of a flat in the arse end of London because Mike was getting acting work and she was selling the odd painting. They were living the dream. It felt like so long ago. 'It would be nice to have a night out together. Maybe once Ruby has got to know your mum better, we can…'

She stopped mid-sentence. There was noise coming from downstairs. Ruby was crying. Screaming, actually. Shooting a look at Mike, she bolted from the bedroom and down the stairs, taking two at a time.

Barbara met her at the door to the lounge fiddling with the locket around her neck. 'I was just coming to get you. I can't stop her crying. I don't know what the matter is.'

Sara knelt down next to Ruby. 'What's the matter, baby? Are you hurt? What is it?'

Mike arrived two seconds later. 'What's the matter with her?'

Sara turned to Barbara. 'Did she just start crying? She didn't fall or anything?'

Barbara shook her head. 'No, she was on the floor the whole time. I just tried to get her to come and have a little more dinner. I know you said she'd had enough, but I couldn't bear to think of her being hungry. It's the mother in me. Children need to eat.'

It wasn't worth getting into that now. Barbara couldn't be expected to know yet what a fussy eater Ruby was. Sara tried to keep her voice light. 'So, what happened?'

'Well, she was playing with those little animals and she wasn't listening to me, so I just said, "Come on, Ruby. Help Granny tidy up," and I started to pack away her things. And then,' she held a hand out towards Ruby, 'then this.'

Well, that would explain it. 'Sorry, Barbara. Mike should have warned you. We never just take her toys away like that. She doesn't understand. It's better if you distract her. Or you take things away gradually so she doesn't notice.'

Barbara frowned. 'Gradually? I'm surprised you get anything done.' She looked at Mike. 'Is that what *you* do?'

Mike perched on the sofa and scratched his head. 'Sara knows her best, Mum. Why don't you pick her up, Sarz?'

Picking her up might well upset Ruby even more. 'Can you get her toys back out, please Mike?' It wouldn't necessarily make Ruby stop crying now that she'd got herself so upset, but they had to try something. As Mike rummaged in the bag for the plastic animals Ruby had been playing with, Sara could feel judgement emanating from Barbara.

'It's probably not my place to say, but you're making a rod for your own back. If you give into her this easily every time she cries, it's no wonder she does it.'

Count to five. 'Actually, Mike, why don't you make a cup of tea? Fewer people in the room might help to calm Ruby down quicker.' It would be rude to ask Barbara directly to leave her own lounge, but Sara would bank on the fact that she wouldn't let her golden boy make his own tea. Sure enough, she bustled out of the room after him, mumbling about spoiled children. *Oh, the irony.*

Exhausted from her prolonged operatics on the way here, Ruby's cries weakened as she lost the energy to keep them going, though she clutched onto a plastic elephant and tiger she now held in each hand. Sara put her arms around her, pressing her lips onto the top of Ruby's head. Her beautiful face was pink and blotchy, eyes puffy. Gently, Sara brushed the hair away from Ruby's eyes, pulling the wet tendrils from her cheeks and tucking them behind her ears. As Sara watched, Ruby's eyelids drooped, each blink getting slower and slower.

'Come to Mummy, Ruby. Let's have a cuddle.' She pulled Ruby onto her lap, laying her cheek on the top of Ruby's head. 'There you go, baby girl. It's all okay now. Mummy's here.' Sara rocked gently forwards and backwards and began to sing softly. 'Blackbird' – the tune still in her head from Mike's guitar.

Once she was sure that Ruby was properly asleep, Sara shifted herself onto her haunches and then stood up. Ruby was getting heavy; she wouldn't be able to lift her like this forever. Slowly, she made her way out into the hallway and up the stairs. When she came downstairs again, Mike and Barbara were back in the lounge with their tea. She paused at the bottom of the staircase to listen to their conversation.

'I'm just saying that you are storing up trouble for yourselves. I know what it's like, Michael. If you don't nip this in the bud now, you are going to really regret it later on.'

'I dunno, Mum. She's only a baby.'

'A baby? She's three, Michael. She's not even a toddler any more. She should be learning appropriate behaviour. You are letting her become a naughty little girl.'

Stick up for her. From her place at the bottom of the stairs, Sara willed Mike to speak up on Ruby's behalf. *Stick up for your daughter.*

But he didn't. 'She is a bit of a handful. Even Sara would admit that.'

A handful? She would *not* admit that. Ruby was just a normal little girl. She'd only just left the terrible twos and everyone talked about those.

'Exactly. And that will just get worse unless you take control. You're her father, Michael. You can't let Sara dictate everything. You must introduce some discipline into the girl's life before it's too late.'

I'm not dictating anything! Surely Ruby was too little for discipline? She was only three. And she was upset. Not naughty.

'It's not Sara's fault, mum. Ruby is just a bit difficult. She gets herself worked up and then we can't get her calm again.'

We? Sara could count on one hand the amount of times Mike had tried to calm Ruby, and on one finger how many times it had worked. He seemed to have conveniently forgotten this. Heaven forbid his mother should think he was shirking his duties as a father.

But Barbara seemed more intent on blaming Ruby. 'Do you think – now don't get cross when I say this – do you think there could be something wrong with her?'

'What do you mean?'

From her position on the stairs, Sara could just imagine Barbara's 'well meaning' expression. She must mean the lack of talking, but Sara was working on that. That's why she'd suggested the preschool. There was nothing *wrong* with Ruby; she was just a bit behind.

'Well, when I was asking her to put her toys away earlier, she didn't even move her head to acknowledge that I'd spoken. Do you think,' Barbara lowered her voice, but her stage whisper would have reached the back of an auditorium, 'do you think… she might be deaf?'

Deaf? Sara almost laughed. Ruby could hear the rustle of a biscuit wrapper two rooms away. But Mike seemed to consider it.

'That might explain why she isn't saying much. Sara is worried about it. Thinks we should start her at a preschool to get some help.'

Sara sank back onto the bottom stair. The carpet was itchy and unpleasant on the back of her thighs, but she had no energy to pick herself back up again. This was harder than she'd thought it was going to be. Was this what other people's mothers were like? Giving their opinions and unsolicited advice? It was a new thing for her; she'd made her own decisions since she was about fifteen. Barbara obviously meant well, but it felt as if she was measuring Ruby – and Sara – against the family next door and they just weren't hitting the right number.

Maybe Sara was being unfair. They'd been there for less than a day. Maybe once Barbara got to know Ruby better she would see things differently. She would grow to love her just as much as Sara did. She would use this week to get to know her way around, find a preschool and maybe some groups that she could take Ruby to, and make some friends for the both of them. Maybe they would even settle in Ashbridge for a while so that Barbara could see Ruby and get to know her granddaughter?

Sara stood and took a deep breath. Preschool. Job. House. She could do this.

CHAPTER FOUR

Dear Lisa,

Well, they're all fully moved in now. I could tell immediately how happy Mike was to be back home. Got himself settled in his favourite armchair and it was like he'd never been away.

Sara barely sat down once. She used the excuse of unpacking every last thing immediately so that she didn't have to spend time with me. Just like when I visited them – I felt so unwelcome. It didn't help that the flat they lived in was so inhospitable. I mean, I expected it when Mike was living with those friends of his – you know what boys are like – but I had hoped that Sara might have brought a woman's touch to their home. They say boys marry girls like their mothers; we couldn't be more different.

It still feels strange to me that he is married. Of course, not having been at the wedding is partly to blame for that. It's all very well that it was a 'last minute thing', but I'm his mother. You think she would have thought to invite me. Pregnant or not.

I'm barely allowed to touch Ruby, either. Sara has so many rules about what the girl likes and doesn't like and you should see the expression on her face if I try anything different. They don't know what problems they are bringing on themselves. It might seem easier to give in to her now, while she's small. But she won't be a small child forever. What about when she's a five-year-old? What will happen when she won't do what they say? Will they still be giving her everything she wants?

Sara is a worker, though. I'll give her that. Apparently, she went back to work when Ruby was only six months old and she won't listen to me when I say she doesn't need to hurry into a new job while they're with me. She's so independent. When I brought the forms home for them to register with my doctor, I could see her biting her lip. But a young child needs a local GP! It's common sense.

I do love listening to Mike learn his lines. He's even asked me to read with him a few times; I read the woman's part and he does his bit. It's just like old times! I remember him learning lines for his school plays – he was so good in them! Ask him to remember his lunch box in the mornings and you could forget it, but he could learn line after line of a script. His drama teacher used to tell me every parents' evening what talent he had. He helped him to get that place at drama school. People used to ask me how I could afford to support him in drama school as a single parent, but you do that for your child, don't you? Sacrifice is part of being a mother. It wasn't as if I got anything from his father to help him out.

I used to go to all his plays in those days. He even did some Shakespeare when he was at college – do you recall me telling you about it? I couldn't even understand most of it, but he was absolutely fantastic. Such a talented boy. And then there was that play at the Edinburgh Festival. He even started to get some bits of TV work – he was in the market on EastEnders *once. Spoke to Ian Beale. It was so funny seeing his face on TV. Almost like having him home.*

I'm so glad he's out there doing it all again. When they had the baby, he seemed to lose interest. It would have been such a waste. And now he has this big part. Could be his breakthrough, he says. Of course, Sara says she's proud of him, but it feels like all she ever talks about is the money. I even heard them having an argument about it. I mean, I couldn't help it when I was walking down the stairs.

Anyway, I told him that he doesn't need to worry about money whilst he is here with me. I'm not going to charge my own son rent, am I? And I can cook their dinners. It's been nice to have someone to cook for again. I'd got in the habit of just having a sandwich or a bowl of cereal. But I know Mike likes his home-cooked food – just like his father did – a real 'meat and two veg' kind of man. I don't think Sara cooks much for him.

And the food she feeds that little girl! Everything is beige. Sandwiches, plain pasta, plain rice – hardly any vegetables either. Once day, when she was out, I made Ruby a lovely plate of dinner, all the colourful veg. Oh my word, what a fuss she made! It was like I was asking her to eat a bowl of cockroaches! And I'm sorry but that is Sara's fault. If she had varied her diet from the start, she wouldn't be having these problems now. I tried to explain that to her, but it's like talking to a stone wall. I'll have to just keep trying.

CHAPTER FIVE

'So, are you going for casual–informal or do you want me to take my top off and try and balance her on my arm?'

After trying various ways to ingratiate herself with Barbara, Sara hit on the idea of a portrait – of Mike and Ruby. She'd wanted to paint them together before, but there just hadn't been the time. Back at the flat, she and Mike passed like ships in the night. At least they had the space to breathe a little now they were here. Thanks to Barbara. Hence the portrait.

Mike stood in the doorway to the lounge, with Ruby on his hip. He grinned at Sara, pretending to unbutton his shirt.

She shook her head and laughed. 'I think shirt on. We don't want to give your mother palpitations. Or nightmares. It's supposed to be a thank you gift.'

Ruby was dressed in a sunshine yellow dungaree dress and a navy-and-white striped top. Sara's attempts to put a yellow clip in her hair had been given short shrift. It didn't matter; she could paint it in later anyway.

Today was just the preliminary sketches. Barbara was likely to be out for a couple of hours, shopping for children's shoes with Lisa and her two perfect children. Why Lisa needed Barbara there was anyone's guess, but Barbara had proclaimed how it was 'nice to be needed' as she got ready to go. This was fifteen minutes after Sara had politely declined her offer to babysit Ruby for the afternoon. They had only been there for four days; it was too soon.

'So, where do you want us? Shall I put Ruby on my lap?'

Sara shook her head. Trying to get a three-year-old to pose for a portrait would be impossible. 'Why don't you just sit down there and play with her?'

'No problem. Playing is my middle name.' Mike picked up two expertly positioned cushions from the sofa and dropped them onto the floor. He sat Ruby on one – which she instantly wriggled off – and himself on the other. 'What are we going to play, Rube?'

Ruby got up and pulled the basket out from under the coffee table.

Mike rubbed his hands together. 'Perfect. I can show off my building skills to mummy. We can build her that house she wants.'

There was something touching about watching Mike play with Ruby. Their dark heads close together, long, dark eyelashes flicking left and right as they chose the blocks for their individual projects. As Mike focused on constructing the walls of a house – stacking the wooden blocks like a master craftsman – his tongue poked out the side of his mouth in a mirror of their daughter's. They were both beautiful.

They'd been in love before they had her, of course, but seeing Mike with Ruby was another level. With her dad beside her, Ruby looked safe, protected, loved. While he was here, everything was okay. It was a sweet kind of joy, worth making sacrifices for. No one's relationship was plain sailing – you had to expect rough periods if you were in it for the long haul. Everyone had blips in their relationship, didn't they?

For the next few minutes, all that could be heard in the lounge was the chink of the wooden blocks and the soft scratch of pencil on paper. Occasionally, Ruby would sigh softly to herself. Sara slipped into a creative space: a world of peace and colour, light and shade, depth and height. Mike's square fingernails as they scratched at his unshaven face, Ruby's curls as they kissed the tops of her ears, the tiny dimples on her knees echoed in his cheeks. Shape and shade and smooth and sharp and shifting movements. From nowhere, a well of feeling rose up within her and caused her eyes to blur. Refocusing, she caught Mike watching her, a smile at the edges of his mouth. He felt it too. They exchanged the proud parent glance. *Look what we made together.*

Mike nodded at the turret of blocks Ruby was building. 'How do you feel about growing your hair? Looks like you might need it if you're going to live in Ruby's tower.'

Sara wiped beneath her eyes with a finger. 'I think yours is more practical. What's the bit behind the box?'

Mike feigned affront. 'That *box* is your dream house, thank you very much. The "bit behind" is the start of your garden. If you're a good girl, and I can snaffle a couple of extra blocks from Rapunzel here, I might even make you a fishpond.'

Sara put her sketchpad down for a rest. 'Talk me through it.'

Mike pointed inside the square model. 'This is the lounge, which will have one of those long sofas you like that curve around the corner.'

Sara peered in. 'With one of those automatic foot rest things that comes up?'

'Of course. This,' he pointed to another corner, 'is a white glossy kitchen, with,' he held up a finger to prevent her from interrupting, 'a breakfast bar where Ruby can sit and eat her Weetabix while I make coffee from a barista-level machine and you get the milk from one of those huge American-style fridges.'

Sara laughed. He knew her so well. 'Sounds amazing.'

'I haven't finished yet. The upstairs will have a large double bedroom for us with a window seat in the bay window and a walk-in wardrobe. At the back will be a bedroom for Ruby with Nemo murals on the walls and a bed with one of those swooshy net curtain things, which you always touch when we're in IKEA's children's bedroom department.'

Sara crawled forwards on her knees and kissed him. 'I love you.'

'You haven't even seen the studio I'm going to build you in the back garden yet.' His eyes crinkled at the edges and he leaned in for another kiss. 'I love you too.'

Sara bent to kiss Ruby on the top of her head. 'And I love you, my beautiful girl. Aren't we lucky to have Daddy?'

In that moment, she really did feel lucky. It had been a tough few months, but – while they couldn't afford a house anywhere near as grand as the one Mike was describing – a small place of their own wasn't a world away. 'I am proud of you, you know.'

'Thanks.' Mike reached out and squeezed her hand.

She squeezed back. 'No, I mean it. It can't have been easy to keep putting yourself out there this year, but it's paid off. I mean, The Gielgud Theatre. *Cat on a Hot Tin Roof.* That's really big, Mike.' When he'd shown her the website with the production details, he'd been so excited. Amy Adams was cast as Maggie. Even though Mike was only playing Gooper, it was incredible.

Mike scratched at his stubble again. 'Yeah, well. I couldn't have done it without you taking on all those extra shifts so I could get to auditions. I know it hasn't been easy for you.'

He was right there; it hadn't been easy. Most of the last year had blurred in a fog of exhaustion. But that was the deal they'd made. 'When you're on the couch on *Graham Norton* you can tell everyone how you only got there thanks to your lovely wife.'

He nodded. 'My *beautiful* wife. No, my beautiful *artist* wife.'

Sara reached behind her for her sketchpad, tore off the page and started a new one. 'Speaking of which. As you were.'

*

Later that evening, Sara laid the sketches out on their bed. They were good. Tracing her finger around the curve of Ruby's cheek, her eyes filled again. Being a mother was such a privilege. She'd been so scared that she wasn't up to the job; worried that her own childhood had denied her the instincts that mothers were supposed to have. She'd made so many mistakes in the first couple of years, mistakes that had almost cost her everything. But they were back on track. The past was the past and she needed to focus on the future. Their future.

Spending this afternoon sketching had felt like a mini holiday. She had Barbara to thank for that. Back at the flat, with rent to pay, she would never have had a week like this. Time to start looking for a job on Monday and that would mean fewer hours for art, but that was okay. There was time to pick that up again later when Ruby was older and money wasn't so tight.

It was all going to be okay.

CHAPTER SIX

Operation 'Make Friends' had not gone well at all.

Mothers seemed to move in packs. A group at the clinic, or the school gates, or just standing chatting at the supermarket. Sara never knew when they all got to meet each other. Were they existing friends who had planned to have babies at the same time? Did they meet at the labour ward? Did they arrange to meet on a mothers' dating app? *I'll be the one wearing puke on my shoulder.*

Making friends had never felt easy for Sara. School had been difficult because her mum had never really encouraged her to bring friends home, even if she *had* wanted to reveal their tiny, rather grubby house to the world. There'd been a small group of art students at college, but everyone had gone their separate ways after graduation and then she'd been temping all over the place to earn enough for art materials, rent and food. In that order. It's hard to forge friendships when you only work somewhere for a few weeks.

After she'd met Mike, it hadn't bothered her so much. He had a group of mates and she'd just shuffled into the pack. Some of the girls were really nice. Then they'd had Ruby and kind of lost touch with them too. So now when she met other mothers… it wasn't that she didn't *want* to be friendly with them; it was more that she had forgotten how to do it. That was probably why Ruby found it difficult to mix with other children. More guilt.

Last night, Ruby had been up so many times that Sara was tired in her bones. Eventually she'd given up and brought her downstairs at some ungodly hour and watched as she played with blocks in the middle of the lounge as if it was the middle of the day. It was almost impressive how Mike could sleep through her cries. Impressive, and unbelievably irritating.

The next person up was Barbara. 'You look very tired, Sara. Why don't you go back to bed? I can watch Ruby.'

She still hadn't left Ruby alone with Barbara. It had been a bone of contention between her and Mike. She would… just not yet. But at least now that Barbara was up, she could give in to Ruby's demands for *Finding Nemo*. 'Thanks. But I'm awake now, I don't think I'd be able to go back to sleep.'

Barbara sniffed her disapproval. 'At least let me make you a proper breakfast. You're going to need more than your usual bit of toast if you're going to keep going all day.'

Sara jumped up. If she didn't get moving, Barbara was likely to start making a full-on breakfast buffet. Not only was she unable to stomach that much food early in the morning, Barbara waiting on her made her feel lazy and uncomfortable. She was quite capable of making her own breakfast; she'd been doing it since she was very young. 'Why don't you let me make breakfast for *you*?'

Barbara was already walking back to the kitchen. 'No, thank you. I know how I like it.'

Had Sara upset her again? Shoving the DVD in, she followed Barbara.

Despite having a decent-sized kitchen, it was difficult for two people to make breakfast at the same time because there was a small table and chairs in the middle of the room, which you had to shuffle around. This morning, whichever cupboard or drawer Sara opened – and there were several as she familiarised herself with what went where – Barbara seemed to be in front of it. There were many tight smiles and pointed looks: the kitchen was most definitely Barbara's domain. And she wasn't keen on sharing.

Once Sara had located the cereals – who puts the cereal in a bottom cupboard? – she opened the fridge to get milk. When she closed it, Barbara was behind the door like the villain in a thriller. Sara jumped.

Barbara's head was tilted to the right and she watched as Sara poured the milk. Was she ready to swoop in at the first sight of sploshing? But, no. It wasn't the milk she was scrutinising.

'I have a good eye cream that takes away dark circles.'

Sara nearly spat out her mouthful of Crunchy Nut. Who knows what she might have said if Ruby hadn't chosen that moment to yell at the trailers for not being *Nemo*.

It didn't matter that Sara flew back into the living room to rectify the mistake. As she pressed the buttons on the archaic DVD remote to get the damn thing to play, Ruby got more and more upset. Sara was tired, overwhelmed and all out of patience. 'For God's sake, Ruby. I'm going as fast as I bloody can!'

And, of course, that was the moment that Barbara had walked in from the kitchen. 'Are you sure you don't want me to watch her? You seem a little fraught. Tiredness makes everything worse, you know.'

Of course she knew. Ruby's overreaction to the film trailers was because of her tiredness. It was her own fault for waking up so bloody early, obviously, but a walk in the buggy might blow the bad mood away. 'Thanks, but I think I'll take her to the park Lisa mentioned. It'll do us both good to get some air.'

Grabbing the usual nappies, wipes, change of clothes from the bedroom – Mike still didn't stir even though she slammed the drawers shut – she also slipped her sketchpad and pencils into the basket underneath the buggy – a habit from baby days rather than an expectation she would get to use them.

According to Barbara's directions, it was only a short walk to the local park. All the houses in this part of Ashbridge looked exactly like the one she'd just left: sixties, brick built, semi-detached. Solid, comfortable family homes. For solid, comfortable families. In her mind, she'd always imagined them somewhere a bit more distinctive, older, characterful. But maybe they would be better in a house like these. If they could ever afford it.

The combination of the early start, fresh air and the movement of the buggy performed a minor miracle as, when they reached the deserted park, Ruby had her eyes closed. A wooden bench to the side of the playground was cold and hard, but Sara could have laid down on it and slept. She reached down to Ruby and tucked a blanket around her. The next best thing to sleep would be some time with her sketchpad. She pulled it out. What was there to draw?

The sky was brightening as the day began to establish itself, but there were a couple of dark clouds in the distance that needed watching. The playground equipment looked newly installed and the primary-coloured swings and climbing frames stood in stark contrast to the greenery around them. Sara kept looking. Just beyond the playground, a large tree stood guard, its branches bare. She'd start with that.

Just the process of sketching could lift Sara's mood. She went somewhere else in her head when she focused on a subject. It wasn't just the sketching; it was the *looking*. The longer you look at something, the more you see. And – for her – the calmer she felt. When Ruby woke, thirty minutes later, she felt a whole lot better. It was probably that, in combination with her guilt for shouting at Ruby earlier, that encouraged her to give in when Ruby pointed at the playground.

This was new. Ruby had never really shown an interest in swings or slides before. Sara hovered with her hands ready to catch her as Ruby climbed the steps – left foot, together, left foot, together – and slid down the slide… then ran around to do it again. The look of concentration on her face as she climbed the steps squeezed at Sara's heart. She grabbed her mobile from the changing bag to take photographs and video to show Mike their grown-up girl. 'Clever girl, Ruby!'

It's a weird feeling watching your child do something for the first time. Pride at their independence coupled with a realisation that they are growing up. Barbara had been right the other night: Ruby wasn't a baby anymore. She wasn't even really a toddler; she was a little girl. A little girl who could walk up a slide on her own.

'Mummy's so proud of you, Rube. You're such a big girl. Careful!' Sara lurched forwards as Ruby misplaced her footing then righted herself. 'Well done, baby girl. Now watch your step. Go slowly.'

Steps. Stages. Milestones. The books tell you what to expect, but they don't tell you how you might feel. The creeping anxiety if they haven't got a tooth yet, or smiled, or spoken, or taken a step. The relief when they do and then the... sadness? No, that wasn't quite right. It wasn't sadness. It didn't make you feel blue. More... turquoise. Pride tinged with nostalgia. Happiness tinted with fear. Love shaded with loss.

As Ruby slid to a stop at the end of the slide, Sara made a grab for her, squeezed her tight, pressed her nose into the warm, soft nook where her neck met her shoulder and breathed her in. 'I love you so much my lovely girl. So much more than you could ever know.'

Ruby wriggled away and back to the bottom of the slide. Sara's laugh caught in her throat.

Ruby was getting bigger and she needed to let her go a little, however much she wanted to hold her tightly, keep her safe. That included trusting Barbara to look after her. Eventually. Sara shook her head and rubbed at her cold cheeks. It was the fatigue making her melancholy. Ruby's independence was a good thing, and this was exactly what she'd pictured doing with her. Trips to the park. Maybe they could try something else next? 'What about the swings, Ruby? Would you like Mummy to push you on the swings?'

But Ruby wasn't interested in the swings. She wanted to go on the slide again. And again. Four times, five times, ten times.

There was no rush to go home so it wasn't a problem. Until another little girl turned up.

The little girl's mum looked as tired as Sara felt, although her exhaustion was veiled by an expertly made-up face. Her expensive-looking coat with coordinating hat and scarf made Sara regret Mike's warm jacket that she'd slung over her washed-out jeans.

But she gave Sara a friendly smile and pretended to prop open her eyes between a manicured finger and thumb. 'Another early bird? I'm hoping to tire this one out enough that she goes back to sleep.'

Start making friends. Sara kept her eye on Ruby, but she nodded and smiled. 'Me too, although I'm not holding my breath. She's like the Duracell bunny.'

With every ounce of her, Sara willed Ruby to play with the little girl. Listening to Barbara reel off all the things that Lisa took her children to and how many play dates they had, brought home what a bubble they'd been living in. Yes, Ruby had been shy with Olivia at the weekend, but that was Sara's fault for not taking her places with other children. Making friends would be good for Ruby. For both of them.

Come on, baby girl. You can do this.

The girl was faster than Ruby at climbing, so she was almost at the top of the steps by the time Ruby got to the bottom of the slide. The problem came when the little girl climbed the steps again – right, left, right, left – because she caught up with Ruby halfway. To be fair to her, she did wait patiently for Ruby. But she got really close behind. Ruby stopped climbing. And froze.

What was Ruby going to do? Sara tried to keep her voice light. 'Come on, Ruby. Keep going. You're making a traffic jam.' She laughed nervously and darted a glance at the other mother. What should she do?

The other mother made supportive noises. 'Maybe she needs some help? Can you help her, Tilly?'

That wasn't a good idea. Ruby's fierce independence made it difficult to help her. 'Oh, thanks but, she's not really good with—'

Too late. Tilly put her hands on Ruby's waist. Ruby turned and put up a hand, straight armed, like a traffic officer. All she was doing was trying to stop Tilly from touching her. But it was easy to see how it might look like a push, especially as the surprise caused Tilly to lose her footing. If it hadn't been for her mother's lightening reactions, Tilly might have fallen.

Sara was pretty sure it was the shock of her mother grabbing her down from the steps that made the little girl cry. It wasn't as if she was actually hurt. But the other mother looked at Ruby as if she was the Antichrist. 'It's okay, Tilly. Some children just don't know how to play nicely. I'm sure her mummy will tell her off and ask her to apologise.'

Ruby was oblivious to all this. Now that Tilly was no longer on the steps, she continued to climb – left foot, together, left foot, together – and to slide. It would have been pointless to ask her to apologise. Especially as she hadn't actually meant to *push* the little girl, she was just trying to ask her not to touch her. How could she make the woman understand without looking like a terrible parent? 'I'm so sorry. She doesn't like… to be hurried along. And she's not really had much experience of sharing things with other children.'

The other mother screwed up her eyes. 'Isn't that what we're supposed to teach them?'

Quickly over her shock, Tilly slid down out of her mother's arms. Straight back to the damn steps. This time, Sara had to say something. The playground had two lots of swings – infant and normal – a slide, a roundabout and a huge climbing frame. With all that choice before her, it had been bad luck that the little girl had chosen the slide.

Sara turned to the other mother, practically pleading with her. This lovely moment with Ruby was disintegrating by the second. 'It might be better to try something else. Ruby is a lot slower so it's going to be tricky. I'm sure she'll get the slide out of her system soon and then it'll be all yours.' *Please. Please don't take this away from us.*

But the other mother had her arms folded. 'Then maybe *she* should be the one to go and play with something else?'

That was going to go down really well. But there was no choice. She couldn't risk Ruby pushing Tilly from the top of the slide. As Ruby got to the bottom, Sara took hold of her hand. 'Come on, Ruby. Let's go and play on the swing. Mummy will swing you up, up and away.' Away from this woman and her judgemental stare boring into the side of Sara's head. *Thanks, lady, for making my morning that little bit more difficult.*

It got worse. Ruby wrenched her hand away and marched to the bottom of the slide, her foot on the bottom step before Sara caught her and took her arm. 'Come on, Ruby. That's enough with the slide.'

Ruby tried to pull free again, but Sara had a stronger grip this time. The weight of the woman's stare caused the muscles in her shoulders to tighten, a wave of heat rose up and flushed out of her face and she tightened her grip as Ruby wriggled and wrestled. 'Come on, Ruby. You can come back to the slide in a minute.' *Please don't do this to me. Please give in.*

At the top of the slide, Tilly had turned and was watching the pantomime at the bottom of the steps. It was wrong to hate a small child who had done absolutely nothing wrong, but – by God – she did in that moment.

Almost as much as she hated her mother, who was keeping up a passive aggressive commentary. 'Keep going, Tilly. Her mummy is dealing with the naughtiness. You are safe to keep going. She won't push you again.'

Sara seriously wanted to push this self-satisfied smugmother herself. Time to get away, whatever it took. Grabbing Ruby around the waist, she lifted her from the ground, arms flailing and legs kicking. Her heels smacked into Sara's shins.

'Shit!'

The intake of breath from smugmother was loud enough for people in the neighbouring houses to hear. Wrapping a showily protective arm around her daughter, she guided her in the direction of the climbing frame. 'Come away, Tilly. Let's find some nice children to play with.'

Now she bloody goes.

It took about five minutes of struggle to get Ruby into her pushchair and bolted in. It felt like five hours. By the time Sara was upright again, two more mothers and their – presumably 'nice' – children were standing by the swings with Tilly and her mother and glancing in her direction. Sara's face burned. If the stupid woman had just listened when Sara asked her to play somewhere else, everything would have been okay. But there was no point trying to explain. She didn't even want to. Taking a deep breath, trying to ignore Ruby pulling on the buggy straps and shouting at her, she held up her head and walked out of the park. Marching home, muttering under her breath, with Ruby screaming and writhing in the buggy, Sara berated herself for going to the park at all. But why shouldn't she? Isn't that what you were supposed to do with a three-year-old? She couldn't keep her at home until she was certain Ruby wouldn't behave like that. How would Ruby learn?

One thing Sara had learned that morning was not to bother making friends with other mothers. Which is why, when she saw Lisa standing again at her postbox, she was less than friendly.

Lisa looked as perfect as usual, smiling as Sara jerked the buggy up the kerb and towards Barbara's path. 'Oh, have you been to the park already? We could have come with you.'

Keep your voice upbeat. 'Yes, we had an early start.'

Lisa wrinkled her nose. 'Ouch. Have you got time to come in for a coffee? I was just about to make some.'

After the smugmothers at the park, the last thing Sara needed was an hour with Perfect Pants and her perfect progeny. 'I promised Barbara we would have a coffee with her when we got back,' she lied. 'Another time, maybe?' Lisa nodded. 'You're so lucky having Barbara to help out. She's been brilliant to us – my two love her like another granny. Do let me know when you're free. I'd really like to get the children together and have a chat.'

Yesterday Sara might have liked that too. But her encounter at the park had reminded her why she didn't make friends with people. She didn't need them. She didn't need anyone except Mike and Ruby. As long as she had them, life would be good.

CHAPTER SEVEN

Much as Sara had loved her Diploma in Fine Art, it hadn't really qualified her for many roles. After finishing college, she had temped in admin, worked in retail and – since Ruby – had worked evening shifts that would fit around Mike and childcare. A juggling act that would make P.T. Barnum proud.

Much trawling of the Internet and the local paper hadn't turned up anything other than some dubious sales jobs that promised *££££££s in commission!*. An actual career was too much to hope for right now; just something to pay enough that they could save up for a deposit would do. She guessed her next step would be to walk into places and try her luck. One useful thing her mother *had* taught her: *If you don't ask, you don't get.*

*

It was way past nine o'clock, but Mike had still grumbled when she'd pulled him out of bed to watch Ruby. He'd got in really late last night after a drink with some of the other actors. Rehearsals were due to start on Monday and they'd met up to introduce themselves. She'd asked if Amy Adams had been there, but she hadn't.

'I just need another half hour, Sarz. Mum will watch her 'til I get up.'

'I don't think it's fair to put on your mother like that when we've just got here.'

The episode at the park had added to Sara's reluctance to leave Ruby with Barbara. Plus, she might strap Ruby into a high chair and force feed her prunes or take her next door for intense lessons on how to be the perfect three-year-old.

'Come on, get up. I've given her breakfast and she's watching her DVD. You barely need to do anything.'

He'd mumbled something under his breath that may or may not have been a death threat to a certain clownfish, but he got up.

*

The High Street was in the opposite direction to the park, and the houses here were older and terraced. One of the preschools Sara had looked at online was around there somewhere, but she'd save that for another day.

The retailers ranged along one side of the road, bookended by residential properties. It was nicer than she'd expected. As well as a small supermarket, a café and a takeaway fish and chip place (none of which were hiring), there was a gift shop full of things like wooden signs that said 'Live Laugh Love', a children's clothes and toy store and, most interestingly, an actual art gallery.

Though they couldn't really afford it, she'd spotted a pretend aquarium in the toy store window, which Ruby would love. Moving along the store front, vaguely searching for its price, she noticed a door with a 'Gallery and Fine Art' sign. The door led upstairs to a room above the toyshop. Once she'd been in the toy store to buy Ruby's gift, she decided to take a look inside the gallery.

At the top of the stairs was a second door with another gallery sign. Below it was the sign she was hoping for: *OPEN*. Pushing on the door had no effect; it didn't move. She tried again, harder. This time it grated against the floor as it opened.

Inside was one of the most silent spaces she had ever experienced. Not silent like a library. More silent like space. Or inside a cloud. Or under a duvet. The walls were white and lined with canvases. Her eyes didn't know where to start. Could she just wander around? What was the form? In the far corner were some sketches, which she'd love to…

'Good morning.'

Sara turned. In the corner behind her was a large, solid wooden desk, behind which sat an elderly gentleman. He took off his glasses and smiled.

'Er… Good morning. Is this the gallery?'

He motioned to the pictures lining the walls. 'It would appear so. Are you looking to purchase something?'

If only. She didn't have enough spare cash to buy herself a postcard, let alone a painting.

'Oh… er… no… I was hoping to just look.'

The man replaced his glasses and returned to the book he'd been reading. 'Of course. Why would you be here to buy? Please, look at your leisure.'

Sara walked past some bright modernist canvases and more traditional landscapes before stopping in front of the sketches. They were nudes: some male, some female. The artist had a preference for bold strokes, which she envied. Her art tutor at college had often urged her to be braver in the marks she made. To be different. To dare.

'You have some lovely pieces.'

The man took off his glasses again and smiled, the edges of his eyes crimped by fine lines 'Those particular sketches came from a local artist, actually. I like to support local talent if I can. Unfortunately, they don't sell as well as I'd like. Hence the move to…' He motioned around the room with his glasses.

The man had looked proud of the pictures and Sara wondered if any were his own work. She didn't like to ask. 'I wasn't expecting to find an art gallery in a town this size.'

The man put down his book and gave her his full attention. 'I used to have a larger place in the centre of Chelmsford, but rents got so high it was no longer viable. The drafty windows and uneven floors make this place pretty uninhabitable as living accommodation, so they let me have it cheap. Unfortunately, that means no one knows we are here so…' he shrugged, 'it's rather a catch-22 situation.'

Sara nodded as she walked slowly around the room, looking at each piece in turn. 'What about Internet advertising?'

The man laughed. 'Yes, I have a website. But no one seems to visit that, either.'

Sara pulled her eyes from a portrait of an old woman where the artist had painted wrinkles deep enough to fall into. 'What about social media? Events? Art trails? That kind of thing?'

At art college, they had often been roped into helping out at local art events in exchange for being allowed to display some of their work. They were usually attended by the same group of people, most of them amateur artists themselves.

The old man laughed. 'That sounds like a young man's game.'

'Maybe you could employ someone to do it for you?' Sara hadn't even dreamed she could get a job working with art. That would be amazing. Could this be the luck she was well overdue?

But, again, the man laughed. 'Employ someone? I don't even make enough to pay myself. This place is a labour of love, I'm afraid. Without my pension, I wouldn't even be able to keep it going.'

Of course, nothing was that easy in life. Especially her life. It would be great to offer to do it for nothing, but there was enough to juggle at the moment and Sara needed to focus on getting a job that paid actual money. 'Labours of love' were a luxury she couldn't afford.

It was hard not to envy Mike, getting to do the job he was passionate about. Of course, she was pleased for him, and he was so much happier now his career was going somewhere, but it was hard not to feel like a Cinderella-wife. If he was happy, everything worked. She needed to keep reminding herself of that. Her time would come.

And, however much it was irritating her, it *was* kind of Barbara to keep saying that Sara didn't need to look for a job while they were living with her. Even if she *did* always follow up by saying how it would be better for Ruby to have Sara at home all day. If nothing else, getting a job would give them all a welcome bit of space from one another.

How nice it would have been to work at the gallery. The quiet, the calm, the beauty; it was good for the soul. 'You really do have some beautiful pictures. I'm just sad I can't afford to buy any of them. Would it be okay to come back and look again?'

The old man replaced his glasses and smiled. 'Of course, my dear. Any time.'

After leaving the gallery, Sara tried to find a different route home that would take a little longer. She wasn't ready to give up the calm of the last half an hour. If only she could do something nice for the old man, find him some customers. Maybe she should ask Barbara's neighbours if they were in the market for some local art. They seemed to have the money to indulge themselves. And Lisa's husband Grant seemed a generous man.

Sara had met Grant the night before while taking out the bins. Barbara had asked Mike to do theirs, but he'd forgotten on his way out. Grant was opening his front gate as Sara was pulling the bin down the driveway.

'Hello!' he'd called. 'You must be Barbara's daughter-in-law?'

She'd walked over to him, rubbing her grubby hands on her jeans. 'Yes, I'm Sara. We're staying with Barbara for a while.'

He'd struggled to get his hands free from the large parcel he was holding. With his rugby player's physique, it almost looked like a sport. Eventually, he thrust a few fingers out from underneath, which Sara managed to sort of shake hands with. 'Sorry. I saw this coat for Lisa and I couldn't resist surprising her with it.'

Any store that put coats into boxes would be pretty pricey. And he was surprising her with it. 'Lucky Lisa.'

Grant smiled. He was a very good-looking man. Thick blonde hair, bright eyes, an easy smile. No wonder their children were so beautiful with the two of them as parents. 'She'll probably tell me off. I buy too many gifts, apparently.'

Sara wanted to bite him, see if he was real. 'Well, if she doesn't want it, I'm only next door.' They had laughed. Sara could have sworn Lisa's front curtains had twitched.

Now Sara was on a street she didn't recognise. She'd give it a few more minutes and then satnav her way home. Turning the corner, she came across a pub. Old-fashioned and a bit grubby, it was just the kind of place her mother would like. She shuddered. A man came out, the landlord possibly. He was sticking a notice up on the window: 'Temporary Bar Staff Required'. It would be the last place she wanted to work, but beggars couldn't be choosers.

'Excuse me. I might be interested in that job. What are the hours?'

The man turned around, looked at her vacantly, then focused, pulled earphones from his ears and smiled. 'Sorry, I was listening to Bowie. I was on another planet. What did you say?'

He was roughly her age, she reckoned. Dark hair, blue eyes, dressed in an old sweatshirt and a pair of jeans. Was he in charge or just a member of staff?

She motioned towards the notice he had just stuck up. 'The bar work. I might be interested. What are the hours?'

'Oh. That. You're quick off the mark. Amy just told me this morning. Her mum isn't well, she's off down to Cornwall for six weeks or so, taking the kids out of school and everything. Trouble is, she does the Friday night entertainment too. You don't sing, do you?'

Sing? What was this place? 'Er… no, I, er…'

The man cracked another smile. 'I'm joking, sorry. You'll get used to me.' He stuck out his hand. 'My name's Kevin. I'm the landlord here at this salubrious establishment, for my sins. I'm looking to cover three afternoon shifts at the moment – Monday, Wednesday and Friday – and some weekends. Amy used to work around school hours with her kids, plus a bit of cleaning in the mornings. There might be some evening shifts too if you wanted to pick those up.'

Morning cleaning and afternoon behind the bar. Three days would suit her plan to get Ruby into preschool. Hours wise, this sounded exactly what she needed. Even if it was the last thing she wanted.

'And the pay?'

Kevin nodded. 'Minimum wage, I'm afraid. We're not the busiest of places. Have you got much experience?'

Experience? How about half her childhood? 'Yeah, I worked behind a bar when I was at college. I'm sure it'll all come back to me.'

'That sounds great. To be honest, you'd be doing me a favour if you took it. Recruitment is not my strong point.' They both looked at the paper advertisement. It was already curling up at the bottom.

Bar work? Did she want to be stuck in here every day, forced to be pleasant to drunk old men? The smell of stale ale seeped out of the door and took her back twenty years. She had been in bars as a customer since then, of course. But only to modern bars: clean, trendy, beers in bottles – avoiding this kind of place like the plague. But she needed a job and they seemed in short supply at the moment.

'Can I come in and take a look around?'

CHAPTER EIGHT

When Sara got home, Mike was on the sofa with his feet up, watching TV. Ruby was playing with her coloured blocks on the floor, positioning them in a straight line. Sara watched the concentration on her daughter's face – her eyebrows low in a frown, tongue peeping out of her mouth – then kissed the top of her head. 'Mummy has a job, Ruby. And I've brought you a present.'

Sara produced the aquarium from its paper bag. Fish, starfish, seahorses and seaweed swished around in a bright blue gel 'sea'.

Ruby placed her palm against the plastic tank, her eyes widened. 'Nemo!'

Thankfully, one of the fake fish was orange and black and could do a passable impression of Ruby's favourite. Sara put the aquarium on the floor and watched Ruby follow 'Nemo' around the tank with her eyes. With a job starting tomorrow, she didn't even have to feel guilty about spending the money on it.

Mike looked up and muted the TV with the remote. 'A job? Really? That was quick. Well done. Where is it?'

Sara focused on Ruby. 'At the pub around the corner.'

Mike widened his eyes. 'The Forester's Arms? But that's full of old men. You'll be lowering the average age by about thirty years. And you *hate* pubs like that.' He laughed. 'When you were going on about getting a job, I thought you were aiming for something a bit better.'

The pub had actually looked more presentable than she'd imagined on the inside. It was small, with a bar running the length of one side, which had been recently rubbed down and varnished. Kevin had explained that he'd only been the landlord there for six months and was trying to make improvements to the décor, but it was a slow process. He'd seemed honest and fair and she needed the work. Especially as he'd said she could start the next day. He'd even suggested a preschool for Ruby; the previous barmaid had had her youngest there so they would have space now, even if it was only until she came back.

Mike was right though; Sara did hate pubs like that. And being at the gallery this morning had served as a reminder of what she *wished* she was doing. But that wasn't possible for her right now.

'We can't all be living the dream. Some of us just need a job to pay the bills.'

Mike sighed. 'Are you trying to make me feel guilty? Yesterday you were saying how proud you were that I was going for it. And we agreed I should be the one to focus on my career right now. You agreed. You're not being fair.'

She shouldn't have said anything. He was right. They'd agreed. Although he could definitely be a bit more considerate of her feelings. 'I know that. But pub work is all I can get at the moment. You don't need to make me feel worse about it.'

He shrugged. 'It was just a joke. Actually, I was just going to suggest we go out for dinner to celebrate.'

Sara's stomach clenched. Although they were living rent free right now, they had credit card debts to pay off and a deposit to save for. Plus, Mike's travel in and out of London every day – and his lunch and drinks after work – didn't leave a lot in the kitty.

Keep your voice light. 'On what? Shirt buttons? How can we afford a meal in a restaurant?'

Mike ran his hand through his hair from the back to the front of his head and looked a little sheepish. 'Mum gave me some money this morning. Said she didn't like the thought of me with nothing in my pocket.'

Sara felt a little bit sick. He was a grown man. 'You can't take money from your mother. She's already letting us live here rent free and cooking all our meals.' Sara had offered several times to at least cook dinner, but Barbara had been adamant that she liked to be in 'her kitchen' cooking for 'her family'. Short of wrestling her to the ground in front of the microwave, Sara had had to give in.

Mike scratched the side of his head. 'She's my mum, Sara. That's what mums do. I know you don't really understand because of, you know, your mum being…'

That was low, using her mother. 'We need to be supporting *ourselves*, Mike. We're adults. We can make our own money.' She rubbed at her eyes with her fingers. God, she sounded whiney. She'd tried so hard these last few months to keep everything positive. No arguments, no judgement. She'd even accepted the move to Barbara's. But Mike wasn't behaving as if this was a temporary pit stop. In fact, he was behaving like a teenager.

He picked up the remote again and flicked the sound back on. 'It's boring talking about money. I'm living my dream right now. That's more important than money.'

Sara thought again of the gallery and the paints in the bottom of the box under their bed upstairs. Their creative ambition was one of the things they'd had in common when they first met. She'd got a couple of days' work painting scenery for a production of *The Cherry Orchard* at The King's Head in Islington and Mike had been around rehearsing the part of Nora's husband Torvald. He'd persuaded her to come back and watch the play, and a week later they'd laid in bed together mapping out their life with him as a celebrated actor and her as a groundbreaking artist. Had she lost her dream? No. But dreams didn't put dinner on the table.

She picked up one of the blocks that Ruby hadn't placed in a line yet. 'Green. Green, Ruby. Can you say "green"?'

Ruby took the block and put it at the end of the line. She was so precise, butting it up against the previous block perfectly. Sara's tongue burned with everything she wanted to say to Mike, but she didn't like arguing in front of Ruby. This wasn't how it was supposed to be. Why did it feel so difficult between them lately? It used to be so easy. Following Mike around the country as he picked up acting work, painting during the day while he was in rehearsal. Watching his performances was an aphrodisiac, his energy and imagination fuelling her own creativity. He'd just finished a really successful run in a three-man show at the Edinburgh Fringe when she'd discovered she was pregnant. He was high on triumph and audition offers. She'd been terrified to tell him: the timing couldn't have been worse.

But he'd been incredible. He got down on one knee and proposed there and then. She'd laughed at him, but he was deadly serious. It was touching. And why not? It was organised in a few weeks; they had a registry office wedding with a few of Mike's friends followed by fish and chips at the pub. Afterwards, she'd turned her slim gold wedding band around and around on her finger. Her baby was going to have everything she hadn't. A father. A family. A proper home.

The front door banged open and Barbara's voice called from the hallway. 'Only me! Oh goodness, I nearly fell over all these shoes that are still here. Anyone want a cuppa?'

'Yes please, Mum.' Mike held out a hand and grinned. 'See, we even get waitress service here.'

He was joking, but Sara didn't laugh. Much as it was kind of Barbara to put them up, she couldn't quieten the nagging feeling that this had been a bad idea. Mike was different here. She'd worked so hard the last few months and she wasn't about to throw in the towel now. The dream she had for Ruby was not one she would ever give up on, whatever the consequences for her own life. Ruby would have the life she pictured for her and, starting tomorrow, Sara was going to earn the money to pay for it.

Starting tomorrow, there was going to be a new routine for all of them. She glanced again at Ruby and hoped that she was going to be okay with yet another change.

CHAPTER NINE

According to *Taming your Toddler*, a child feels safe when they have a clear routine. The authors recommend a 'bath and story and bed' evening routine, then a 'breakfast and teeth and dressed' morning routine. This particular morning started to go downhill at breakfast when Sara discovered they were all out of Weetabix because Mike had fancied a late-night bowl of cereal.

'Can't you give her something else?' Barbara was pulling boxes of cereal from the cupboard. 'I have Bran Flakes and All-Bran and Oat Bran.'

Sara knew very few adults who liked any of those, let alone a stroppy three-year-old, and there were also serious concerns for Barbara's bowel movements if she needed that lot every morning.

'Weetabix is the only cereal she likes. Don't worry, she can have toast.'

Barbara did The Smile again. It was appearing more and more and always preceded some 'well meant' advice. 'Well, it's up to the parent to encourage the child to try new things, I always think.'

The toast popped up just in time to prevent Sara tipping the damn cereal over Barbara's head. She quickly buttered it and cut it into soldiers, saying a silent prayer to the god of three-year-olds that that it would be accepted in lieu of Weetabix. It wasn't.

Getting dressed had also not gone well. It was always a struggle to get Ruby out of her pyjamas and into proper clothes. She would wriggle as if they itched her and then pull on them. Sometimes she was distractible. Her favourite DVD usually worked, but Mike refused to let her watch *Finding Nemo* on the living room TV.

'I am not watching that again. It burrows into my head.'

Sara could most definitely live without listening to dozy Dory again, but Ruby loved it. She would sit in front of the TV screen captivated by every scene. She had even started to repeat more of the lines from the dialogue. That must be a good sign, surely?

Despite Sara's remonstrances, Mike wouldn't budge. It didn't help that Barbara backed him up. She stood at the lounge door and repeated one of her favourite mantras. 'It's not good for her to be watching that much TV. Her speech would come on a lot more if we were talking to her rather than letting her sit there staring at the box.'

What did Barbara think she'd been doing? Ignoring her child for the last three years? She *did* talk to Ruby. All the time. But sometimes it was a relief to let her watch her film again. A one-way conversation could be exhausting.

At 10.00 a.m. Sara had no choice but to leave for work. Ruby was breaking her heart. This wasn't a tantrum, whatever Mike said. Not being allowed to see Nemo was like being kept away from a friend. More guilt that she had not found any friends for Ruby. She needed to be around children her own age. Maybe that was the problem? Sara decided to bite the bullet tomorrow and speak to Lisa next door again.

She put her head to one side to try and catch Mike's attention. 'Can you sit down here on the floor and play with her? I've got to go and it'd be a lot easier if she was distracted.'

He waved that damn script at her.

Then Barbara jumped in. Again. 'I'll play with her. It'll be nice for me to have some uninterrupted time with her.'

Sara could just imagine how that would turn out. When Barbara went out to the kitchen, Sara hissed at Mike. 'You need to play with her too. Ruby isn't used to your mum yet.'

Mike sighed and slid down onto the floor. Ruby got louder.

*

Now Sara was at the pub, wiping down the bar area and restocking the fridge with mixers. Kevin was sitting up at the bar with a ledger, recording sales figures and working out an order. He had offered her a drink, but she opted to get on with work.

'I hate this part of the job.' He threw his pen down and ran his hands through his hair. It stood up in tufts like a young boy. 'Maths was never my strong point.'

The hard-backed ledger he was writing in looked like something from another era. He was the same age as her, wouldn't he rather do this electronically? 'Why don't you do it on the computer? Set up a spreadsheet?'

He put an elbow on the bar and rested his cheek in his palm. 'Yeah, I should. I inherited this method from the previous owner. Might be why he went out of business. I will get it all onto the computer at some point. I just never seem to get around to it.'

'I could do it for you.'

Sara was pretty proficient on Excel, thanks to a temp job she'd had just before she fell pregnant with Ruby. Maths had never been her strongest point either, but she could manage a simple formula.

'Really? That would be great. I can clean; you can add up.' Kevin grinned at her.

He was very easy to be around. When he'd let her in that morning, he'd shown her what he needed her to do and then let her get on with it. She never thought that cleaning would be an enjoyable job, but some furious wiping this morning had done wonders for her mood. It was also nice to be on her own without Ruby. How awful was that? She loved her daughter, of course she did, but sometimes motherhood felt relentless.

'Okay. The bar is done. Shall I make a start on the tables and chairs?'

Kevin closed the ledger and pushed it away. 'Good plan. I'll put some music on.' He disappeared behind the bar, crouching down to the CD player. Sara took her cloth out into the main seating area.

Why should she feel bad for enjoying some time away? It wasn't as if Mike felt guilty when he went out without them. It would be good for him to spend some time with Ruby on his own for once; it would force him to actually look after her. Ruby's first six months had been okay. He'd made all the right noises when she was born, had got up in the night with her when she'd cried, changed nappies. Ruby was a fractious baby, and a full night's sleep had been nothing but a rumour, but between the two of them they had coped. It was when Sara went back to work that it got more difficult.

Kevin's voice called out from behind the bar. 'What kind of music do you like?'

Sara kept on wiping. 'Anything, really. I don't have a particular favourite band.'

Kevin stood up and looked at her as if she'd just said she ate small children for breakfast. 'What do you *mean*, you don't have a favourite band? What kind of monster are you?'

Sara laughed. 'I'm just not really a music person. I like it in the background but…'

Kevin leaned on the bar dramatically as if to steady himself. 'Background? *Background*? Music is *life*! Come on, you must have a genre. Rock? Classical? Dance?'

She had to give him something. 'Okay. If you pin me down, I'd probably have to say One-Hit Wonders of the Nineties.'

He held up a finger, 'Chumbawamba it is!' then disappeared downwards.

The lyrics started up. *I get knocked down…*

Kevin stood up. 'What the lady wants…'

Sara laughed. 'I can't believe you actually have this! I haven't heard it in years.'

Kevin's mobile rang. He looked at the number and frowned. 'Sorry, I need to get this.' He pressed to connect. 'Hi.'

Sara moved to a table further away to give him some privacy and rearranged four chairs around it, unable to keep her mind off of how things were going back at Barbara's. Approaching Ruby's second birthday, she and Mike had been back on track for a while. They'd sorted out a decent routine, Mike working for a call centre during the day – amusing himself by practising different regional accents on the callers – and she had a permanent job as an evening receptionist for a budget chain hotel. But then Mike decided to get serious about his acting career and started auditioning again – often during the day when he should have been at work. Eventually he lost that job, and then the next. Her money hadn't covered their outgoings and they'd racked up credit card debts. Also, the more he pursued his acting, the less interest he seemed to have in Ruby. It was like the novelty had worn off of a new toy. And the less he did for Ruby, the more Sara had to do. Until now she had been doing, well, everything.

Kevin was pacing up and down as he spoke on the phone, so it was impossible not to overhear his conversation. 'But you promised. We've had this arranged for two weeks. Mum is looking forward to it.'

Whatever the person said on the other end, it didn't make him happy. 'Look, you've made your decision. It's nearly midday. I need to get ready to open up.'

He scowled as he turned off the phone. 'Do you mind if I change the CD? I'm in the mood for some heavy rock.'

He looked more in the mood to *wield* a heavy rock. 'Fine by me.'

Kevin was quiet for the rest of the morning – in stark contrast to his music choices – until he opened the doors at twelve. Sara's first afternoon shift passed quickly. There weren't many customers, but she kept herself busy reorganising everything behind the bar and setting up a spreadsheet for Kevin on his laptop. When

3.00 p.m. rolled around Sara was ready to go home so she could sit down with a cup of tea.

*

Sara heard the screams before she even got to the end of the path.

When she walked into the lounge, it was bedlam. There was an upturned potty – where had *that* come from? – and toilet paper everywhere. Ruby was sitting to one side, distraught, flapping her hands by her sides like a baby bird whilst Barbara hovered around her, wringing her own hands. And no Mike.

'What happened? What's going on?' Sara bent down to Ruby and tried to pick her up, but Ruby just pushed her away. She was fixated on the potty, eyes wide in terror. Sara could smell urine on her. Where the hell was her nappy?

Barbara started to pace up and down. 'I found Mike's old potty in the loft so I thought we'd make a start on potty training. It's time she started to try. Lisa next door had both hers potty-trained by two.'

Potty training? Who potty-trains someone else's child without their permission? Unless…

'Where is Mike?'

Barbara didn't meet Sara's eyes. 'He… er… he popped out.'

Rage was darting around Sara's body for so many different reasons that she didn't know where to start. What was Mike doing going out and leaving Barbara to look after Ruby? Hadn't they agreed to wait until Ruby was more settled? And potty training? She didn't even know where to begin with that one. More important than any of that was Ruby. Sara needed to calm her down, make her feel better. Where were her blocks? 'Do you know where Ruby's toys are?'

Barbara pointed to a basket under the coffee table. 'I tidied them away.'

Sara pulled the basket out from the table perhaps a bit more roughly than was necessary. She pulled out the blocks and placed them in front of Ruby. 'Look, Ruby. Here are your blocks. The blue ones are here. They're your favourites.' She pushed them closer.

By now Ruby had stopped screaming and she was moaning to herself. Rocking backwards and forwards. Barbara was still wringing her hands and staring at Ruby as if she was a wild animal. Sara really wanted to punch her.

'What exactly happened?'

Barbara's hands fluttered up to her locket. 'I brought the potty out to show her. I wasn't actually going to put her on it, but she seemed really interested. She sat down on it, so I thought it might be worth giving it a go. I took her nappy off and she was still okay. She sat down again and then it happened.'

'What happened?'

'She did a… She went to the… You know, she did a…' Barbara lowered her voice, '… poo.'

For goodness' sake. 'And?'

Barbara started pacing again; she was making Sara feel sick. Or maybe that was the smell of the crap everywhere. 'She seemed terrified of it. She flipped the potty over, she screamed at me, she just, well, this.'

Ruby had a blue block in each of her chubby fists and she was slowly soothing herself. Her eyelids drooped. The force of her upset had tired her out. Sara took the opportunity to put her arms around her and – slowly, slowly – pull her onto her lap. Ruby rested her head on Sara's chest and quietened down.

They heard the front door bang. And Mike's whistle. He walked into the lounge and then stopped in his tracks. 'Whoa! What happened here?'

Sara stood slowly and walked towards and then past him. 'What happened,' she hissed through gritted teeth, 'was that you couldn't look after your own daughter for a measly few hours.'

Mike followed her and stood at the bottom of the stairs, talking to her retreating back. 'I only popped out for a while. Sara, stop walking away. Sara!'

She ignored him and continued to ignore him as he swore under his breath and returned to the lounge. What she wanted to do was pack up her things and leave, taking Ruby with her. But then what? She'd take her daughter where exactly? She was working towards giving Ruby a better life, not a worse one.

Sara placed Ruby gently on her bed and very carefully put a fresh nappy on her. A wave of exhaustion hit Sara and she lay down next to her daughter. Ruby's breathing became more regular as she fell asleep, but there was still an occasional sob. Sara wanted to cry too. Every time she left, something seemed to happen. Was she the only one who knew how to look after Ruby? She could just imagine the conversation downstairs.

There was a gentle knock on the door and Mike put his head in the room. 'Is she okay?'

Sara didn't look at him. 'No thanks to you. Why did you have to go out and leave Ruby with your mother?'

Mike seemed to take her response as permission to come in and perch on the edge of the bed. 'I was only gone for a couple of hours. And she's going to have to get used to my mum at some point, isn't she?'

Sara opened one eye. 'Why?'

'Well, for a start, she's her grandmother. And secondly, when we're both at work, Mum will be looking after her.'

Sara opened her other eye. 'But this is temporary, Mike. We won't be living here forever. We can't rely on – or expect – your mum to look after Ruby.'

'Yeah, yeah. Of course. But we'll be here for a bit and then I've been thinking we might stay nearby. I mean, it makes sense to, doesn't it? With Mum able to babysit if we want to do stuff.'

Sara could admit to herself she had no desire to move back to London. At least, not to the area they'd been living in. But close to Mike's mum? They hadn't discussed that. Why did he want to be near her all of a sudden? Another wave of exhaustion washed over her and Sara closed her eyes. 'Let's talk about that tomorrow.'

She waited for Mike to close the bedroom door behind him before opening her eyes to look at Ruby, laying a hand on her shuddering chest. 'I'm so sorry, baby. You don't have to worry about that stupid potty until you're ready.'

Was three too old to still be in a nappy? The books had been a bit vague about it and, to be honest, it was one of those things that had kind of slipped through the net. Even more reason to find a preschool where they could help Ruby – and Sara – to learn new things. It was clear that Mike couldn't be relied on to look after Ruby when she was at work. And she definitely wasn't going to rely on his mother after today's adventure. She hadn't had a chance to show Mike the preschool Kevin had suggested, but she'd give them a call now. She'd been putting it off because the idea of letting strangers look after her daughter had felt scary. But after today, trained strangers were a much more attractive proposition.

Sara stroked her daughter's hair and pressed her nose into her neck. 'We'll find somewhere you'll love, Ruby. I promise.'

CHAPTER TEN

All around them was a constant shift of sound and movement; everywhere Sara looked, children were running and yelling and singing and skipping. Ruby kept glued to Sara's side as they entered. The walls were painted in bright, primary colours, interspersed with kids' paintings and poster-sized canvases of happy, smiling, active children.

When she'd called BumbleBees Preschool on Friday, she'd explained their situation and had been relieved to hear they had space for Ruby. They'd even suggested she come in as early as that coming Monday to see how Ruby took to the place. Mike had his first full day of rehearsals that day in London so they'd wished each other luck on the way out this morning.

Now Sara was sat in front of the sand and water table, another mum opposite her, the silence between them almost painful.

The woman smiled and nodded at Ruby. 'Is it her first day?'

'Yes, we've, er… we've just moved here. Temporarily. We're looking around, and then this is a sort of introduction session for Ruby. I'm not sure yet how many sessions she will do.' It had been such a relief to find out that Ruby was eligible for thirty free hours of childcare. It would have been barely worth going to work otherwise.

Beneath the chaos there was order: specific toys in specific areas. A book corner where a member of staff was reading aloud to two enraptured boys. A playhouse played host to two kids mid-disagreement as to whether the door should be open or closed. A table strewn with DUPLO blocks in every shape and size. It was overwhelming.

Ruby just stared ahead. At one point, when a boy had run past her shouting after his friend, she had put her hands up to her ears. Sara knew exactly how she felt.

The other mother nodded. She was scooping up sand in a tea strainer and watching it filter through the holes. If Sara weren't so nervous, it would have been humorous: two grown women, playing with sand.

'I'm here on a Home Contact day. They encourage parents to come in once a term and play with their kid.' She pulled a face and laughed.

Well, that sounded positive. Maybe it wouldn't be so bad leaving Ruby here if Sara could stay with her sometimes? The curtain of impending doom she'd felt all morning lifted a little. This was going to be a good thing. She wasn't abandoning her; she was helping her. Sara picked up a small cup filled with sand and offered it to Ruby. 'Look at this, Ruby. Feel it.' Ruby just turned away from her. She had touched the sand when they first got there, but had quickly brushed it off of her fingertips. She didn't like anything sticky on her hands.

Sharon, the preschool manager, had talked through the organisational side of things when they first got there and had then encouraged them to just wander about and get familiar with everything. Ruby hadn't been interested in the books or the dolls or the dressing-up box. Sara had spied some wooden blocks, but she'd managed to avoid Ruby seeing them; if she let her play with those, they would do nothing else but that for the rest of the session. That's when she'd tried the sandpit. It wasn't going well.

Now Sharon was walking towards her with a younger woman in tow. 'Me again. This is Ellie. She'll be Ruby's key worker.'

Ellie held out her hand and Sara shook it. Slim, blonde and young. Sara had been hoping for someone with experience.

Someone who could help Ruby catch up with her speech and her socialising.

'Hi. This is Ruby.'

Ellie crouched down next to Ruby. 'Hello, Ruby. I'm Ellie. Do you like the sand?'

It was as if she hadn't even spoken. Ruby continued to stare at the sand in front of her, almost as if she was waiting for it to start moving.

'It can be a bit overwhelming for them to start with,' Sharon smiled reassuringly. 'Give her a few sessions and she'll be running around with the rest of them.'

Sara really wanted to believe that, but she wasn't convinced. Ellie continued to talk to Ruby, picking up different plastic animals and placing them in front of her. After a minute or so, Ruby frowned and picked one up.

'That's great, Ruby.' Ellie sounded so pleased. 'That's an elephant.'

Ruby ignored her and pushed sand away from the edges of the box to make a clear space for the elephant to stand in. Sara knew what was coming next. She watched as Ruby picked up a giraffe and put him behind the elephant. Then picked up a camel.

Sara wanted to talk to Ellie about her concerns for Ruby, but she didn't want to do it in front of the other mother. She had mentioned to Sharon that Ruby was behind on her speech, but Sharon hadn't seemed overly worried. *We'll keep an eye on her and let you know if we have any concerns.* Watching these other children playing and talking had made Sara feel even worse.

Sara could see the other mother watching Ruby. Appraising her. Did she think there was something wrong with her? Her own son was happily making sandcastles and decorating them with oddments from the tray, chattering away the whole time. Not all of it was intelligible, but his mother seemed to know what he was saying and she answered him and passed him anything he needed. When she made a funny face in the sand, he giggled. A child's infectious giggle. Sara wanted to ask her how old he was, but was afraid to hear the answer.

Milestones. That's what they called them. Those stages that every child is supposed to hit at a certain age. First smile, first tooth, first word. Of course, everyone repeats the mantra, 'Every child is different. They all get there in their own time,' but no one really believes it.

After Sara's first scan when pregnant with Ruby, she'd scoured those library books so often that Mike asked if she was planning to train as a midwife. She'd never been around babies, didn't know what to expect. But she was damn sure going to find out. Every week she consulted the book to find out how big the baby would be, what features could be seen, what parts of the body had been developed. When they went for the second scan, she knew all the right questions to ask the sonographer.

For the first twelve months or so, Ruby had hit all her milestones. Apart from the erratic sleep patterns, she was a textbook baby. It had been so reassuring for Sara to tick each stage off, know that everything was okay, know that she was being a good mother. Ruby had taken a while to walk, but Sara had read some online forums and there were plenty of children who were walking later than average. Ruby had also been quite withdrawn lately, but that was just her shyness and the changes at home. Online research confirmed that communication was the key. If they could just help Ruby's speech development, everything else would fall into place.

Ellie was still chatting away to Ruby, leaning towards her, passing her animals. A couple of times, she picked up plastic tools and encouraged Ruby to play with the sand. She may as well have spoken to the chair for all the reaction she got.

Mike always told Sara she was overreacting. Maybe she was. It was just a bit of delay in Ruby's speech, after all. And Sara had once overheard a conversation at the doctor's about a boy who didn't speak until he was four and then no one could shut him up. There were the tantrums too, though. But doesn't everyone joke about the terrible twos? And one of the girls she worked with at the hotel had said it went on till the Fecking Fours. Ruby was only three. Not much more than a baby. The preschool would help. They were professionals. Now Ruby was here, it would all be okay.

CHAPTER ELEVEN

Dear Lisa,

Well, Sara has found a preschool that will take Ruby from tomorrow. If you ask me, it can't be a good sign that they had spaces available. But no one does ask me, of course.

I had secretly hoped that there would at least be a waiting list, to give me time to show her that I can look after Ruby. But Sara is adamant that she wants someone professional. Professional? How can a young girl be better than me – Ruby's own grandmother? Of course, Sara tried to say it was because she wants Ruby to be with children her own age, but she could play with Olivia and Stanley, couldn't she? I said that, but she rolled her eyes at Michael behind my back, thinking I couldn't see her.

Michael would like me to be more involved in Ruby's upbringing – I know he would. I've heard him tell her, 'Mum can do it'. But she keeps on at him, telling him that he *should look after Ruby more. She needs to be careful, nagging him like that all the time. Men don't put up with that for long. And bringing up a child on your own is not easy. I should know.*

If only I'd had someone on hand to help when Michael was young! Things might have turned out very differently. It's scary when you have a new baby. Surely it's nice to have advice from someone who has been there? And here I am, offering her the benefit of my experience and all my time and she doesn't want to know. I even tried to make a joke of it. 'Michael turned out all right, didn't he?' I said. More eye-rolling was all I got for that.

She might want to keep her eyes on Ruby rather than rolling them at me. If you don't keep an eye on your children at all times, things happen. Things you can't repair. I know that better than anyone.

CHAPTER TWELVE

For many children, preschool is the first time they are away from their family. It can be hard for the child to make that break. It can be hard for their mothers too. From that moment on Monday, when the preschool confirmed that Ruby could start on the Wednesday, Sara's stomach had been tumbling with apprehension. And now the day was here. And they were running late.

Mike had had a late night in rehearsal and had stayed over in town so he wasn't there to help.

Sara tried to prepare Ruby for what was happening. It was always best not to spring things on her. 'We're going back to the preschool today, Rubes.'

She was brushing Ruby's hair. Long, rhythmic strokes. It was something Ruby enjoyed. Actually, it was something they both enjoyed. Ruby had her eyes closed and her hands on her knees. It was one of the times she was most calm. She mumbled to herself. 'Where you, Nemo?'

'You'll get to meet lots of other girls and boys and be able to play with them.' Sara hoped desperately that this was true. *Please let them play with her.*

Ruby's eyes stayed closed. 'Nemo?'

'Do you remember all the toys we saw there? All the big toys, the sandpit and kitchens and building blocks? You liked the big building blocks. Do you remember?'

Who was Sara trying to persuade here? This was going to be a good thing for Ruby. There was no need to feel guilty about it. Or sick. These people were professionals. They would be able to help Ruby. Once her speech caught up, she would probably find it a lot easier to play with the other children and if she could communicate what she wanted, she would get less upset about things. Sara had repeated this to herself so many times that she was almost starting to believe it. Almost.

Ruby decided her hair had been brushed enough, got up, walked to the basket of toys and pulled out her wooden blocks. She put the first two down on the floor and made sure they were straight. *Dammit.* That was Sara's fault for mentioning the building blocks. She'd hoped to get out the door before the blocks came out. Getting Ruby away from them now would be tricky.

Sure enough, Ruby did not take it well when it was time to leave. The extrication process wasn't helped by Barbara hovering at the lounge door.

'Why don't you leave it today? There's no rush for her to start, is there? If you want to go out and about you can always leave her with me.'

'Out and about' made it sound like Sara wanted to go on a shopping trip or lunch with friends. 'I'm sure she'll be fine when she gets there.' But she wasn't.

When they finally got to the preschool, they were fifteen minutes late and the gates to the parent entrance at the back were already closed. Ellie, Ruby's key worker, met them at the front door with a smile and was very kind. 'It'll be better actually because now I can give Ruby my full attention.'

For once, Ruby didn't want to get out of her buggy when Sara unbuckled it. She'd have to lift her out. But when Sara tried to put her down again, Ruby clung on like a limpet, fingers entwined in Sara's hair and her legs clamped around Sara's waist like a vice.

'Come on, Ruby, we're going to have some fun!' Ellie looked even younger today than last week, but she had a lovely calm manner. Leaning around Ruby, she lowered her voice. 'You can stay today if you like, but it's usually easier to just leave. It's the leaving part that the children find most difficult. She'll be fine once you've gone and she's playing with the toys.' Now Ellie turned back to Ruby. 'We've got lots of coloured blocks, Ruby. Mummy said you like playing with coloured blocks.'

Why hadn't they said she'd be allowed to stay again? It was impossible to wait now, because she'd promised Kevin that she'd definitely be on time today; he had the accountant coming and was super proud to show off the shiny spreadsheet she'd made for him. There was no choice. She had to leave now. Again, she leaned down and tried to make Ruby stand.

If anything, Ruby clung tighter and she pushed her face into Sara's neck. 'No. No.'

Sara swallowed hard. Her throat was tight and the backs of her eyes were beginning to burn. God, this was unbelievably difficult. Ruby's body was pressed so tightly against her she could barely breathe. A sudden memory of Ruby's birth, her naked little body against Sara's chest, skin against skin, heart against heart, the overwhelming knowledge that this tiny creature was of her and from her and part of her forever. She hadn't wanted the nurse to take her then and she didn't want Ellie to take her now. Ruby was scared and she was scared. It was too soon. They weren't ready.

Ellie took a step forward and placed a gentle hand on Ruby's back. She lowered her voice again. 'Do you want me to just take her from you?'

Take her? Was there a choice? She had to get to work, but, *take her*? There was no way she could say those words aloud, but there was nothing else for it. One tiny nod of her head and Ellie put her hands firmly under Ruby's armpits to pull her away. But Ruby was strong and Ellie, with her size six frame, was no match. Sara tried to help, but that would involve actually pushing Ruby away and she couldn't do it. Just couldn't do it. Eventually, Ellie called to a colleague to come and help. An older lady came over and gently uncoiled Ruby's legs from around Sara's waist. Now it was just her fingers that needed untangling from Sara's hair.

The pulling on her hair was painful, but it wasn't the pain that made the tears come. This felt wrong. So wrong. She was letting strangers take her baby from her. People she'd only just met. Ruby was distraught. Traumatised. It was all right for Ellie to say that this was normal, but it was awful. Two more late mothers were dropping off their children and they were openly staring at Ruby and Sara. Like they were some kind of freak show. She wanted to scream at them to look away. Why wouldn't they just go?

Why in heaven's name hadn't she just taken the morning off work? She was so stupid. She could have taken Ruby home and tried again another day. Any day but today. *Picture her in a few months, chatting and playing with the others. Be strong for her. Be strong.*

Finally, Sara was free and Ellie turned around and moved Ruby's hand into a wave. 'Say, "Bye, bye, Mummy! See you in a few hours."' And she turned and took Ruby away, leaving Sara's stomach to lurch as if they were still attached by an invisible cord.

Over her shoulder, Ruby reached out for Sara. 'Where Nemo?'

Sara couldn't do this. It was too hard. She took a step after them, but was stopped by the older lady placing a gentle hand on her arm. 'It'll be easier for her if you just go. Honestly.'

Sara could barely see her way to the door through her tears. The other mothers – with their perfectly calm offspring – were still looking at her, but she didn't care. It felt like she was giving Ruby away. Like she didn't love her or want her. It was as if someone had just ripped out her heart and she was leaving it behind.

At the door, one of the other mums approached her. 'Hi, I'm Jo. Are you okay? Do you want to go for a coffee?'

Go for a coffee? This Jo woman was probably trying to be nice but did she really think Sara would abandon her daughter in this way if she was just going to pop out for a coffee? 'No, thanks. I need to go to work. Thank you, but I'm fine.'

*

Sara was ten minutes late for work, but Kevin didn't comment. He also didn't comment on the fact that her face looked as if it had been for a spin around the washing machine and then taken out early. 'How did it go?'

Sara took a deep breath. Actually, she didn't want to talk about it. Didn't want to tell Kevin how awful it was leaving Ruby with strangers. How she wanted with every inch of her body to run back there and snatch her child up and run away. Right now, she wanted to block it out of her mind for a few hours and take it out on the beer rings on the counter and the stubborn marks on the floor.

'It was fine.'

'Good. Look, I'll only be in the back for an hour or so with the accountant and then I'll come out and give you a hand. Do you want a coffee before he gets here?'

Sara thought of the mum who had offered her a coffee back at the preschool, who had only been trying to be nice. This was why Sara had no friends; she wasn't able to talk to people like a normal person did. 'You go and get yourself set up in the office. I can make my own coffee.'

Despite rubbing the counter hard enough to almost set it on fire, it was impossible to stop her mind from wandering to Ruby. What would she be doing right now? Would she be playing with the blocks? Dare Sara hope that she might have made a friend? What if she was all alone? Still crying? What if she was reaching out for Sara, calling for her, needing her? How was this going to affect Ruby, thinking that her mother had just abandoned her? Tears splashed onto the counter, diluting the polish.

Kevin was true to his word and was only the hour he said he'd be with the accountant. When he joined her back in the bar, he brought out another coffee and placed it on the plastic drip tray.

'Do you want to talk about why you're so upset or are you just really angry with my tables?'

Sara picked up the mug and leaned against the bar. 'I'm just thinking about my little girl. First days are always hard.' Ellie had kindly called thirty minutes ago to reassure her that they'd managed to calm Ruby down in the sensory room and that she was now playing with her blocks quietly. It meant Sara could actually breathe, but she wouldn't be happy until she'd seen her and held her again.

Kevin sipped at his coffee. It was in a huge mug with the name of the brewery stamped on the side. Wearing a navy suit to meet with his accountant, he looked out of place somehow. 'According to my mum, I cried every morning until Christmas when I started school. Sensitive soul, me. How old is your little girl? Ruby, isn't it?'

Sara had both her hands wrapped around her coffee mug and she stared in at the treacle-coloured liquid. She should have made the coffee herself. 'Yes, Ruby. She's only three.' Her chin wobbled. 'It feels too young.'

Kevin reached into his suit pocket and brought out a packet of digestives, laying them on the bar. 'I've got a son. Callum. He's six.'

Sara looked up. She couldn't really imagine Kevin as a dad. And he lived above the pub, so where was he hiding a child? 'Really? Is he with your…' *Wife? Girlfriend? Partner?*

'He's with his mum. We're not together. I don't see that much of him.' He sipped at his coffee, not meeting her eye.

Sara put her mug down and picked up the cloth again, moving across to start on the tables. Kevin had seemed such a nice bloke. But what sort of man walked out on his family? 'That's a shame. For your son, I mean.'

Kevin scratched a welded piece of crisp from a table with his thumbnail. 'Yeah, it is. His mum, she's… Well, it's difficult.'

Wasn't this always the mantra of men like this? *It's not me, it's her.*

'Difficult? In what way?'

Kevin kept scratching at the crisp and didn't look up. 'She's got someone else; they've been together for a while. Since before we split up, actually.'

That was not what Sara had expected to hear. 'I'm sorry. That must have been tough.'

He still didn't look at her. 'Yeah. Not great. Anyway, he's pretty much taken Callum on as his own. They always have plans at the weekends and it's tricky for me during the week with this place, so… it's just difficult.'

That's what could happen when parents weren't together: the dad just drifting out of the picture. Her own included. Ruby was never going to wonder where her dad was, though, because Sara was going to bend over backwards to make sure he was there for her. Kevin was her boss, but she wanted to shake him. Who gave up that easily on their own child?

'But you're his dad. I'm sure he wants to see you. And don't you want to spend time with your son?'

Kevin sidestepped around the tables, slotting chairs into place. 'That's what my mum says. She goes up the wall about it. Wants to see her grandson. I just don't want to make it difficult for Kelly. That's my ex-wife. She's a good mum, and she's doing all the hard work of parenting. And he's a great kid, which is down to her. But I'm working on it.'

Working on it? This was his son. 'You need to get a move on. If he's six, he's going to remember that you weren't around.' Sara pictured Ruby's distraught face as she left her this morning. Her hand reaching out for Sara. Would she remember that?

Kevin leaned on the back of one of the chairs. 'I know. I do see him. Just not as often as I should. When we first broke up last January, I was at my mum's and he used to come over some weekends. But since I took on this place six months ago, I've been living upstairs and Kelly doesn't want him coming here.'

Sara could understand not wanting to bring a child into a pub, but if his dad was living here? This defeatist attitude was irritating in the extreme. He needed to step up and be a proper father. 'Well, you're the only person who can sort that out. Take him to your mum's. Take him away for the weekend. Just make sure you see him. And it needs to be regular. Kids need to know where they are.'

For God's sake, she was sounding like Barbara. *Stop speaking to your boss like that, crazy woman.* It was almost laughable, her dishing out parenting and relationship advice. It wasn't Kevin she should be speaking to like this.

But he took it well, gave her a mock salute, then smiled. 'I know you're right. I will. I'll speak to her.' He pulled a mobile from his pocket. 'In fact, I'll call her right now.'

As he left, Sara checked her own mobile. No call from the preschool must be a good sign? Another hour and she could collect Ruby. How had her day gone? *Please let her be okay.*

CHAPTER THIRTEEN

BumbleBees was only four streets away from the pub. Sara had to prevent herself from running all the way there at 3.00 p.m.

Although Kevin had let her leave work a little early, there were already a couple of other mothers waiting when she arrived. One of them had a baby in a pram and the other was pregnant. Maybe it was easier to be away from your child if you had another one to cuddle.

Parents had to queue along the side of the building, next to a large window with blue vertical blinds, hand-painted with clouds and rainbows. One of the slats was bent or broken leaving a chink exposed. Sara shuffled closer and peeked in. Where was Ruby?

Inside was a hive of activity, children buzzing around laughing and chasing one another. Mismatched fancy dress meant that a Spiderman princess was chasing a spanner-wielding Little Red Riding Hood. But where was Ruby?

Another table seemed to be full of something that looked like shaving foam. Children were pushing their fingers into it and pulling them out, rubbing their palms together. A small boy in a pair of red shorts started to rub it into his hair before one of the preschool teachers spotted him and wiped him over with a cloth. Ruby wasn't there either.

Eventually, Sara spotted her, off to the side, sitting on the floor with a few plastic animals in front of her. They must be very English-minded kangaroos and elephants and giraffes because they were in a queue. Obviously.

The noise around Ruby wasn't affecting her one bit. She was fully focused on what she was doing. Goldilocks and Batman chased past and she didn't even look up, much less react or try to join in. A little boy holding dinosaurs came to sit next to Ruby, adding a dinosaur to the end of her line.

Sara held her breath. What would Ruby do? Without looking at the boy, Ruby picked up the dinosaur and threw it away. If Sara hadn't been so desperate to see her playing with another child it would have been comical.

Another wave of guilt about not taking Ruby to any of those groups when she was a baby. It had been so difficult to get out in the morning after her late stint at the hotel. She should have made more effort; found a group they could go to.

The boy wasn't giving up. He took a few moments to select another dinosaur from his collection and placed that down instead. Sara wanted to kiss him. Thank you for trying. She stared at Ruby, willing her to play with him. *Come on, Ruby. Just give it a chance. Play with him.*

But Ruby just swept the second dinosaur away with her hand and then she pushed the little boy. Ellie appeared and bent down next to her. Then the side gate opened and the parents were being called in.

Some of the mothers were walking interminably slowly and Sara had to squeeze her hands into fists to prevent herself pushing them out of the way. Ellie was knelt next to Ruby, holding her little coat. Just behind Ellie was the mother – Jo? – who had invited Sara for a coffee earlier. Sara should apologise, but right now all she wanted to do was reach down to pick up Ruby so she could hold her tight and breathe her in. It was so good to have her back.

But Ruby didn't seem desperate to see Sara. Was she angry with her? Or was it a good sign? She took Ruby's coat from Ellie. 'So, she settled okay after I left? Thank you for calling me.'

Ellie smiled down at Ruby. 'Yes, we had a lovely time in the sensory room, didn't we Ruby?'

Ruby turned her head and buried it into Sara's thigh. Sara placed a hand on her head and stroked it. 'How was she with the other children? Did she talk at all to them? Did she play with anyone?'

Ellie folded her arms, her head to one side. 'I think today was more about her settling in and getting to know her new surroundings, really. She did great.'

Now Sara felt like a tiger mother, pushing her child's progress. All she wanted to know was that Ruby was happy and the other kids had accepted her. 'But did she play with the other kids?'

Ruby had started to butt her head against Sara's thigh; she wanted to leave. But Sara really needed to know whether the preschool was a good idea. If they couldn't help, it was ludicrous to put them both through this every time. But her enquiries were fruitless. All she got from Ellie was a generic-sounding response. 'It's normal for children to sometimes just play alongside each other at this stage. Playing together will come.'

But Sara had seen from the window that Ruby wasn't even playing alongside that little boy. She clearly wanted nothing to do with him. 'What about talking? Did she talk at all?'

Ellie frowned. 'Not a great deal. Is she normally quiet with new people?'

Sara knew what Ellie was going to say. *She's just shy. She's a quieter child.* Mike had said them all. 'She used to talk, but she seems to have stopped.'

Sara's hand hovered over her pocket. Should she get her mobile out and prove it? Show Ellie the videos of her happy, smiling baby, wriggling on her play mat, softly mouthing, 'Mama, Mama, Mama'? Her throat constricted. She had said it. She *had*.

Ellie glanced down at Ruby. 'Some children are more introverted. They just take time. It doesn't mean they are behind their peers, just that they need to think things through, take it all in, before they act.'

Sara crouched down and dipped her face this way and that, trying to make eye contact with Ruby. 'Are you taking it all in, Rube?'

Ruby stared ahead at the wall of photographs in front of them. Photographs of children playing together, interacting with each other. What was she thinking as she looked at them? Was she desperate to join in but couldn't make the move? Was she just anxious? And did she get that from Sara?

Now Ruby started to pull at Sara's hand. It was definitely time to go. Sara stood up again and smiled at Ellie. 'Is there anything I can do at home to help her?'

'Just keep talking to her all the time. Not asking questions, just chatting so she can hear your voice. And when you do speak to her, use short, clear sentences.'

Rocket science, this was not. 'Short sentences. Keep talking to her. Anything else?'

'Routines are important. All children feel safe with routines. And give her time if anything is about to change, like she has to stop playing with her toys or you want to go out or bedtime is coming. Warn her beforehand that you are going to do it.'

All of that sounded achievable and most of it Sara was doing already. But maybe Ellie was right; maybe Ruby just needed time to adjust. She had had a lot of change in her little life already. A lot of coming and going.

On the way home from the preschool, Sara kept up a running commentary.

'Look at that pretty flower… I can hear a bird… What a pretty song.'

Ellie had said to just keep talking to her without expecting a response. Which was probably for the best, as she wasn't getting one.

Mike had got cross with her again the night before, saying she was looking for 'excuses' for Ruby. He thought they should stop giving in to her so much. She would bet her favourite paintbrush she knew where that idea had come from. Maybe they did need different rules now she was getting older, but Sara couldn't shake off the feeling that there was something more, something they were missing. If she was honest, she had been hoping that the preschool would be able to tell her what it was and how to fix it. But it was possible that everyone was right and Ruby just needed more time. She took a deep breath and let it out slowly. Her head was a tangle of thoughts. It was exhausting.

'I think we've both earned a treat on our first day, haven't we Ruby? Maybe some sweets for you and some new pencils for me.'

A trip to the High Street would delay their return to Barbara's and give her an excuse to visit the gallery again. There was something about that place which she hadn't been able to get out of her mind.

CHAPTER FOURTEEN

Taking a tired child into a noisy supermarket was not a good idea. Doing it after her first day at preschool was an even worse one. Sara nearly gave up on the idea of going to the gallery to buy pencils because Ruby was being an absolute nightmare.

It started when she refused to sit in the seat at the front of the trolley. The Tesco Metro had kindly provided a buggy park so parents could use a trolley, which *should* have been easier than navigating the aisles guiding the buggy one-handed with a basket slung over your other arm. But Ruby just kicked her feet every time Sara tried to thread them through the leg holes until Sara gave in and sat her in the main part of the trolley instead. There wasn't much to get anyway. It would be fine.

It wasn't. Sara threw a multipack of Mike's favourite crisps into the trolley and Ruby leaned on them and exploded the whole lot. It made such a loud bang that an old lady standing in front of the cheese biscuits further up the aisle jumped and put her hand to her heart. Sara made a swift exit past her, apologising profusely as the old lady shook her head and Ruby threw Quavers from the trolley like confetti. In a different life, Sara might have laughed. Today she wanted to cry.

Then there was the cereal aisle. Maybe she could distract Ruby with the packaging. 'Which cereal shall we try, Ruby? The one with the monkey? Or the tiger?' As she picked them up, Sara looked at the ingredients to see which ones had the least sugar or additives. Not that Ruby was likely to actually eat anything other than Weetabix but she had to try.

In the few seconds that she was reading the box, Ruby stood up in the trolley, reached out and cleared a whole shelf of Oat So Simple with one swish of her arm. Less than two steps away, two women with prams watched as Sara tried to keep Ruby in the trolley with one hand and pick up the cereal boxes with the other. It was impossible. As fast as she was picking them up, Ruby was grabbing them and throwing them back. In the end, Sara just walked away under their disapproving glances. What the hell did they want her to do? How about some bloody help?

Somehow, they had made it out of the supermarket, but Ruby was now screaming and straining at the straps on her buggy to be released. All Sara wanted was to get home, away from the staring strangers and judgemental mutterings. But she wasn't going home. She was going back to Barbara's, with the prospect of a whole evening of more raised eyebrows and knowing looks ahead of her. Sara turned back towards the gallery to get the pencils. She would be in and out.

There was room for the buggy at the bottom of the staircase, just inside the front door. Ruby leaped from it as soon as the straps were undone and started to clamber up the stairs. Thankfully, she couldn't open the door on her own, so Sara managed to clamp on to Ruby's hand before pushing hard like last time.

The old man was sitting in the same place as he had been the other day, completing a puzzle in a newspaper. He looked up at the tempest breaking in through his front door. Sara attempted to drag Ruby over to the desk, but somehow Ruby twisted her hand free from Sara's grip and started to run around the gallery.

Sara felt sick. There was no way she could afford to replace any art that Ruby knocked from the walls.

'Ruby! Stop!'

Sara made a grab for her as she ran past, but Ruby swerved and kept going. She should have known this was going to happen. Why had she risked it? Running after her, Sara called back at the old man, 'I'm so sorry. She's just overtired. I just came in to buy some pencils.'

But he was laughing. 'She doesn't look very tired to me. It's fine. The most excitement I've had in here all week. Leave her. She'll probably stop running if you stop chasing her.'

Leave her? Was he insane? Did he have any idea how much damage a three-year-old could do in less time than it took to go to the toilet on your own? Suddenly, Ruby stopped in front of a Warhol-esque canvas: four prints of the same cow in red, yellow, blue and green. She was mesmerised. It was the perfect opportunity to make a grab for her hand, but Ruby managed to pull it away again.

'No!'

'Let her look, honestly. It's nice to have someone in who enjoys the art.'

Sara appreciated the sentiment, but really didn't think he knew the implications of what he was saying. 'I can't afford to pay for anything she damages.'

The man shrugged. 'I won't make you.' He opened a drawer in his desk and brought out a sketchpad and some pencils. 'Does she like to draw?'

'Oh thanks, but, no, she…'

Sara watched in amazement as Ruby made her out to be a liar by taking the pad from the man's hands. She sat on the floor and began to flick through the pages. He got up from his desk and laid the pencils beside her. Ruby didn't look up as she reached a hand out for a pencil and began to move it across the page. He must think Ruby was so rude.

'Sorry. We're working on "pleases" and "thank yous".'

He waved his hand to show he didn't care. 'When the muse is strong, you have to get to work immediately.' He returned to his desk and picked up his newspaper, frowning at the puzzle page. 'You can look in peace now.'

Sara's throat tightened and tears pricked the back of her eyes. Did he know how much this meant to her? This simple act of kindness? This moment of calm he had gifted her? Less than fifteen minutes ago she had felt a tightness in every muscle in her body. And now? Now she could breathe.

Ruby was completely absorbed by the motion of the pencil across the page. Was it the line or the soft sweeping sound? Who cared? It was keeping her quiet. Slowly, carefully, Sara moved away from her. Ruby didn't react. Sara could have another look at the nudes she'd seen last time. Something drew her towards them. How wonderful would it be to own something like that? To be able to look at it every day. It would be out of her budget. Cost nothing to ask, though.

'Excuse me. How much are these sketches?'

The man looked up and frowned. 'Sorry. Those ones aren't for sale.'

Not for sale? Then why were they on the wall? And it didn't look as if he could afford to be turning away custom. He'd returned to his paper and Sara didn't want to push it, especially as he'd been so kind to Ruby. She pulled her eyes away from them and continued to walk slowly around the gallery.

Although the walls were less than smooth, it was a beautiful room. It must have covered most of the top floor of the building, although there was a door ajar in the corner apparently leading to a kitchen and another that was marked as being a toilet. How lucky he was to spend every day here. In perfect peace.

He looked up as she was paused in front of a shelf of art materials. 'Do you paint?'

Sara could feel the warmth in her cheeks. 'A little. Mainly I sketch. Pencil drawings. Though nothing as good as those.' She nodded back at the nudes.

He smiled as he looked at them. 'Yes. They are rather unique.' He nodded at Ruby. 'Looks like you might have another artist in the family.'

Ruby was still moving the pencil across the page, now in swirling movements. Sara was amazed. She had never shown a huge amount of interest in drawing before, although she had only given her chunky children's crayons before. And cheap paper. The man had given her proper textured paper and what looked like a soft 2B pencil. Clearly her girl had standards.

Ruby's fringe was getting long, it fell down in front of her face and cast a feathery shadow across her cheeks. Her face was beginning to lose the softness of babyhood, her nose was a little sharper, her chin more defined. Sara wiggled her fingers; they wanted to pick up a pencil and draw her beautiful daughter. But she was too self-conscious to ask for a piece of paper for herself and she knew better than to take one from Ruby's pad.

Instead she turned back to speak to the gallery owner. 'Thank you. She's really enjoying that. She's… Ruby, she's…' What should she say? How could she describe it to him?

He turned his head to one side. 'She's rather unique, too?'

Sara's eyes filled and she bit her lip as she turned back to her daughter. 'Yes. She's rather unique too.'

He turned back to watch Ruby draw. 'Well, Ruby, I'm Leonard. And you and your mummy are welcome here any time you like.'

He reached into his desk and pulled out another sketch pad and pencil and offered it to Sara. She could have hugged him. Settling onto the floor, a few feet from Ruby, she started to draw. With every pencil stroke, the muscles in her shoulders began to loosen. For a while, she could lay down her worry, and just breathe. The worry would be there waiting for her to pick it up again in a short while, though. Then she would need to go back to Mike and ask him to help. Because she couldn't do this alone.

CHAPTER FIFTEEN

Dinner time on Friday was remarkably painless, because Barbara was having dinner with Lisa – Grant was away for the night – so she wasn't home to see Ruby reject every single coloured vegetable on her plate and eat only the breaded chicken and four frozen chips.

Mike was on good form, though. That afternoon they'd had a first full run through of the play. It must have gone well because he'd come home with a bottle of red wine to celebrate. After dinner, when Sara started to clear away, he put his hand over hers. 'Leave them for a few minutes. Let's sit in the lounge with Ruby. Make the most of our family time while Mum is out.'

Sara sipped her drink. She rarely drank wine; it was too strong for her. If she drank anything, it was a beer or – more often these days – shandy.

'Wouldn't it be lovely to have this every night, Mike? Just the three of us like this?'

Mike laughed. 'What are you suggesting we do? Bump off my mother and keep the house?'

Sara dug him in the ribs. 'Don't be awful. No, I mean when we get our own place.'

Mike took a deep breath. 'Can we leave off talking about that tonight? This is the nicest evening we've had in a while, Sarz. Don't spoil it.'

His words stung. She wasn't trying to spoil anything. She was trying to work out how they could have this all the time. This was what she wanted more than anything. Ruby was content, too – surely that was because she and Mike were relaxed and happy?

The last two nights, Mike had got in after Sara had collapsed exhausted into bed. So, other than a short text on Wednesday, they hadn't had a conversation about Ruby's first days at the preschool. Sara hadn't hung around at Friday pickup because Mike was getting home early and she wanted to pick something nice up for dinner. Still, the difference between Ruby and the other children had been etched on the insides of her eyelids; she needed to talk to him about it. 'Ruby's keyworker is really nice. She's given me some ideas of things to do at home to help her speech.'

'That's great. Do you feel better now?'

Did she feel *better*? What did he mean? 'Well, it's a start. I still think we might need to get some specialist help. I've been looking online. There are speech and language therapists who make really great progress with kids who have speech delay.' Sara had googled so many different sites about speech that she was getting to know all the jargon. 'I'm not sure if the preschool can refer us or if we have to go to a doctor.'

'A doctor? Bloody hell, Sara. Don't you think you're taking this a bit too far?'

Here we go again. 'She's not speaking, Mike.'

He shook his head. 'She's only just three. Kids all do things at different times. My mum was saying that just the other day.'

Take a deep breath. 'I know that. But look at Lisa's little girl. How much she was speaking. And she's younger than Ruby.'

Mike shrugged and slid his arm away from her shoulders. 'That doesn't mean anything. She's probably advanced.'

He wasn't there. He hadn't seen the difference. 'And at the preschool this week. All the other children were playing and running around and chatting and laughing.'

'For God's sake. It was her first week. Give her a break. To be honest, we've been wondering if…' He trailed off and scratched at his new beard.

We? 'Who's we? Wondering what?'

Mike turned in his seat so that he was facing her. 'I mean *me*. *I've* been wondering. Look, don't take this the wrong way, but I'm starting to think you're making more of this than there needs to be. You're becoming a bit… obsessed with it.' He held his hands up. 'I'm just saying.'

Obsessed? *Obsessed*? She couldn't even look at him. He hadn't been there Wednesday or today. He wasn't the one who had to go to work feeling as if he'd been turned inside out. He wasn't the one who… *Oh, what's the point*?

She slid down onto the carpet and tried to take Ruby's hand. Ruby just frowned and pulled it away. 'Can Mummy play, Ruby?'

Mike groaned. 'See? This is what I mean. You're always on at her. Why don't you just leave her alone while she's quiet? Come and sit back up here with me. Maybe I phrased it wrong. Let's not talk about this now when we're both tired.'

Absolutely typical. Open up a can of worms and then sit back and leave her to deal with them all. How could they start talking about this and then go back to cuddling on the sofa? *Don't argue in front of Ruby. Swallow it down.*

'I'm just playing with my daughter.'

'For a start, she's *our* daughter. And, no, you're not. You're testing her. Leave her to do what she wants to do. Come up here and have a cuddle. That's what I want to do. It was nice talking together before we started on this.'

Why couldn't he understand? Wasn't it obvious that something wasn't right? That Ruby needed help? It *was* nice being together, but it wasn't about them right now. It was about Ruby. Sara's whole life had changed. She had to work a job she never wanted and live in a house where she didn't feel welcome, but if that's what it took, she would do it. What had changed for him? He wasn't working towards their future; he was thinking of his acting career. Months of supressed rage bubbled in her stomach. *Just focus on Ruby.* 'Can Mummy play?'

No response. Try a different tack. Sara picked up the blue block. Ruby watched her.

'This is the blue block, Ruby. Do you remember? You used to say blue. Blue block. Can you say blue?' Ruby reached out for the block and Sara held it just out of her reach. 'Say it for Mummy, Ruby. Blue. *Blue*.' Maybe it was the reminder of perfect Lisa next door. Maybe it was seeing the other kids running around together in their dress-up clothes at preschool. But she needed to start working with Ruby. She clearly needed help to catch up and Sara was going to do her damnedest to give her that. 'Come on, Ruby. Blue. Block. You know this! It's blue! It's the blue one!'

Mike leaned forwards and put a hand on her shoulder. 'Sara! What's got into you? You're acting crazy! Leave her alone.'

Sara felt a roar begin in the pit of her stomach, trying to climb her throat and out of her mouth. *Breathe. Just breathe*. 'I can't leave her alone, Mike. She needs our help. Why won't you see it?' Hot tears spilled down her face. Damn them.

Mike stood and began to pace, gesticulating as he spoke, dramatic as always. 'What do you want from me? I don't know what you expect me to do.'

Stay calm. 'I want you to take an interest in helping your daughter. I want you to listen when I tell you my concerns. I want your help.'

Mike clenched and unclenched his hands. He closed his eyes. 'For God's sake, Sara. I didn't sign up for all this.'

Sara felt a cold trickle down her back. This was feeling familiar. This sounded like last summer. This was what she had been working so hard to avoid. 'All what? What do you mean?'

His answer was so predictable. 'Nothing. It doesn't matter.'

Again. Not talking about it. Like last time.

Don't raise your voice. Remember Ruby. 'Of course it matters. You can't say that and then clam up.'

Mike sat back down but was still waving his hands around. 'This *drama*. This hassle. Normal people don't have all this hassle just because they've got a kid. Why is it always like this with you? I know you didn't have a good example, but…'

Sara put her wine glass down on the table and stood up. She was trying so hard not to fight, but he was pressing every single bruise she had. 'Don't you dare bring that into it. That's always your go-to. Your mum was clearly a frigging saint and that hasn't done much to sort you out, has it?'

'This is so typical of you, Sara. You started this and now you are lashing out at me and slagging off my mum.' He picked up his glass.

She wanted to pour the contents over his head. How did he manage to twist her words so quickly? It was okay for *him* to make comments about her mum, and even to make comments about his own, but she was not allowed? Enough was enough. Any longer and she'd say something that couldn't be taken back. 'I need some air. I'm going for a walk.'

Mike laughed sarcastically. 'Great idea. Perfect timing too. You go out and I'm the one that has to try and get Ruby to bed. Well played, Sara. You know how difficult that is.'

Now she wanted to pour the rest of the bottle over his head. How dare he! She was the one who always put Ruby to bed. Every. Single. Night. In the early days, they used to take it in turns, but these days Ruby always wanted Sara and it had become a routine they hadn't been able to break. She hadn't had the energy to break it; it was easier to put her to bed than to listen to her cry when Mike did it. And he'd never put up much resistance, spending the evenings watching crime dramas on TV while Sara sang 'Twinkle, Twinkle, Little Star' over and over and over again. Just once, let him put his own daughter to bed.

Without speaking, Sara stood and walked to the hallway where her jacket was hanging. When she opened the front door, Barbara was standing there with her key, about to put it in the lock.

Since they'd arrived in Barbara's house, Sara had kept her lips buttoned, not reacted, not commented in front of Barbara. But right now she was raw and uncontrolled. 'Perfect timing. Your son is probably just about to ask you to put your granddaughter to bed. After which, if you could read him a bedtime story and tuck him in, I'm sure he wouldn't say no.'

Barbara's eyes widened, but Sara didn't stop to explain or to hear her reply. She stalked past and into the street. It wasn't until she got outside that she realised that she had no clue whatsoever where she was going to go.

CHAPTER SIXTEEN

With nowhere else to go, Sara ended up back at the pub.

There was only so much wandering about she could do, especially since she shoved her feet into a pair of boots without socks. Sara had been striding so fast at first that she barely noticed it, but now there was a definite blister coming up on her right heel. Great.

As she approached the pub, her pace slowed. Was it a good idea coming here? Working in the pub was one thing, but as a customer? One of the regulars, Sid, pushed open the door and stood outside to light a pipe. Swaying slightly as he held a match to the tobacco – looking like a figure from a Hogarth painting – he shook his hand to extinguish the flame and glanced up in her direction.

'Hello, love. You got an extra shift tonight?'

She shook her head. 'Not tonight. Just having a walk.'

'That's a shame. Kev's run off his feet in there. Alan rang in sick, apparently. Don't let him see you or he'll have you behind that bar.' He held the door open for her.

She ducked under Sid's arm to go in. A shift behind a busy bar might be just what she needed right now. No time to think – of the past or the future.

Sid hadn't been wrong about the bar. It was normally quiet in the afternoons when she worked, so it was unusual for Sara to see it so full on a busy Friday night. Kevin caught her eye as he posted change into the top pocket of a young guy who was trying to juggle three pints of beer.

Kevin frowned. 'Did we get our wires crossed? You're not due in tonight.'

Lifting up the flap, she slipped behind the bar. 'I heard you needed help.' She mimed a Superwoman pose then turned to face the customers. 'Who's next, please?'

The next few hours were busy enough that Sara didn't have time to consider what was going on at home. Or to answer the phone, which kept vibrating against her hip. It could only be Mike and she wasn't ready to hear the apologies or the remonstrances or the complaints about putting Ruby to bed. It was about time he pulled his weight. Of course, there was a distinct possibility that he had left Barbara to sort out Ruby, but she couldn't think about that right now. Every time his face came up in her mind, she felt another wave of anger. *I'm too young to be dealing with all this. What a complete tosser.*

Before Sara knew it, Kevin was ringing the bell for last orders and then calling time. Once he'd locked the door behind the last customer, Kevin returned to the bar where she was stacking the last few glasses into the washer.

'That was a result, you turning up when you did. I don't know what I would have done. Sid might have started a riot.'

Sara grinned at the idea of eighty-seven-year-old Sid starting anything. It took him twenty minutes to make it to the bar from the front door. 'You're welcome. It was just what I needed tonight.'

Kevin put a bottle of wine down on one of the tables and motioned for her to come and sit down. 'On the house, to thank you for saving me.'

Sara's feet ached. It would be good to sit down for ten minutes. She'd already had one glass at home, and it wasn't usual for her to have more than one, but she'd been here a couple of hours so a small one wouldn't hurt. She was in no rush to go home to Mike and Barbara who had probably crowned her the worst mother in the world by now.

'Okay. Just one. I had no idea how busy it gets on a Friday night.'

Kevin smiled proudly as he poured her a drink. 'It's been picking up each week. Tonight was particularly busy, which is why I got caught out on the staffing. Good job Superwoman was on hand.'

Sara picked up her glass and chinked it against his. 'You're welcome. How come someone your age is running a pub like this full of old men? Wouldn't you prefer some trendy bar in town?'

Kevin sat back in his seat, rubbed at his eyes with his free hand. He looked as tired as she felt. 'This is the first time I've run a pub, actually. I used to be a manager for a couple of bands. Great job, but it takes over your life. Well,' he paused as he filled Sara's glass, 'it *is* your life.'

That explained why he was into his music. 'You sound like you enjoyed it?'

Kevin grinned, ruffled his hair with his hands. He looked five years younger when he spoke. 'I loved it. Traveling around the country, different venues, different people. Everyone loving the music. We'd have a drink after the gigs and just talk crap about our favourite bands for hours.' His eyes glazed for a moment as if lost in a memory. Then he shook his head. 'But when you have a family, life has to change, right?'

That was it in a nutshell. If only Mike could see that. You couldn't just do what you wanted when you had a child to think about.

'Yep. Life changes.'

They sat quietly for few moments, both lost in different worlds. Sara stared into the ruby-coloured wine in her glass, so it took a few moments before she realised that Kevin was gazing at her. He coughed.

'So, how come you ended up here tonight? It's not usual for you to be here outside of your shift.'

Sara picked up her wine and took a sip. It tasted good. 'I just needed to take a walk. Clear my head.'

Kevin nodded. 'A walk can be good for that. I don't want to pry, but is everything all right… at home?'

It felt disloyal to talk about Mike to another man. But Barbara was a different matter. 'Well, I'm living with my mother-in-law. Let's just say it's a little bit fraught.'

Kevin pulled a face. 'Yikes. I can imagine. Is she a bit of a tyrant?'

Tyrant wasn't the right word. But what was? What was it about Barbara that annoyed her so much? The fact that she treated Mike like the messiah? Her 'helpful' comments about raising a child? The comparisons to her perfect next-door neighbour? All of the above?

'She's a little judgemental.'

Kevin smiled. 'And that's not easy to live with. I know that from my ex-wife. I can't imagine you do anything to annoy her though?'

Sara shrugged. 'I'm not a Lisa.'

Kevin frowned. 'Lisa?'

It felt as if barely a day went past without Barbara regaling Sara with something wonderful that Lisa had said, done or breathed. 'My mother-in-law's perfect next-door neighbour. Super Mother. Master Baker. General all-round perfect human being.'

Kevin held up the wine bottle to ask whether she wanted a top-up. 'Oh.'

She shouldn't have another glass, but it wasn't as if she was driving. She pushed her glass towards him. A *little* more wouldn't hurt. 'I'm being mean. She's probably perfectly nice.'

Kevin topped up his own glass too. 'You don't strike me as a mean person.' He smiled. 'So how long will you be with your mother-in-law?'

Sara shrugged. 'Hopefully not long. I am just trying to save up enough so that we have a deposit for a little house and a few months' rent in the bank.'

Kevin leaned forwards in his seat. 'Tell me to shut up if I'm being nosy, but you make it sound like you are doing this all on your own. Isn't your husband working? Didn't you say he was an actor?'

It probably was disloyal, but she needed someone to talk to. 'He is, and he's getting paid, but,' she sighed, 'he needs to focus on the play and that means I'm having to do most of the Ruby stuff.'

'You mean he's not pulling his weight?'

'No. No. It's not that.' She didn't want to sound like she was moaning. 'We agreed that he would focus on the play. It's a really big deal. It's just a bit harder than I thought it was going to be.' She didn't mention how heartbroken she'd felt watching Ruby at the preschool. That was too personal.

Kevin sipped at his wine. 'Maybe he doesn't realise how you feel. Looking back, I wasn't a great dad when Callum came along. I found it pretty difficult, to be honest. Kelly was a natural. She knew what Callum wanted, how to stop him crying, how to get him to sleep. Any time she left me to look after him on my own it was carnage. There was a particularly spectacular fail in the disposable nappy department, which I won't share while we're drinking.'

This was the kind of irritating comment that Mike might make. '*She's better with you. You know what you're doing with her.*'

'It's not like mums get a shot of parenting hormones as the baby whooshes out of the birth canal, you know. If you spend a lot of time with a child, you get to know what works. It's not an epiphany; it's practice.'

'Fair point. Kelly used to say much the same thing, with a few choice swear words thrown in.' He smiled.

Sara glanced at the clock behind the bar. It was past midnight. 'Actually, I probably should be getting home, really. Thanks for the drink.'

'My pleasure.' Kevin picked up the two glasses with his finger and thumb. 'Are you okay to get home?'

Sara picked her denim jacket up from the back of her chair and slipped it on. 'Yeah. It's only a couple of streets away. I'll see you tomorrow morning.'

Kevin followed her to the door and locked the bolts behind her. As she walked away, she glanced back and saw him at the window. He raised a hand in farewell.

*

When Sara let herself into Barbara's house, it was in darkness and quiet. She gently pushed open the door to the lounge. Empty. Everyone must be in bed. Quietly, she crept up the paisley-carpeted staircase and into Ruby's room.

When she was asleep, Ruby looked like a tiny baby again. Her long, dark eyelashes rested on the tops of her cheeks and her soft pink mouth pouted and twitched. Sara laid her face on the mattress next to Ruby and watched her little chest rise and fall. When she was first born, Sara would check on her every hour, placing her hand on Ruby's tiny body to make sure she was still breathing.

It wasn't Ruby's fault, but everything was so much easier when she was small. Strolling in the park with the pram, enjoying playing the role of 'new mother' – she'd been so proud of her beautiful daughter. Everything had been better with Mike, then, too. He had really stepped up. She'd had almost six months off work and he had supported them; working six days a week, turning down auditions and even missing out on a small TV role without mentioning it to her. That's partly why she'd agreed to support him now. So why was it so hard?

Ruby murmured and turned onto her side. A pudgy arm flopped out of the bed. Sara held her breath; she didn't want to wake her. 5.00 a.m. would come soon enough.

Everything was different now. Ruby was hard work. There were days when it felt like nothing Sara did was right. Dinner, toys, talking; everything seemed to upset Ruby. What was the right thing to do? Give in? Set boundaries? Sometimes she lost her temper with her; it was all just so overwhelming. But she had never done what she did tonight – just walk out and leave her. Obviously, she had left her with Mike, but it still felt wrong.

Barbara had a laundry cupboard in this room. That woman had a drawer or cupboard for everything. Slowly and quietly, Sara pulled out a pillow and a blanket. So, Mike 'didn't sign up for this'? Really? She was still too angry to sleep with him tonight. How could he throw that at her again after all the sacrifices she'd made? With the pillow on the floor next to Ruby's bed, Sara lay down, pulling the blanket over her. Reaching out, she touched her fingertips to Ruby's.

'Mummy is sorry for leaving you, little one. We will sort this out, I promise. Mummy will do everything she can to make this okay.'

CHAPTER SEVENTEEN

Sara woke up to the sounds of Ruby clapping her hands together. At least she was starting the day happy, even if it was – she squinted at her phone display – 6.15 a.m. Wow. A lie in. This was a treat.

'Morning, gorgeous girl. Shall we just stay here and play for a while? Look, here's your aquarium.'

No one would be up yet anyway. Pre-Ruby, Sara would still be snoring at this time on a Saturday. Then she or Mike would take it in turns to make the coffee and bring breakfast back to bed and they would lie there and watch whatever box set they had on the go.

While Ruby was mesmerised by the aquarium, Sara thumbed through her phone. Never a good idea. Smiling pictures of other people's Insta-perfect lives aren't conducive to happiness. Especially if they've posted videos of children Ruby's age naming their colours or counting to ten or drawing a passable circle. It was impossible not to compare.

She swiped social media away. Now 7.00 a.m., light was coming in through the chink in the curtains. Might be a good idea to get a blackout blind fitted if they were going to be here much longer. Sara pulled one panel aside and peeked through the net curtains into Lisa's garden. It looked like an advert for a garden centre. Flowerbeds, an immaculate lawn, furniture that wouldn't look out of place in a lounge. Of course. What else would Lisa have? As she watched, Lisa appeared in the garden where she was met by Barbara at the fence. Barbara passed something over to her and Lisa appeared to thank her. What were they doing at this time of the morning? And how were they so close? For all her generosity at letting them stay, Barbara wouldn't be Sara's first choice of someone to spend time with. Although maybe Barbara didn't feel the need to tell Lisa the best way to do things because Lisa was already doing it.

Lisa and Barbara walked back inside their respective homes. Sara let the curtain fall closed again. Ruby must have found her animals at the bottom of her bed – she was lining them up on the floor. No time like the present.

'Hello, Ruby.' Sara dipped her head to try and catch Ruby's eye. 'Hello, Ruby.'

Ruby wasn't paying her any attention. Was it because she was engrossed in her game or was there something else? It would be so easy to believe that Mike was right, that Ruby would catch up. But she couldn't ignore this feeling. A feeling it was something more. 'Hi, Ruby. It's Mummy.'

Ruby reached out and patted her hand. Tears pricked at Sara's eyes. Why wouldn't she speak? A wave of exhaustion washed over her and she lay down on the floor so her body was curled around Ruby's back. She could feel the warmth of Ruby on her stomach and she let her eyes close. Just for a moment.

When she woke up, Ruby was gone.

Like she'd had a shot of adrenaline, Sara was wide awake. She had no idea if she'd been asleep for ten minutes or two hours. Surely, Ruby hadn't gone down the steep stairs without someone walking in front of her? She opened the door and listened. From the kitchen she heard Barbara's voice.

'There you go, Ruby. Granny's special breakfast.'

When Sara walked through the kitchen doorway, Ruby was sat in a chair with a plate full of toast soldiers. Barbara had her back to Ruby, chopping onions and meat and throwing them into a slow cooker. The whole time, keeping up a running commentary. 'When your daddy was a boy, he loved toast soldiers. And a dippy egg. He would have lived on egg and soldiers if I'd let him.' She didn't wait for Ruby to respond, just kept chattering away whilst Ruby chewed on her toast.

'Why didn't you wake me up?'

Barbara turned around with a large, sharp knife in her hand. A pink tendril of raw beef dangled from the end. 'You were obviously tired. Though why you were on the floor, goodness only knows. Is that some kind of modern yoga thing?'

No. Sara wanted to say. *It's a very old-fashioned, avoid-your-arsehole husband thing.*

'Is Mike still in bed?'

Barbara raised an eyebrow as if to suggest that Sara should be the one to know about that. 'I would imagine so. I went to get Ruby so that the two of you could have a lie-in. I almost had a fit when I saw you on the floor.' Barbara turned back to the chopping board. 'That's Ruby's fourth slice of toast. The poor thing must have been starving.'

Sara didn't allow Ruby to have that much toast in one go because, once she started on it, she just kept eating and eating. It had taken her long enough to get her to try Weetabix and now she was also obsessed with that. It wasn't important enough to start the day badly, though. It couldn't hurt this once.

According to the clock on the wall, it was nine thirty. Sara hadn't slept this late in months. Maybe years. 'I'll go and wake him up.'

It would be better for her to see him alone upstairs anyway. He could say what he wanted to say about last night – and so could she – without his mother listening in to their conversation. She wasn't looking forward to it.

But when she opened the door, Mike's bed hadn't been slept in. The bed was made. At home they always used to leave the quilt scrunched up wherever they had thrown it, but here Barbara made the beds every day. It was a little bit icky. Or it would have been, if they had actually had sex in the bed. Where was Mike? Maybe he had gone out early and Barbara had made the bed already? Confused as to why Barbara hadn't mentioned that, Sara returned to the kitchen. 'His bed has been made. Did you make it already?'

Barbara put the lid on the slow cooker and frowned. 'No. I was up at six thirty. He hasn't been down here since then.'

Sara turned her mobile back on. It pinged immediately. On some level, she knew before she even read the message.

Sorry, but I need some time. I need to get my head straight. I'm not performing in London. I'm part of the touring cast. I've been meaning to tell you, but there's never been a good time. And I can't seem to talk to you these days without you taking it the wrong way. I'll be in touch.

Barbara was staring at Sara's face and she must have seen the colour drain from it. Sara slid down into the seat next to Ruby's high chair. On tour? But *Cat on a Hot Tin Roof* was on at The Gielgud. He'd shown her the website. She'd seen it with her own eyes.

Barbara was wiping her hands with a tea towel and she stepped forwards. Worry lined her face. 'What is it? Where is he? Is everything all right?'

'Gone.'

Barbara's hand clasped her throat. 'What do you mean "gone"?'

'He's left.' Sara held up the phone. 'He said he's sorry.'

Barbara slid into the chair opposite. Her hand continued to flutter around her throat, fiddling with her locket. 'What happened? What did you do?'

Sara was so shocked by Barbara's response that she nearly laughed. What did *she* do? 'Mike is part of the touring cast. Not in the West End. Obviously, he didn't see fit to clarify that.'

Her mother-in-law looked confused. 'But the tour doesn't start for another two weeks.'

Sara narrowed her eyes and leaned forwards. 'You *knew* about this?'

Barbara blanched, then started to organise the breakfast table. Short of getting a set square out, the tablecloth couldn't have been any straighter, but Barbara seemed intent on trying. 'I'm not the person you should be speaking to about this.'

Sara stood and her chair flipped backwards and hit the cabinet behind her with a clatter. She stepped away from the table.

'You bloody knew.'

Barbara stopped fiddling with the cloth and frowned. 'Please don't swear, Sara. Especially in front of Ruby.'

Sara started to pace. 'When did he tell you? How long have you known that he was going to…' Everything began to slot into place. The move here. His insistence that they let Barbara start looking after Ruby. The fact that their rooms had been made so ready for their arrival. 'Was this the plan all along?'

Barbara got up from the table and began to fill the kettle. 'Let's just have a cup of tea and talk about this calmly.'

'No!' Sara banged her fist down onto the table so hard that a knife bounced onto the tiled floor. She didn't care. 'I don't want a cup of bloody tea. Was this the plan all along?'

Barbara sighed and turned to face her, leaning back against the counter top. 'I knew that his play was going on tour, yes. It's a great opportunity for him.'

Sara spoke through gritted teeth. 'When? When did he tell you that the play was going on tour?'

Barbara looked embarrassed. 'It was always going on tour. He told me that when he came to ask me about moving in here.'

Sara's mind was spinning, trying to make sense of all this. 'He came here to see you? I thought he called you?'

Barbara shook her head. 'No, he came here. More than once. Stayed for his dinner. It was lovely to see him, and to give him a home-cooked meal.'

Sara's fingernails bit into the tablecloth. When had this happened? Why hadn't he told her? First things first. 'So, he was never going to perform in the West End?'

Barbara pulled at her earlobe. 'The West End? No. There was a short run in the West End with lots of famous actors but it was in its final week when you moved here. Maybe that's why you're confused? Michael is in the new cast, the one that's touring the country.'

No, the reason she was confused was because Mike had wanted her to be. He'd told her that he was part of a new cast but had never said *anything* about a change of venue. She wanted to slap that proud expression from Barbara's face. How was she not embarrassed? Sara didn't expect any sympathy for herself, but what about Ruby? 'And it doesn't worry you that Mike has left his daughter without a backwards glance?'

Barbara turned and started to fill the sink with hot water. She held her hand under the tap to test the temperature. 'Michael hasn't left her. He knows I'm here. I can look after Ruby when you're busy.'

Busy? Doing what? Working, that's bloody what. How convenient that they were living with Barbara. She had a sudden memory of Mike the other night.

'She needs to get used to my mother.'

Oh. My. God. She put her elbows down on the table and let her head fall into her hands. She'd been such a fool. 'You planned this between you.'

The rumbling of the ancient kettle was getting louder. 'Sorry, dear. You'll have to speak up.'

Sara raised her head. Her chin began to wobble and she waited to get it under control. 'I said: you planned this between you. Mike moving us all in here. You both knew he would be leaving.'

Barbara turned off the tap and turned to face her. 'Now you're just being dramatic, again. He hasn't *left* you. He is working for a theatre company who have gone on tour. I agree that he should have told you but he's never been very good with confrontation. He had a very different upbringing than… some people have. There were never arguments in this house and if he hasn't told you to your face, it's only because he was trying to avoid this kind of unpleasantness.'

Sara wanted to unleash a whole other level of unpleasantness. 'I can't believe you're defending him.'

Barbara looked cross. 'I think we should leave this conversation for now. You're obviously upset. It's not as if he has run off with another woman, for goodness' sake. That's one thing he'd never do.'

Oh. So there were *some* things Barbara didn't know about her son.

CHAPTER EIGHTEEN

In the shower Sara cried the tears she hadn't wanted to shed in front of Barbara. Tears of anger. Of frustration. Of grief.

Twelve attempts at calling Mike's mobile, but he hadn't answered any of them. Was this revenge because she hadn't answered his texts last night? Had he been planning to tell her before he left? She should have answered them. Eventually he sent another text.

Can't speak now. Will call soon.

Just like the last time he'd left.

*

When Ruby was around a year old, things had been particularly bad between them. Ruby hadn't been a good sleeper since they got her home from the hospital. Sara had been expecting to get up in the night with a newborn, but one year later and Ruby was still waking at least twice and took forever to settle back to sleep.

The first six months had been okay because Sara could catch pockets of sleep during the day when Ruby did. But once she went back to work, she had to get by on a handful of broken hours of sleep. Moving zombie-like through life, many times she had found herself standing in front of a kettle, minutes after it had boiled, just staring into space. Her body moved as if wading through treacle. Everything was such an effort, like being a used dishrag that someone had wrung dry.

Mike would reach for her in bed and she would turn on to her side, facing the opposite wall. Even being touched was too much. After an hour of persuading Ruby to eat a pot of mush, wrestling her into her pyjamas, trying to shush her to sleep, she was completely spent. There was nothing left to give. Mike couldn't understand. For him, sex was a pleasure she was denying herself. And him.

'I just want to hold you. I don't need anything else.'

That was a lie. If she let him hold her close, he always wanted more. She would feel his hardness pressed into her hip, his hands would move, stroking her, his mouth would whisper into her ear. She couldn't respond. She didn't want more. She just wanted to sleep. To block out the rest of the day.

He started to stay out later. Drinking with old mates from drama college days. In some ways it had been a relief, she could collapse into bed alone, be asleep – or pretending to be asleep – when he came home. But then she began to resent the fact that it was always her stuck at home, changing nappies, cooking and mushing carrots and apples, worrying about why Ruby was only just beginning to sit up on her own without help.

Their rows had been horrific. Many cruel things were said, by both of them. He'd call her cold and unfeeling. She'd accuse him of being lazy and selfish. Once, in a rage, she'd yelled that she should never have told him about the pregnancy.

'If I hadn't had Ruby, I wouldn't still be here with you.'

That stopped him dead in his tracks. 'Are you saying you wouldn't have had her? You wish you hadn't had Ruby?'

'Of course not.' But she had. In that moment she had wished that the whole of her life had been different. And the guilt afterwards was monumental.

That was the night he left, with nothing more than a text saying he 'couldn't talk now'. She'd had to miss shifts at work because she didn't have anyone to look after Ruby. If it had been difficult before, it felt impossible on her own. Mike hadn't helped much around the house, but he had been physically there to watch over Ruby when Sara went to the hotel. It was the only job she could get that had hours outside Mike's working day. She was always looking for a more creative job that would pay enough to cover childcare, but hadn't had any luck, so the 'temporary' receptionist job had become permanent. Now, with no Mike there, she had to call in sick. There was only so long the hotel would put up with that.

After six nights, Sara had got to the end of her tether. Ruby had been crying on and off all day. There was nothing in the house for Sara to eat, but she couldn't face peeling off her pyjamas and getting Ruby into the buggy to go to the supermarket, nor could she afford a takeaway. In the end, she had defrosted two of the purees she'd made for Ruby and eaten those. When Ruby had finally cried herself to sleep, Sara had crawled back into bed, pulled the duvet over her head and let everything wash over her. She was living in a small, dark rented flat, her husband had gone, her daughter wasn't sleeping, she had no friends, no support and, if she didn't manage to turn up for her next shift, she might have no job. This was not how it was supposed to be. This was her childhood repeating itself. This was more than she could bear. She'd sobbed, deep, animal, uncontrollable sobs, until her exhaustion won out and rendered her unconscious.

That night, by some miracle, Ruby had slept for eight hours straight. Either that, or Sara had been in such a deep level of unconsciousness that she hadn't heard her. Sara hadn't slept for eight hours since before Ruby was born. When she woke, she felt strange, wired somehow. Like she'd drunk ten cups of black coffee. But she was scared. That last night had frightened her. She'd lost control, lost sight of the plan. And she couldn't do that. She owed it to Ruby.

So, the first thing she'd done was take a shower and get dressed. The upside of her misery had been her losing a little weight and she was able to fit into clothes she hadn't worn in a long time. Putting them on had reminded her of the art student with the big ideas. The one who Mike had fallen in love with. Maybe their problems *had* been just as much her fault as his.

She'd called him then, and begged him to come home. There'd been a female voice in the background. *Of course there's another woman.*

Sara had chosen to close her eyes, to focus on their future. Picture the life she wanted. And that's what kept her going. The picture of their future. A house of their own. Steady work for them both. Stability for Ruby so that she could catch up with other children her age. Whenever Mike had done something selfish or she was annoyed about his lack of help with Ruby, she had focused on that. The future.

To be fair to Mike, things had got a lot better between them for a while after he came home. They'd talked through their problems, he made more effort with Ruby, she made more effort to pay him attention and to support his acting career. Life had seemed to be getting back on track.

It's just that the track didn't go anywhere.

That was the first time Sara realised they were never going to get a deposit together for a house, even if they could have paid the mortgage. So that's when Sara changed the plan, edited the picture. They would find a proper house to rent. But even that had been impossible on the money they had between them. Especially when Mike started to miss shifts to go to auditions. Just when Sara had managed to save a little bit of money towards a deposit on a better place, Mike lost his job and they had to use the money – and credit cards – to tide them over until he got something else.

The girls at work had told her back then that she was better off without him. If she was on her own, she might get some help from the council. But those very words spun her back twenty years to a damp flat with one bedroom. Plus, Mike was Ruby's dad. And she did love him; they did still have times when things were good between them, when he would make her laugh and they would lie in bed and conjure up that fantasy scenario where he was a famous actor and she was an artist and they had a huge sprawling house in the country where Ruby could have a garden swing and a dog and maybe even a sibling. It was those days that had got her through.

When he'd got this latest role, he'd been so happy about it: the opportunity, the possibility. It was hard not to be infected by his happiness. To picture their future again. How was she to know that it would end up with them all moving in with his mother?

*

And now he had gone again.

What was she going to do? Could she and Ruby stay at Barbara's without Mike? Or would Barbara want them out now that the perfect son had done a bunk? Her head fell back and the water from the shower ran over her face. The pressure of the water made a kaleidoscope behind her eyelids. Her toes, resting on the plughole, felt the water drain away. How long had she been in there? Crying. Worrying. Giving up. No home. No Mike. No…

No.

Opening her eyes, she poured shampoo into her hands and rubbed it roughly into her hair. There was nothing for it but to keep going, get Ruby sorted out, find a house for the two of them. Barbara had offered to look after Ruby many times and, in the short term at least, she was just going to have to swallow her pride and let her do it. All she needed was a deposit and one month's rent. The worst had happened and she was still standing. This was as bad as it was going to get.

Once she got out of the shower, Sara checked her phone to see if Mike had called. He hadn't. But when she checked her voicemail, she found one from Friday that she had somehow missed.

'Hi, Sara. This is Sharon, the manager at BumbleBees Preschool. Do you have some time after Ruby's session on Monday so that we can have a chat?'

CHAPTER NINETEEN

Dear Lisa,

Michael has moved out. I knew he would be leaving soon, of course I did. But not two weeks before the play even opens. When he first told me that the role was going to take him away from home, he was so worried about leaving them alone in that flat, bless him. If that's not proof of how much he cares about them, I don't know what is. But he couldn't let an opportunity like this pass him by, which is why I suggested they come and stay with me.

He should have told her from the outset. I told him that. It was wrong to mislead her – and very awkward for me at times – but it wasn't my place to tell her. Understandably, she's upset. I know how she feels. Trevor just up and left me, too. Not that he sent me a text message, of course. This was way before mobile phones. No, I got the back of an envelope. A gas bill. 'I'm leaving. You only have room for one man in your life and it's not me.'

It's not easy bringing up a child on your own. When Michael was small, I was like a social outcast. Everyone else had a husband at home except me. Money was tight too. Trevor did keep paying the mortgage until it was finished, I'll give him that. And he sent money every month towards food and bills. It was difficult to get a job until Michael started school anyway, and I could get a few hours of office work. Still, we managed. And I paid for all his drama clubs too. I never missed a performance.

Sara asked me last night whether it is okay for them to stay for another few weeks, and I said of course, as long as you need.

As if I would turn my own granddaughter out into the street! And I know Sara means well. Deep down I do. Still, I'm glad I get to spend more time with Ruby on her own now, as I think Sara will have no choice but to leave her with me a bit more now Michael's not around. Ruby's easy most of the time as long as we just stay home together. I say to her all the time: 'I'm not going anywhere, Ruby. Granny is staying right here.' She never replies, but I'm sure she understands.

CHAPTER TWENTY

A text arrived from Kevin early Sunday, asking if Sara could work an extra shift. She'd assumed she would begin by clearing the debris from a rowdy Saturday night, but when she saw his son with him, she wondered if he had other ideas.

Callum was sitting up at the bar as Kevin filled a pint glass with lemonade from the mixer tap. The combination of the drink, and the packet of salt-and-vinegar crisps next to his glass, was a flashback to Sara's own childhood. As was the fact that neither of them was talking.

'Good morning.'

'Hi, Sara. This is Callum. His mum just dropped him off and we're going to have a drink before deciding what to do with our afternoon. Have you got any ideas for us?'

The look of pleading in his eyes told her that he hadn't a clue what to do with his son. The poor boy was balanced on a stool that was far too high for him, sipping his drink through a straw. The mood she'd been in since Mike's departure didn't dispose her to helping out another dad who couldn't be bothered to consider his child. Still, it wasn't Callum's fault.

'Have you been to the park?

Kevin smiled nervously. 'We thought we'd do that later when the weather warms up a bit, didn't we Callum? Is there anything *inside* that we could do?'

How would she know? She'd only just moved here. 'I'm not the *Ashbridge A to Z*, you know. And can I at least get my coat off?'

She walked through to the hallway behind the bar and Kevin followed her. He lowered his voice. 'Kelly called this morning and asked if I could take him. I didn't want to say no and give her more ammunition, especially when I've been bugging her about letting me see him more often. Sorry. I've called Alan and he said he'll come in and give you a hand this afternoon while I'm with him. I wouldn't leave you on your own.'

Sara sighed. 'No, I'm sorry. That was rude of me. I'm not in a good way today.' She pressed her lips together. Might as well tell him. 'Mike left.'

'What?!' Kevin's voice was loud. He glanced back towards Callum in the bar and lowered it. 'What do you mean "left"?'

She mimed a walking motion with two fingers. 'Left as in, packed a bag and has gone to live somewhere else.'

Kevin frowned. 'But what about his play?'

'It's a tour, apparently. Not that he told me that. But that's not where he is. That doesn't start for another two weeks. I have no idea where he is right now.' What she meant was, she only had her suspicions. Not evidence. Nor any specifics. Like her name.

Kevin closed his mouth, which had gaped open. 'I'm so sorry. Are you okay?'

She shook her head and bit her lip. *Do not cry. Deep breath.* 'Not really, but I can't even think about that right now. The preschool wants to talk to me about Ruby.'

'Dad?' Callum's uncertain voice came up the hallway. 'Can you help me get off here?'

Sara waved Kevin away with her hand. 'Go and help him. I'm fine. I'll be out in a minute.'

After hooking her coat and bag up, Sara leaned against the wall and closed her eyes. Every muscle in her body felt tight. Since Mike's departure, she and Barbara had been sidestepping around each other like two queens on a chessboard. If it had been awkward to share her home before, it was impossible now. More than ever, she wanted to find somewhere else for her and Ruby to live. She reached into her rucksack.

When she walked back into the bar area, Kevin and Callum were sat opposite each other. Kevin was asking him about school and whether he liked his teacher. Poor sod.

'Do you like drawing, Callum?'

His dark hair flopped up and down as he nodded at her. 'I love drawing. 'Specially cars.'

From behind her back, Sara brought out the sketchpad and pencils she'd taken from her bag. She still took it everywhere with her: old habits die hard. 'I have some really professional drawing materials here, which are for highly skilled artists. I'm sure your dad can help you to find a picture of a sports car on his mobile that you can copy, if you're up to the challenge?'

Callum twisted in his seat. 'Yes! Can I, Dad? Can you help me find a picture?'

Kevin pulled out his phone. 'Of course. Coming right up!'

Sara tore three sheets of paper from her sketchpad and laid them on the table, along with the pencils. Callum hopped off the chair and stood close to his dad, their dark heads bent over the phone as Kevin thumbed through a selection of Porsches, Lamborghinis and Ferraris.

Kevin looked up at her gratefully and mouthed, 'Thank you.'

Once Callum was focused on his drawing, Kevin came to the bar to get him another drink. Sara stopped mid-wipe as he reached for the mixer tap. 'I think that huge lemonade was probably enough for one day, unless you really hate his mother and want to keep her up all night?'

Kevin replaced the tap. 'Ah, good point. I'll do him some water. Thanks. Again. You've saved me this morning'

'No problem. I just appealed to his male competitiveness with the "highly skilled" and "professional". You're all the same.'

Kevin laughed. 'Great work.' He paused. 'We're not, though. All the same, that is.' He looked at her for a moment and then turned back to his son.

Rain stopped their trip to the park in the end, so Kevin and Callum decamped upstairs at opening time. The rain kept most of their older regulars away too, so Sara barely needed Alan there.

An hour into the shift, Kevin appeared behind the bar.

Sara stopped composing a vitriolic text to Mike. This was her fifth one. She wasn't sending them, but there was something cathartic in typing the words 'selfish' and 'heartless' and 'prick'.

'What are you doing here? Not more lemonade?'

Kevin shook his head. 'Callum wanted to go home so I called Kelly and dropped him back.'

Sara put her phone in her back pocket. 'Why? Couldn't you have found something else for him to do?'

'I tried.' Kevin shrugged. 'He got bored of drawing so we watched some car videos on my phone and then he said he wanted to go home.'

'Didn't you persuade him to stay? What did Kelly say?'

'She wasn't best pleased. She was out shopping and had to come home, but I didn't want to upset him. If I'd made him stay and then he'd gone home miserable, I would have been public enemy number one.'

A customer in high-vis jacket and paint-strewn trousers appeared at the bar with an empty pint glass. 'Same again, please, love. Might as well. Can't work in this rain.'

After she'd served him, Sara turned back to Kevin. 'Maybe you should get some stuff in that he'd like to do. Some craft stuff, a couple of games, a few DVDs – ask Kelly what he likes. She's not going to want him to come if he goes home early every time.'

Kevin ran his hand through his hair. 'I know. I know.' He looked at her pleadingly. 'Can you help me make a list?'

It was hard not to mock his ineptitude. 'I'm no expert on six-year-old boys, but I can ask at the preschool for some ideas if you like?'

He looked relieved. 'That would be great. Speaking of the preschool, what did they want to talk to you about?'

Sara's stomach flipped over at the thought of their meeting tomorrow. 'I don't know yet, but I did ask them for some help with Ruby's speech. She doesn't really talk very much and I was hoping for some advice.' She couldn't shake off the feeling that it might be something else, though. Otherwise why would they leave a voicemail?

Kevin nodded. 'She's only little, though, isn't she?'

He sounded like an echo of Mike. 'Yes, but she should be saying something by now. Well, she *was* saying things. I don't know. I just want to do the best thing for her, you know? If they tell me I don't need to worry, I won't.' That was a blatant lie, but she might dial the worry level down a bit. It was all very well Mike – and now Kevin – suggesting Ruby was young and it would be okay, but she wanted to hear it from a professional. To know either way. And tomorrow morning, she would.

CHAPTER TWENTY-ONE

We will help your child to be the best that they can be. That's what it said on the BumbleBees Preschool website. Although Sara had been hoping for their help, her heart had flip-flopped when she heard Sharon's voice. What could be so serious that she would leave a phone message rather than having a quick chat at drop-off?

That morning, Sharon hadn't been available to speak to her and Ellie had been vague about a 'plan' for Ruby, saying Sharon – as preschool manager – would explain when Sara collected Ruby later. It was on Sara's mind the whole day. Maybe it was a good thing and they had managed to secure some speech and language therapy? A 'plan' suggested help, didn't it? There was no need to worry. Was there?

As always, she was one of the first at the preschool for pickup. When the door clicked open to let the parents in, she readied herself. What kind of day did Ruby have today? But when she saw the children sitting on the carpet ready to meet their parents, Ruby wasn't among them. Then Sharon touched her on the arm.

'Hi, Sara? Ruby is in the sensory room with Ellie. Could we have that chat?'

Sara followed Sharon to the office in silence. This felt oddly formal. Why weren't they letting her see Ruby first?

Sharon opened the door to her office and pulled out a seat for Sara before sitting behind her desk. 'Ruby is absolutely fine. She got a bit upset this afternoon, so Ellie has taken her in to look at the bubble tubes. She likes it in there.'

It was a relief that Ruby was okay, but it didn't quieten her anxiety. What else was Sharon going to tell her?

'The thing is, I wanted to have a chat about Ruby. I know that you've had conversations with Ellie about her speech and we've been trying a few things, which we'll continue with. We also think it may be time to get some other professionals involved. We can get the ball rolling from our end, but it might speed things up if you also speak to your doctor.'

Doctor? Did they think Ruby was ill? 'I'm sorry. I don't understand. Is this for speech therapy or do you think there is something physically wrong with her? Because she *is* able to say words. I mean, she *was* talking.'

Sharon nodded slowly. 'Speech and language therapy would definitely be one area we could explore. But we think there might be a bigger picture to look at here. There are various behaviours and signs that Ruby might need support in other areas.'

Other areas? 'Do you mean the "parallel play"? Ellie explained that. She said a lot of children play alongside each other rather than with each other at this age. Is that not right?'

Sharon smiled and twirled a pencil between a finger and thumb. 'Yes, Ellie is absolutely right. But it's not the parallel play that's the issue. I'm not an educational psychologist; I don't want to make an amateur diagnosis here. We just think we should explore whether Ruby has any additional needs.'

Diagnosis? Additional needs? Sara's heart thumped. What did that mean? 'What do *you* think she needs?' She held a hand up to stop Sharon from repeating herself. 'Please. I'm not asking for medical advice and I won't hold you to it. I just honestly don't know what you mean. Why do you think I need to see a doctor?'

Sharon placed both her palms flat on the desk. She looked at Sara for a few moments as if making a decision whether to speak and then gave a small nod. 'Well, from what we've seen in her first two sessions on Wednesday and Friday, Ruby is exhibiting a lot of classic autistic characteristics. I'm not saying,' she added hurriedly, 'that she is autistic. But I do think it's worth you speaking to your doctor about getting a referral to a paediatrician…'

Was it possible for your heart to actually stop? For the world to freeze in front of you? For your blood to stop pumping and your skin to turn to ice? It was as if the volume button on the world had been flicked to zero as Sharon's lips continued to move, but no sound came out, then immediately twisted back to maximum as the blood rushed back in so fast it thumped in Sara's ears.

'… I know it seems like we're being rather quick off the mark, but we know how long the process can take.'

Autism? Wasn't that a thing that boys had? Sara had known that there was something not right about Ruby's behaviour, but surely it wasn't as serious as that? They must have it wrong. Sharon was still looking at her, obviously expecting a response. What should she say? 'These autistic… er… characteristics. Is it the tantrums? Because she has had a very unsettled few months, her father and I…' she trailed off as Sharon shook her head.

'They are not just tantrums. Believe me, we get enough of those in here.' Sharon smiled and pulled a face. The fact that she was being so gentle made this even worse. More frightening. Like on TV when they send the kindest police officers to inform the family of a road traffic accident. 'With Ruby, it isn't a case of her being petulant. She really can't cope with certain situations. She gets very stressed. It's also very difficult for her to do anything outside her routine and her play is… well, it is fairly classic play for an autistic child.'

But all of those things could be explained by the fact Ruby couldn't communicate, couldn't they? Was it the lining-up thing? But that didn't mean she was autistic, either. Barbara said that Mike had done the same as a child. They'd laughed about it. Not that they would be laughing now. She felt sick.

The atmosphere in the office was thick and hot. For some reason, she couldn't get her lungs to take in enough air. Time to get out of the room and find Ruby. Take her home. *Get the facts. Think about it later.*

'Okay, so how do I go about this? What do I say to the doctor?'

Sharon opened a file on her desk and took out a printed sheet. 'I've already written a letter for your GP with our suggestion that you seek a referral. If you make an appointment and go and speak to him, he can get the ball rolling.' She took a deep breath. 'You need to be prepared for it to take a while.'

What would take a while? The appointment? It was as if Sharon was talking to someone else and Sara was listening. 'Do I tell the receptionist what it's for so that I get a longer appointment?'

Sharon smiled kindly as she pushed the letter across the desk. 'No, I mean the process. If your doctor refers you, it will take a while to get an appointment with the paediatrician. There are other agencies we can get involved from here, but let's take it one step at a time for now.'

One step at a time? Sara would barely be able to step at all; her legs were jelly. She took the letter from Sharon and looked down at the words on it. Methodical play. Difficulty in interaction. Resistance to breaking routine. The words blurred and a fat tear dropped onto the page.

'Oh, sorry. I'm sorry.' A sob escaped. Damn. She needed to get it together. Ruby needed her to be strong.

'It's fine, honestly.' Sharon pulled some tissues from the box on her desk and passed them to Sara. 'Take your time. It's a lot to take in. But we only want to make sure that Ruby gets all the support that she needs.'

Hadn't Sara been saying the same thing to Mike for months? That Ruby needed more help? That she wasn't hitting her milestones? That she was getting left behind? Even last week, when she'd tried to talk to him about Ruby's speech, he had shut her down, told her she was overreacting, being dramatic. She'd known there was something else. She'd known it deep down in a place she couldn't articulate, hoping all the while that she was wrong.

But autism? It couldn't be autism. That was serious. That was incurable. That was… forever.

'I need to see Ruby.'

Sharon stood. 'Of course. Of course. I'll take you to the sensory room and you can speak to Ellie too. Let us know when you've spoken to the doctor and we can take it from there.'

Sara nodded mutely and followed Sharon to the room in the corner, which was full of coloured tubes and lights. It took all her strength to put one foot in front of the other. *One step at a time.*

When Sara saw Ruby, another sob threatened to escape. Sitting in front of a light box, reaching for squares and circles as they lit up, her little shoulders still twitching – a giveaway of being newly recovered from an upset. Sara kneeled down and put a soft hand on Ruby's back. 'Hey, Rubes. Mummy's here.'

Ruby turned and looked at her. Her big brown eyes were huge. Her face dappled pink as it was cooling down. Sara reached out and stroked her face. 'Shall we go home, baby girl?'

The whole way home from the preschool, the letter Sharon had written weighed heavily in Sara's shoulder bag. Doctor. Referral. Autism. The words went around and around her head like a carousel. If only she could walk to the doctor right now. Demand that they look at her daughter and tell her what to do.

What was Mike going to say? Would he believe her now? That they needed to get some help? Like a wave, she remembered that he'd gone. He wouldn't be there for her to tell.

She would call him. Whatever was going on between the two of them, it would be wrong to do this without Mike. He was Ruby's father and he loved her. Surely he'd come home for this? They had problems, but they were a family. They would face this together.

*

When Sara turned the corner into Barbara's road, she spied Lisa in her front garden. Probably ironing the damn grass. She was the last person Sara wanted to see right now.

Lisa stood and smiled as Sara approached. She had gardening gloves on, but the floral pattern of Joules or Laura Ashley had been barely marked by the soil. The dirt probably wouldn't dare. Lisa brushed imaginary grass from the front of her designer jeans. 'Hi, Sara. Hi, Ruby.'

Sara forced on a smile. 'Hi, Lisa.'

Lisa seemed intent on conversation. 'Just thought I should do something with these weeds before they take over and the neighbours start to talk about me. The children are at their grandmother's tonight so it seemed like a good idea at the time.'

If Sara had some child-free time at home, she could think of a hundred things she would rather be doing than gardening. Sleeping, for one. Right now, that's exactly what she wanted to do – go to bed and not get up again. 'Good for you.'

Sara turned the buggy up the path, but Lisa followed her, still talking.

'They're only there because we're going out to dinner. The new Japanese restaurant in town. Grant has to entertain some associates from their US office.'

Sara felt a stab of jealousy. Lisa's perfect children were probably behaving perfectly at their perfect grandmother's house so that their perfect mother could go out for a perfect dinner with her perfect husband. She gripped the handles of Ruby's buggy tightly. 'Lucky you.'

Lisa shrugged. 'I'm not actually that keen on Japanese food. I don't really like fish cooked, let alone raw.' She paused, fiddled with her gardening gloves. 'Sorry, I'm wittering on. What I actually want to say how is how sorry I am to hear about Mike leaving. That's really crappy.'

Sara froze. How did Lisa know about his departure so soon? Had Barbara gone straight next door and told her the same day? She could imagine how she'd been cast in the retelling. Well, she wasn't going to be pitied. 'He's just gone on tour. It's his job. We're fine.'

Lisa nodded and stood back. 'Of course you are. I just wanted to say that I'm here if you needed a chat or anything. I'm sure you have your own friends, but, you know, I'm knocking around in that house all day.' She motioned back towards her front door. The knocker shone like a new pin.

As if Sara needed reminding that Lisa was a lady of leisure. And as if she was likely to tell her what had happened with Mike. It would have been nice to talk to someone, but Lisa was definitely not the right person. 'Thanks. I'll remember that.' She nodded down at Ruby. 'Better get her indoors.'

As Sara fumbled in her bag for the door key, she could feel Lisa's eyes on her back. Was she judging her ripped jeans and the fact that she was wearing an ancient coat? Or had she noticed the puffy eyes caused by a tearful walk home? Whichever it was, Sara just wanted to get out of her line of sight.

Barbara was in the kitchen, unloading two shopping bags. If Sara hadn't been annoyed that she'd spoken to Lisa about Mike, she would have told Barbara straight away what the preschool had said. Instead, she just stuck her head round the door. 'We're home.'

'Good. I am making a casserole for dinner. I'll have it ready for five thirty so we can all eat together.'

Barbara was being kind, but there was no way Ruby would eat casserole. Sara didn't have the energy for that conversation right now. 'I'm just going to give Ruby a quick bath. She's covered in paint from preschool.'

'Okay, dear. Whatever you think is best.'

Sara turned on the bath taps, making sure the water ran tepid because Ruby liked to hold her hand in the stream, wiggling her fingers. 'Shall we have some bubbles, Ruby? Shall we spoil ourselves?'

Ruby was transfixed by the water. 'Keep 'wimming. Keep 'wimming.'

More quotes from *Finding Nemo*. Was that an 'autistic characteristic' too? 'We're not swimming, baby girl. We're having a bath. Can you say "bath"?'

Ruby wiggled her fingers again, watched the water move. 'Look out! Sharks eat fish.'

A painful lump rose in Sara's throat. When she'd googled about Ruby's speech delay, autism had come up, but she had scrolled past it, discounted it. 'It's a bath, Ruby. You love your bath. Can you say "bath" for Mummy?'

Sara stroked Ruby's hair; it was long enough for a proper ponytail. Mike had teased her when Ruby was first born and she had bought special hairclips online for babies with very little hair. Of course, Ruby had pulled them out within seconds and Sara had put them away in a box to try again when she was bigger. Wasn't that half the fun of having a little girl? The accessories and the pretty things.

Ruby let Sara stroke her hair, but she was no longer listening to her. She was humming to herself as she watched the water. Tears dripped down Sara's face. 'What's going on in there, Ruby? What are you thinking, baby? Please let Mummy in.'

Sara's life had never been perfect; she'd never asked for it to be. All she'd wanted was Mike and Ruby. Now the little she'd had was disintegrating in front of her.

She would call Mike tonight once they'd had dinner and Ruby was in bed. But if she couldn't get hold of him, she would have to move forward alone. Whatever happened, she was calling that doctor tomorrow and getting some help. After her conversation with Lisa earlier, she'd also made up her mind to call someone else for help tomorrow. Someone she never expected to ask.

CHAPTER TWENTY-TWO

Back in East London, GP appointments had been almost as difficult to come by as affordable housing, so there were upsides to living out in Essex. When Sara couldn't get hold of Mike, she called the local Medical Centre, silently thanking Barbara for being so insistent that they register with her doctor. Their appointment was for the following Monday morning. Then she had made another appointment, for that coming Thursday, which also made her anxious: a visit with her mother.

The fact that Barbara had known about Mike's intentions had been bad enough, but her conversations with Lisa about it had been final confirmation: Sara and Ruby needed to get their own place as soon as possible. Sara's contact with her mother was intermittent – maybe once or twice a year – but Jackie liked to tell Sara that she could always come to her if she needed help. Not that Sara had ever taken her up on it. Now she didn't have much choice.

The drive to Harlow on Thursday was under an hour. She'd planned to meet Jackie at home, but her mother had sent her a message just before she left to say that she had to run an errand. *Meet me at the pub instead.* What a surprise. Sara had toyed with the idea of leaving Ruby with Barbara, but was already going to have to rely on her a lot more in the next couple of weeks until she could arrange more hours at the preschool. Plus, maybe the sight of Ruby's beautiful face would persuade Jackie to be generous.

The pub was exactly as Sara remembered it. Unfortunately. The afternoon was warm, so she was able to meet her mother in the garden and avoid having to take Ruby inside. She'd dressed Ruby in a beautiful yellow sundress with a pink cardigan. It would have to be a cold-hearted person who didn't think she was absolutely adorable. When they arrived, Jackie was already there.

'Hello, darling. How are you?' She kissed Sara and ran a hand over Ruby's dark brown hair. 'Hello, Ruby sweetheart. Is it nice to see your Granny Jackie? Mummy never brings you to see me, does she?'

Sara took a deep breath. Must start off on the right foot if she was going to ask her mother for money. 'It was a bit of a drive, especially with a baby, Mum. You would be welcome to come and visit us whenever you want, though. You know that.'

Jackie waved a hand in the air. 'I don't like to be a burden, sweetheart. You have your own life. I know what that's like. I used to have one too.' She laughed. A tinny, unconvincing laugh that ended in a chesty cough. That would be the Marlboro Lights.

'Anyway. What would you like to drink? Are you still teetotal or are we on the grown-up drinks these days?'

Sara took a deep breath. *Don't rise to it.* 'I'll have a shandy. I'm driving.'

'Goodness, I am honoured. And what about Ruby? A lemonade?'

Sara blinked hard. The déjà vu was killing her. Half her childhood had been spent in this garden with a glass of warm lemonade, trying to make it last. 'No. She has a beaker of water. She's fine thanks.'

Jackie disappeared back into the pub and Sara got Ruby settled on a blanket next to the table. She'd brought an array of toys to keep her occupied. Nemo, obviously, some of her blocks and a drawing pad and pencils. Since meeting Leonard, Ruby would sit happily for an hour at a time, just drawing swirls and circles on paper, all different colours. It was quite soothing to watch.

Jackie was chuckling when she came back out from the pub, holding their drinks. Her glass of wine looked as if it held a third of a bottle. 'Phil's in there with a couple of his friends, he said we can join him.'

If Sara remembered correctly, Phil was her mother's current boyfriend. She'd been talking about him at Christmas when Sara had spoken to her last. 'Thanks, but I wanted to talk to you about something. Something personal.'

'Crikey. Sounds like I did the right thing getting a large drink.' Jackie picked up her glass and took a gulp. Then another. 'Hit me. Mike has left you, right?'

That put Sara on the back foot. How had her mother known? Surely Barbara hadn't spoken to her, too? 'He's just… working away at the moment. How did you know?'

Jackie took another gulp of her wine and smiled. 'I know the look. Seen it in the mirror enough times.'

For a moment, Sara felt some sympathy for her mother. She hadn't had it particularly easy, bringing up a daughter on her own. According to her, Sara's father had stayed around long enough to change one nappy and then disappeared. Since then, there had been a string of 'uncles', but no one who stayed very long. That wasn't going to happen to Ruby.

'Yes, well, I don't really know at the moment how long he'll be… away, but I do know that I need to sort out my living arrangements. At the moment, Ruby and I are staying with Barbara.'

'The mother-in-law?' Jackie grimaced. 'Ugh. That can't be a lot of fun. I hope you're remembering to use a coaster?' She winked.

Sara smiled. Barbara and Jackie had met once, not long after Ruby was born. In the first flush of motherhood, Sara had thought she could bring their single mothers into the family fold so that Ruby would have at least female grandparents. It hadn't been an occasion she ever attempted to repeat.

'It's not ideal, no. But I don't have enough saved for a deposit. I was wondering if…'

Sara was interrupted by a moan from Ruby. A spider had made its way across her blanket and she was trying to brush it away, getting more and more upset when she couldn't get rid of it. Sara bent down and picked her up. 'It's okay, Ruby. It's just an incy wincy spider. He can't hurt you.' She put Ruby on her lap and tried to distract her with a pile of beer mats that someone had left on the table. Thankfully, Ruby was interested enough to take them and start putting them together in a line, focused on fitting them together perfectly.

Jackie reached out and put a hand on Sara's. 'If you were going to ask me to help you out with a deposit, I'm afraid I can't help you. I only have a couple of thousand in the account and that's destined for my holiday.' She beamed. 'Phil is taking me to Gran Canaria!'

It would have been bitchy to point out that he wasn't actually taking her if she was paying for herself, so Sara didn't. 'I wouldn't need the money for long. I have one job and I'm looking for another one.'

Jackie supped again. 'What about Mike? Didn't you say he's working? Isn't he paying for his daughter?'

Sara swallowed. She didn't want to tell her mum that she had no clue where he was. It would be like admitting failure. And this was hopefully a temporary setback. If she and Mike managed to sort things out, she didn't want her mum holding this over her and reminding her about it for the rest of her life.

'Like I said, he's working away at the moment.'

Jackie squinted at her and nodded slowly. 'I see.'

Sara kept going so as not to give her mother the chance to pry. 'So, if I could borrow just a few hundred pounds to help with a deposit, I will get it back to you before you need it.'

Jackie swilled the wine around in the bucket-sized glass and then took another large sip. 'I would love to help you out, you know that. But I really can't risk it, Phil and I need this holiday. We've had a few problems lately and we need some time together.'

Sara wanted to ask if their problems had originated at the bottom of a bottle of whiskey, but she bit her tongue; she hadn't come here for a fight. It was her turn to lay her cards on the table.

'The thing is, Mum…'

Ruby started slapping Sara's hand. She wanted the beer mat Sara was turning around in her fingers. Sara gave it to her daughter and watched her slot it into a line with the others.

Jackie tilted her head. 'Ah. I remember when you were that age. So beautiful.'

From nowhere, Sara's throat constricted, tightened by emotions that were never far below the surface at the moment. Her mother never spoke about her as a child. Other than to say how difficult it had been for her to raise Sara alone after her dad did a bunk. Now she was a mother herself, she understood more than ever before how hard that must have been. Was history repeating itself? No. She wouldn't let it.

Ruby slapped Sara's hand again. She wanted more beer mats. She'd been so good since they got there; it was a small thing to ask.

'Can you just watch Ruby for a minute, Mum? I'm just going to find her some more mats.'

As quickly as she could, Sara mineswept the other tables for discarded beer mats. Thank goodness they were the only people out here. She would have looked like a total nutter. When she got back to the table, a broad man in jeans and a polo top was giving her mother a glass of wine.

Jackie was beaming. 'This is Phil, just bringing me out another drink. He asked if you wanted one. Isn't that nice? Phil, this is Sara.'

Phil turned to face her and looked her up and down in a way that made her want to take a shower. He was typical Jackie fodder. 'Your girl don't talk much, does she?'

When she does talk, she'll be grammatically correct. Sara didn't even bother making eye contact. 'She's still young.'

Phil shrugged. 'I'll be inside, Jack. Get that down your neck and then we'll make a move.'

Jackie looked at him like he was a movie star. She raised her glass to show him the contents. 'I'll be as quick as I can.'

As soon as he'd gone, Jackie turned to Sara. 'He's right, you know. I tried to speak to her while you were getting those beer mats. She didn't even look at me.'

That's because she's a good judge of character. 'Like I said to… your friend: she's still very little.'

Jackie tipped the dregs of one glass of wine into the new one. 'When you were her age, you were a right little chatterbox. My mum used to say there was a hole at the back of your head, and when the wind blew it would waggle your tongue.'

Sara was surprised that her grandmother had taken her cigarette out of her mouth long enough to say such a long sentence. 'All children are different.'

Jackie shrugged. 'Still. You might want to get her checked out. Y'know. Make sure she's *all right*.' She lowered her voice at the last word as if this was a medical term. Sara dug her nails into the table.

Ruby had made her way through the last of the beer mats and was tapping Sara's hand again. It was a good time to go, but she would need to do it slowly. And without an audience. 'Actually Mum, we need to make a move and get her some lunch. Why don't you go and join Phil and your friends and I'll just get packed up here and head home?'

Thankfully, her mother was predictably quick to agree, stand up and step out from the bench seat. You had to give it to her; she still looked good for her age. Too good for that meathead she was about to join. There was a vulnerability about Jackie, though. And an uncertainty, like an anchorless ship. She'd never been able to be alone.

'Okay, love. Well, you take care of yourself.' She paused, moved as if to hug Sara and then thought better of it. 'Let me know if you need anything.'

Why? Sara wanted to say. *So you can say 'no' again?*

Watching her mother walk back towards the pub gave Sara another moment of déjà vu. She'd asked Jackie about her father many times. Refusing to believe her mother's disparaging comments, Sara had fantasised about him collecting her from a pub garden like this one, taking her back to his house where he would have decorated a bedroom pink for her. But when she'd plucked up the courage – at about fourteen – to say she wanted to try and find him, Jackie told her that she didn't know where he was. In fact, she didn't even know his surname. Sara was a couple of years older before she realised that she must have been the product of a one-night stand. Even the 'changing one nappy' story had been an exaggeration of his involvement. She'd grieved the loss of this imaginary father as if she'd actually known him. No one was going to rescue her. There was no pink bedroom in a house with a garden.

Well, that wasn't going to happen to Ruby. Whatever happened between her and Mike, she wouldn't let him ignore Ruby. She took her phone out of her bag and tried him again.

CHAPTER TWENTY-THREE

The next morning, Sara finally got to speak to Mike.

She'd tried his number so many times since he'd left that she wasn't expecting it when he actually picked up. 'Hi, Sara.'

'Mike.' She sat up straighter. 'Where are you?'

He didn't answer immediately. 'I'm staying with a friend.'

Sara bit back the question of whether his friend was an attractive woman. It had taken too long to make contact to risk him hanging up. 'How long are you going to be there? Are you coming back before the play opens?'

There was a long pause at the other end. 'I think we just need a bit of a break, don't you? Everything has been a bit intense.'

His utter, utter selfishness knew no bounds. 'What about Ruby? Don't you miss your daughter?'

Mike sighed. 'Of course I do. I love Ruby. I love you both. But I can't get my head around this play while you are telling me to save up a deposit and sort out Ruby and do all the other things you keep asking for. I need space to become the character, Sara. Learn my lines. Get stuck in to the part.'

Sara sucked her bottom lip in hard. There were parts of him she would like to get stuck in to. With a baseball bat.

Focus on Ruby. 'I've made an appointment with the doctor. For Ruby. Next Monday. There was a cancellation and they could fit her in. I thought you might want to be there.'

A long sigh at the other end. 'You're not going to let this go, are you? What does my mum say about it?'

It was like being fifteen again. 'Your *mum*? I haven't asked your mum, funnily enough. But the preschool thinks it's a good idea. They think she might be… autistic.'

It was so hard to say the word out loud.

There was a brief silence. 'You have got to be kidding me.'

Finally, he realised the magnitude of the situation. 'I'm not. They asked me to go in and speak to them. Gave me a letter for a doctor.'

But that wasn't what he meant. 'Ruby's only been there five minutes. Shouldn't they be teaching her rather than sending you to the doctor? What had you said to them?'

'Me?' Because of course this was her fault. The tears that never seemed far away filled her eyes. 'I didn't say anything apart from being concerned about her speech. This came from them.'

'Of course it did. You've been on about this for months, Sara. It's like you *want* something to be wrong with her. She's fine.'

How could he say something so awful? Did he not know her at all? This conversation was making her feel worse. 'I need to go. Are you coming to the appointment on Monday or not?'

Another silence. When he spoke again, his voice was cold, resolute. 'If you want to waste your time with this, Sara, knock yourself out. Right now, I need to focus on the play. This is my opportunity to get somewhere in this business. You can't just let that pass you by.'

Sara felt sick to her stomach. But she needed to know where she stood. It was the not knowing that was messing with her mind. 'So, you're leaving me. Us. Me and Ruby. That's it?'

Now there was a big sigh at the other end. 'I haven't left you, I'm just working. Plenty of men go away to work – some are on oil rigs for half the year. Would you feel better if I was on an oil rig?'

Actually, she would. And not just because that would give the possibility that he might fall into the icy sea and drown. 'Men who work on oil rigs get paid a ton of money, Mike. I don't think you can make that comparison.'

Mike coughed out a bitter laugh. 'Money. It always comes down to that with you.'

How could she make him understand? Of course, it had to be about money. Money was security. Money was safety. Money was a small house with a garden and a bedroom for Ruby. 'You can't just run out on us whenever you get an opportunity, Mike. You have responsibilities. You have a child.'

'Oh, for God's sake, Sara. You'd think I'd left you in a bedsit with no heating. My mum's house is comfortable. She'll even look after Ruby for you. Look, I have to go. The others are waiting for me. I'll call you.'

And he hung up.

*

Although Sara didn't officially start work until nine thirty on Friday, she'd got into the habit of going straight there after dropping Ruby at preschool. After hanging up her coat and bag, her first job would be to make a coffee for herself and Kevin. Then she would wipe down all the surfaces before getting the hoover out. If Kevin wasn't sorting out an order or tapping at his computer with one finger and a confused look on his face, he would give her a hand.

Today he was revarnishing a couple of the bar stools. With his sleeves pushed up to his elbows, he was painstakingly guiding the brush around every curve on the ornate legs.

Without looking up he called out to her. 'Did you have a nice day off yesterday?'

Sara pulled her eyes away from his hands and resumed the wiping. 'Yeah, it was okay.' Actually, after failing in her quest to borrow some cash, she'd spent most of the evening searching the Internet for jobs, flats and information about autism. 'I went to see my mum.'

Kevin righted the stool and stood it on the newspaper pages he had spread on the floor. 'That's nice.'

Nice was not the word Sara would have used. Painful? Humiliating? Depressing? 'Not particularly. We're not close.'

Kevin leaned his face towards the stool and frowned. He dipped his brush in the tin and started to dab varnish into a crack. 'That's a shame.'

Sara wasn't in the mood for discussing her mother. 'It is what it is. I've been trying to find a flat too. Now Mike has gone, I really need to move out of Barbara's. But there's not much around here in my price range. Unless I want to live in a shoebox and sit on my bed to eat dinner.'

Kevin sighed and shook his head at the stool. Tilting his head to one side and then the other, he dabbed at it randomly. 'Does this look done to you?'

Sara put down her cloth and took the brush from his hands, unable to watch his ineptitude any longer. 'You need to go with the grain of the wood.'

Even though this was hardly art, the rhythmic strokes of the brush were soothing. She needed to make more time to paint; it was therapy.

Kevin sat back and folded his arms. 'You've got a knack for that.'

Sara smiled. 'It's not my first rodeo.'

He raised an eyebrow. 'You restore furniture?'

Sara squirmed a little. She never told people about her painting. After the post-college rejections, she'd kept it purely to herself. It was less painful. 'I paint a bit. Just a hobby.'

Kevin looked impressed. 'I'd like to see those. Have you got any pictures?'

She did have some photos on her phone of ones she was proud of, but wasn't about to show them to Kevin. 'Not with me. I don't get much time to do it these days. When I was younger, I didn't go anywhere without my sketchpad.' She felt a pang at the thought of her younger self in the park, sketching strangers as they sat on a bench eating their lunch. Life was so easy then.

'So that was your sketchpad you gave to Callum? I assumed it was Ruby's. No wonder you were so well equipped.'

Sara wiped the excess varnish from the brush on the side of the tin and laid it next to the stool. She held out a hand like a magician's assistant.

Kevin clapped his hands. 'Impressive. You're making yourself indispensable round here. Look, I know it's not ideal with a little one, but if you need to get out of your mother-in-law's place, you're very welcome to stay here. There's a couple of spare bedrooms in the apartment upstairs. You'd have to share a bathroom and kitchen with me, of course, but it's very handy for work and the rent would be cheap.'

Bring Ruby here? With the meet up with her mother still fresh in her mind, the last thing she wanted to do was raise Ruby in a pub.

'Thanks, I appreciate it, but I've got something a bit more child-friendly in mind.'

Out the window this morning, she'd watched Lisa's children running about the garden next door squealing with delight as their dog chased them around the swing and slide. Why couldn't Ruby have that, too?

'Fair enough.' He picked up the stool and carried it across the bar. Returning with another, he winked at her. 'While you're on a roll?'

Sara smiled and picked up the brush again. 'How about you? Did you do anything yesterday?'

'Actually, I spent a few hours with Callum again.' He stood back and watched her with his arms folded and a smile on his face.

Sara stopped mid-stroke and looked at him. 'Really? That's great. What did you do?'

Kevin's smile widened. 'I went to watch him play football after school. Then I took him out for something to eat. It was good.'

'That's great.'

'Yeah. It really was. I'd love to bring him back here for the night, but Kelly won't hear of it. She thinks it isn't good for him to stay in a pub.' He raised an eyebrow at her and she regretted her 'child friendly' comment.

She could see Kelly's point; she didn't want Ruby staying here either. But on the other hand, Kevin was Callum's dad. And it wasn't as if he was a drunkard. Whenever Sara was around, Kevin rarely drank anything other than coke or coffee. 'That's hard for you. That means you can't have him for a whole weekend?'

Kevin picked varnish from the side of his finger. 'Nope. That's probably part of it. I don't think she trusts me to look after him for longer than a few hours. Him wanting to leave here the other day didn't help much.'

'It just takes time. You've got to build up his trust. And Kelly's. Show her how serious you are about looking after him. Did you get some of those games and toys we looked at?'

'Yeah. They came yesterday from Amazon.'

'Good. Well, maybe his next visit he'll want to stay longer. Eventually he might be asking to come.'

'Maybe.' Kevin looked up at the clock on the wall. 'Nearly time to open up. I'd better get cracking. Give me a shout when you've finished that one.'

He was obviously upset that he couldn't spend more time with his son. Kelly didn't know how lucky she was to have an ex who actually wanted to spend time with his child. Kevin staggered back into the bar with a crate of beer. 'I was thinking: you should bring your sketchpad in with you next time. You could get some drawing done when we're quiet. Maybe you could draw the regulars? They're not pretty, but they are interesting.'

Sara gave the leg of the stool a final sweep of the brush. Maybe she would do just that.

CHAPTER TWENTY-FOUR

To begin with, Sara thought Ruby was pulling her towards the toyshop. She really didn't have the energy for that today. There was no spare money to buy a toy and no spare energy for the meltdown that would ensue when she told Ruby that she couldn't have one. 'No, Ruby. No toys today. You can look in the window, but we're not going in.'

But Ruby wasn't interested in the toyshop window. She continued to pull at Sara's hand until she was in front of the door to Leonard's gallery. Then banged on the door with her flat palm.

The other option is going home to Barbara, Sara thought. *So, why not?*

Sara knew now to push the door firmly to get in and Leonard smiled as he looked up from his desk. 'Hello, Ruby. Have you come back to do some drawing?' He pulled paper and some pastels from a drawer. Ruby didn't look at him, but she took the gift and sat in the corner with them, getting to work immediately.

Sara breathed out slowly. What was it about this place? It was so calm and peaceful, even Ruby felt it. She looked at her daughter – head down, hair fallen forwards, concentration etched into Ruby's frown and the tip of her tongue, which protruded from her lips. She was so calm here. It was almost magical.

'Coffee?'

Sara turned to look at Leonard, who was holding up a mug. He smiled tentatively. 'It's only instant, I'm afraid.'

'Er… yes, coffee would be great, thanks. Are you sure we're not stopping you from…?' She trailed off. What was she stopping him from doing?

Leonard laughed. 'Exactly. The only thing you're keeping me from is cheating on the crossword in the paper.' He disappeared into the tiny kitchen.

While he was gone, Sara walked the gallery again. There was nothing new, but the light coming in the window gave everything a different feel. She stopped again in front of the nudes. They really were something special. Last time he'd said they weren't for sale. Were they his work?

Leonard walked back in with two mugs on a tray, a carton of milk and an open packet of sugar. 'Do you want milk and sugar? And would Ruby like a glass of milk?'

'That's fine. She's okay with her water beaker. Just milk for me, please. I love these. Did you say the artist was local?'

Leonard slid the tray onto his desk, sloshed some milk into a mug and brought it over to Sara. 'My wife.'

Sara raised an eyebrow. He hadn't mentioned a wife before. 'Wow. She's very talented.'

He stood beside her, mug in hand, and gazed up at the drawings. 'Yes. She was. I'm afraid she's not around anymore. This was *her* dream, really, the gallery. We talked about it when we were first married. She had big plans for it. I would run the gallery and she would paint and maybe run a tea shop alongside.' He held his coffee mug up. 'Some tea shop.'

He looked so sad that Sara wished she hadn't asked. 'I'm sorry. I didn't realise you'd lost your wife. You started the gallery together?'

Leonard shook his head. 'Unfortunately not. She never saw it. When she died, I was rather lost. We didn't have many close friends, you see. She was all I needed so when she went, I wasn't sure what to do with myself. We'd been saving up, planning to start a family. Well, that wasn't going to happen so I used the money to start the gallery.' He nodded at the nudes. 'Those sketches were the first things I put on the wall.'

Sara was confused. Starting a family? Would it be rude to ask? 'How long ago did you lose her?

'It'll be thirty-seven years this September.'

Thirty-seven years? Had he been on his own that whole time? Sara sipped at her coffee. Leonard continued to look at the sketches, lost in thought. Then he transferred his gaze to Ruby. For a few moments, they both watched her in silence.

Only the most avant-garde art critic would find a discernible form to Ruby's picture, but she was certainly enjoying dragging the pastels across the page, every so often sitting back to admire her work before reapplying herself.

It would feel rude not to say something. 'Thirty-seven years is a long time to be on your own.'

Leonard's face changed as he spoke about his wife. 'She was impossible to replace. I'm not the sort of man who collects a lot of friends, anyway. I only ever needed her. Although it would have been nice to have children.'

Sara could identify with the 'not many friends' part. She wasn't a great example of that, either. Didn't he have *anyone*? The silence rested between them for a few more moments.

Leonard sipped at his coffee. 'Sandy had a congenital heart condition. Her doctor said she should never attempt to have children, but Sandy was… well, let's just say that Sandy had an artistic temperament.' He smiled. 'She didn't react well when people told her what to do.'

The pride in his eyes when he spoke about his wife made Leonard's face come alive. Sandy must have been a very special woman.

He turned back to the nudes and sighed. 'Sadly, it turned out the doctor was right. Sandy died giving birth to our baby girl. She was only halfway through the pregnancy. I lost them both.'

The quiet in the room seemed to deepen. From Leonard's face, Sara could see that thirty-seven years wasn't long enough to get over what had happened. She left it a few more moments before speaking gently. 'So you opened a gallery in her memory.'

Leonard crouched down on the floor beside Ruby, looking at her picture. Sara held her breath for Ruby's reaction, but she didn't seem to notice that he was there. He moved his head this way and that to get a different perspective. 'Yes. I opened the gallery in her memory. Shame I can't make a better job of getting people to visit it.'

The defeat in his voice was heartbreaking. Someone as kind as Leonard deserved something good to happen to him. Though, short of accosting people on the street to buy art, she had no idea what she could do to help. But she really wanted to. Sara almost laughed at herself. As if she had nothing else to be sorting out right now.

CHAPTER TWENTY-FIVE

Kelly was stunning. Long, thick brown hair, immaculate make-up and a manicure, which she tapped on the surface of the bar. She checked her watch. 'What time did you say you were expecting him in?'

Sara stopped wiping the surface and looked at the clock. 'I didn't. But we open up at twelve so I'm sure he'll be here by then.' This was another Sunday shift that Kevin had asked her to cover. It was becoming a regular thing. Was he doing it for his benefit or Sara's?

Kelly sighed and perched on the edge of a stool as if it was carrying something contagious. She pressed a number into her mobile, tucked her hair behind her ear with her middle finger and put the phone to her ear. 'Hi. Yes… I'm here now… I agreed you could take him to football practice as long as I could collect him from here at 11.00 a.m. I know, but Callum and I have somewhere to be, Kevin. You can't change the plan… I don't really care, to be honest… just hurry up and get him back here.'

Kelly placed the mobile face down on the bar, sat still for a moment, then picked it up again and began to swipe her finger downward. She frowned. Smiled. Frowned again. Sara could hear the tap of her fingernail on the screen.

There is nothing more irritating than unsolicited advice, especially from a stranger. But Sara couldn't help but feel sorry for Kevin. She also wondered if his ex-wife knew how much he wanted to spend time with his son. He seemed almost scared of her. If Mike were half as keen to spend time with Ruby right now, Sara's life would be a hundred times easier. When Kelly sighed and put her mobile down on the bar again, Sara saw her opportunity.

'Kevin loves seeing Callum.'

Kelly's head flipped in her direction. 'Excuse me?'

Sara carried on wiping the table. 'Kevin. He talks about his son all the time. How he wishes he could spend more time with him.'

Sara hadn't meant that to come out as judgemental as it sounded. She wanted to stuff the words back into her mouth when she saw the expression on Kelly's face. 'He told you that, did he?'

Sara coughed. 'I have a little girl. We chat about being parents and…' She trailed off as a smile played across Kelly's lips.

'I see.'

That sounded dodgy. 'No, nothing like that. I'm married. It's just, you know. Once the doors are shut at night, you get chatting about stuff and I feel a bit… sorry for him, I guess.'

Kelly's eyes glinted. 'I see. Poor Kevin. All alone. Evil ex-wife. That kind of thing?'

'No. No. He never said anything about you. Just that, you know, it's hard for him to see Callum because…' Oh, God. She was making a complete hash of this. It was none of her business anyway – a thought that clearly occurred to Kelly too.

'He loves a late-night chat, does Kevin. Used to have them all the time when he was out on the road. Obviously, I was completely in the wrong to expect him to come home to his wife and baby at one in the morning, when he would much rather be *chatting* to his *band*.' She raised an eyebrow at Sara.

Kelly's condescending tone would normally put Sara's back up, but she'd probably asked for that by sticking her nose in in the first place. Still, she'd started now so she may as well say her piece. 'I didn't know about that. But now I guess I just think it's got to be hard that Callum can't have a bit more time with his dad.'

Kelly laughed. She wasn't smiling. 'Time with his dad? You say you have a little girl – how much time does her dad spend with her?'

Sara bristled. 'He's working away right now. It's complicated.'

Kelly nodded slowly. 'It always is. I'm assuming you've had the full sob story from Kevin. His side, obviously.' She laughed again. 'He really doesn't change.'

Just then the back door opened and they heard the sound of little feet running before a mop of dark hair appeared at the bar.

'Mummy! Daddy bought me a racing car! Look!' Callum shoved a red plastic sports car at his mother and waved a remote control.

Kelly slid from her stool. 'That's lovely. It's the one you wanted for your birthday, isn't it? Why don't you go to the toilet quickly and then we'll be off?' She scowled at Kevin as she waited for Callum to leave the room.

Kevin smiled. 'Sorry we were late. He couldn't choose between the red one and the blue one.'

Kelly's fingernails were tapping the bar again. 'And you didn't think to check with me?'

Kevin frowned. 'About buying a car for my son?'

Kelly closed her eyes, took a deep breath and breathed out slowly. 'We've already bought him that car. For his birthday. He saw it last week and we told him he had to wait to see what he got for his birthday.'

Kevin looked dejected. 'I'm sorry.'

Kelly's hands clenched at her sides. Sara could almost feel the knot in Kelly's stomach. Sara had felt similarly on many occasions. 'I just ask that you run things by me. I know you are playing "Dad of the Year" right now,' she glanced at Sara, 'but I'm the one who has to deal with the day-to-day.'

Kevin's hands went to his temples. 'You have to give me a break, Kelly. I'm trying. I really am.'

Callum reappeared from the toilet. 'I washed my hands, Mummy.'

'Good boy. Now say goodbye to Daddy and let's go.'

After seeing them out the back door, Kevin came back in and shrugged at Sara. 'I got it wrong again.'

She felt for him, but was now more than a little curious to hear Kelly's side of the story too. 'She does seem to be quite angry with you.'

Kevin sighed and ran his fingers through his hair. 'I probably deserve it. I was a pretty crap husband when Callum was a baby.'

Sara kept wiping and didn't look up. She wanted to hear this story, but she didn't want to know anything that would make her change her opinion of Kevin. 'In what way?'

He pulled out a chair and sat down. 'I was so focused on the bands I was managing, the whole music scene with the gigs and the scouts and recording demos. I loved it. Kelly used to tell me all the time that I needed to be home more, that I was missing out on Callum, but I didn't listen. I thought he was just a baby, that it made no difference to him whether I was there or not. And Kelly was miserable, and then it was just arguments the whole time I was home so I just… didn't come home. I'd stay out for most of the night, kip at a friend's house, pop home for a few hours in the afternoon. I never cheated, but God, I was an absolute arse. I couldn't see it, though. All the time I would tell her, "I just need to get this tour sorted, then I'll be at home more. We just need to get this demo down and then I'll be home more. Next week, next month, next autumn, it'll all calm down and I'll be at home more."'

He stood up and walked around the bar, straightening the tables and chairs. Sara would have to move them again in a minute to vacuum the floor, but she didn't interrupt.

'I don't blame her for meeting someone else; I really don't. And I don't blame her for being reluctant to let me spend too much time with Callum. In her head, I'm sure she's expecting me to go AWOL again and leave Callum upset. Now he's older, it would be even worse.' Kevin was near to where she was wiping now. She couldn't avoid looking up at him as he gripped the back of a chair and looked at her. 'But I won't, Sara. I really won't. I love that boy and I am so angry – not at Kelly, I mean. But at the old me who didn't realise what he had. Really bloody angry. And I just want her to realise that I am here for good, and I'll never let Callum down ever again.'

So Kelly had been left to look after Callum while Kevin was living his dream. That was uncomfortably familiar. Kelly wasn't an unreasonable ex-wife, she was a woman who was protecting her son. 'I can see how it's hard for her, Kevin. I don't want to make you feel worse, but you need to earn her trust.'

Kevin slumped onto the chair he'd been holding. 'I know that. But I have been trying and nothing seems to work.'

'It will take time. See it from her perspective. Callum is the most precious thing in her life. If she's effectively been a single mother, that must count double. It's terrifying to entrust your child to someone else – even if that person is his dad.'

'I get it. I do. But how can I prove to her that I can look after him if she never lets me have him for more than a few hours at a time? I want him to stay overnight. Or come for the whole weekend. Or even go away on holiday together. I want to get to know him. I want to be a good dad. I know it's a huge responsibility. But I am up for that. I'm ready for it.'

Everything he said about Callum was what Sara wanted to hear Mike say about Ruby. She wanted Mike to *want* to be a good dad. To *want* the responsibility. But it had clearly taken Kevin some time to realise the error of his ways. Did that mean there was still hope for Mike?

'Just keep going. Keep being there. Show her she can trust you with her baby boy.'

The early shift was always quiet in the pub, but this particular afternoon was almost silent. For the first hour, the only person was Sid.

Kevin practically plucked the old man's glass from his hands after he'd drained the last of his beer. 'Same again, Sid?'

'Better make it a half. Don't want to upset the missus. It's her birthday.'

Sara stood up from where she'd been turning the mixers so their labels faced front, desperate for something to occupy her. 'Her birthday? What are you doing here, then? I hope you've at least bought her a very good present.'

Sid took the beer from Kevin and slurped off the froth. 'Ah, she doesn't want me under her feet. She's got her sister over. And I'll pick up some flowers on the way home.'

Kevin laughed. 'Some flowers? You can do better than that, surely? Actually, Sara's an artist. What about asking if you can commission her? I don't know what her rate is, but I bet she could do a lovely sketch of you for Mrs Sid.'

Sid sat up straight on his stool. 'Would you really, love? I could even pick up a frame from the cheap shop on the way home. She'd be made up with a proper picture for the wall, I reckon. I'd pay you, of course.'

The sketchpad and pencils were in her bag on the off-chance of some time to draw, but she hadn't envisaged an actual customer for her work. But they were so quiet and it would help the time go by, so why not? 'Okay.'

Sid sat up even straighter on the bar stool, licked a finger and smoothed his eyebrows. For the next half an hour he was rigid – didn't even move to sip his beer. While Sara drew, a couple of locals arrived for a lunchtime drink and made jokes at Sid's expense.

'Aren't you supposed to have your kit off, mate?'

Sid ignored them and she followed his lead. Kevin kept popping over between customers, looking over Sara's shoulder as she drew. She ignored him too, feeling a little thrown by his revelations about Callum and Kelly.

All this time she had thought he was a properly good guy, had even felt sorry for him. Now that she'd seen it from the other side, maybe she'd got it wrong. It was so easy to judge when you didn't have the full story. He was only her boss, after all; it was none of her business. But she couldn't shake off a feeling of disappointment.

Normally drawing made Sara relax. It was the one thing guaranteed to absorb her mind and protect it from whatever else was going on. Today it wasn't having that effect. It wasn't just the awkward atmosphere with Kevin; it was Ruby's doctor's appointment tomorrow, hanging over her like a dark cloud. A creeping fear of what he might say. What it would mean for Ruby. For their future.

No amount of concentration on the folds in Sid's cheeks could take that off her mind.

CHAPTER TWENTY-SIX

The waiting room was full of people. Sniffs and coughs filled the air and Sara tried not to breathe in. A bout of the flu would be the final straw right now. Gripping Ruby's hand tightly, she registered their arrival on the machine at the entrance, standing in front of it for about four minutes trying to remember Ruby's date of birth. Exhaustion wasn't good for the memory.

When their appointment was announced by the digital display, Sara tried to pull Ruby away from the toy area. 'Come on, Ruby. We'll play after.' Though she purposefully kept her voice upbeat and light, Ruby didn't want to cooperate.

'No!' Ruby frowned, pulled her hand from Sara's grasp and sat back down with the blocks.

Sara tried again, the display still scrolling: *Ruby Lucas to Room 1.*

Sara picked up a handful of blocks and then took Ruby's hand again. 'Come on, Rubes. We'll take them with us.'

'No!' Ruby pulled her hand away. She was surprisingly strong for a three-year-old. Several pairs of eyes were on them; Sara's face began to burn.

An announcement came over the tannoy, 'Ruby Lucas to room one, please.'

This time Sara would just have to go for it. She grabbed Ruby around the waist and pulled her up to her hip.

A well-meaning woman of grandmotherly age nodded and smiled at her. 'They can be a handful at that age, can't they?'

Sara attempted a smile, which was probably more like a grimace. *You have no bloody idea.*

The doctor was typing into his computer as Sara and Ruby came in. Was that for his last patient or had he diagnosed Ruby from a camera in the waiting room?

He didn't even look up when he spoke. 'Good morning. How can I help?'

Where should she start? 'It's for Ruby. My daughter.' Sara offered him the letter from the preschool. 'She doesn't seem to be making the expected progress. Her preschool suggested I bring her to see you.'

Finally, the doctor turned to look at them. He wheeled his chair around and smiled. 'Did they, now? Hold old is Ruby?'

'She's three.'

'And what is it particularly that concerns you?'

All the time they were talking, Ruby was squirming on Sara's lap like an eel. Hitting Sara's hand. The hitting got harder and harder, but Sara didn't dare release her. Then Ruby leaned forwards, and bit. Sara yelped and let go, whereupon Ruby slid to the floor and started to cry. Sara looked at the doctor. Did she even need to say anything? But he was still waiting for a response.

Sara tried to swallow over the huge lump in her throat. She coughed. 'Erm, well she is not really speaking. Other than "no", obviously.' She laughed, hollowly. Even though it wasn't remotely funny. 'And she struggles with anything outside her routine. And she won't try new foods, but those she likes she just eats and eats and we… I can't get her to stop and…'

Now that she'd started, the words just came tumbling out. All her worries. All the things that hadn't felt right. All the times Mike had told her she was overreacting. Some of the words surprised even her – how much had she supressed these last few months? But beneath the words was a huge well of guilt. This doctor was a stranger. And here she was telling him everything bad she could possibly think of about Ruby. Her beautiful girl, who was weeping on the floor right now… breaking Sara's heart.

The lump got higher and higher in Sara's throat until it threatened to cut off her voice. *Mustn't cry. Mustn't make him think I am a hysterical mother. Must make him hear me.* '… and she, she can't make friends. She doesn't want to be near other children.'

The doctor nodded. He returned to his keyboard and typed. Sara desperately wanted to know what he was writing. 'Bad mother'? 'Attention seeker'? 'Hypochondriac'? He unfolded the letter from Ruby's preschool and gave it a cursory glance. He turned back to face Sara.

'I understand your concerns, but your daughter is very young. I could make a referral to a paediatrician, but it would be a very long wait.' He paused and looked at her.

Was she supposed to respond? Make a decision whether it was worthwhile or not like they were at a funfair, deciding whether to join the queue? 'So…?'

The doctor sighed. 'You need to understand. Autism is a lifelong diagnosis. You have to consider how useful it is to label your daughter in that way. If you want me to make the referral, I can do that. Alternatively, you can give her a few more months, watch her development, see if she catches up on her own.'

Catches up? So, Ruby wasn't autistic? Had the preschool got it wrong? Was Sara being too dramatic? Had Mike been right all this time? Was she the one with the problem? What should she do? It was so hot in there and Ruby's cries were getting louder and louder. The doctor was looking at her for a decision. What should she say? 'Okay. Thank you. I'll… erm… speak to the preschool and… I'll… er…'

She bent to pick up Ruby, who was now biting her own hand. Surely that wasn't normal? But the doctor just gave her another cursory nod as she backed out of the room and walked the long corridor back to the waiting room and the sea of eyes that followed them out towards the front door.

By the time she got home, Sara was exhausted. She had had to fight Ruby to get her back into her buggy outside the surgery. Ramrod straight, it was impossible to make her sit and bolt her in. No one came to help Sara; they just watched. Eventually, she had to lie across Ruby horizontally and push her down before quickly clipping the seatbelt into place.

An older man coming into the surgery had held the door open for her and 'joked' that Ruby was too big to be in a buggy. 'No wonder she's upset, she wants to be walking herself.' Sara had had to resist ramming his legs from under him.

Ruby's screams were Sara's soundtrack for the whole walk home. She passed at least three mothers with their perfectly happy children in their prams or buggies. What was she doing wrong? As much as she hadn't wanted to accept that Ruby might be autistic, at least that would explain why she was behaving like this. If not, it must be something that Sara was doing. Or not doing. Or should be doing. Her head swam.

By the time she put her key in the front door, Ruby's wails had subsided into the odd sob – her face swollen from crying, her eyes red. Safely inside the hallway, Sara unclicked the harness and lifted Ruby from the buggy. She took her through to the lounge and sat her down on the floor, before sinking down onto one of the armchairs and letting her head fall back.

Have I made the right decision?

The doctor hadn't seemed overly concerned about Ruby's behaviour and he must have seen many children with special needs. But so had the preschool. Why would they write the letter if there wasn't something more to it? She covered her face with her hands. 'Oh, Ruby. This is so difficult. I can't make this decision on my own.'

The front door banged followed by the rustle of shopping bags as Barbara made her way up the hall. Tins clonked onto the kitchen worktop, the squeak of a tap, water filling a kettle, the loud click of an electric switch. Barbara came into the lounge.

'Oh, you're home already. What did the doctor say?'

Barbara had been very quiet when Sara told her what the preschool had recommended; not giving away whether she thought it was a good idea or not. What had the doctor said? Sara could barely remember. Had he really said anything at all? 'He said we should give her some time.'

Barbara nodded, as if she'd known that all along. 'Very sensible. Would you like tea?'

No. What she wanted was a large glass of wine. Or a bottle. And sleep. For about a week. 'Actually, would you mind keeping an eye on Ruby for ten minutes? I could really do with a shower. It might wake me up a bit.'

'Why don't you have a bath? Take your time. Ruby's okay with me for a while. I got some of her favourite biscuits at the shop. We'll have a cuppa and a biccie, won't we Ruby?'

Sara was about to say she didn't need that long, and that Ruby didn't need a sugary snack right now, but the offer was too tempting. Thirty minutes alone in the bath would be heaven. 'Thank you.'

As Sara lowered herself into a hot bath, she kept sliding until her whole head was under the water. Silence. Complete silence – closed eyelids shutting out the world until the need to breathe forced her back up. At some point, she would need to let Mike know what the doctor had said. She would send a text, not wanting to hear the smugness in his voice at having been proved right.

But why wasn't she happy that the doctor didn't think Ruby was autistic? Like he said, autism was a lifelong condition. No one would wish difficulties on their child. Everything a parent did was about making their child's life better, easier. So why did she feel so… so… sad? Disappointed even. Was Mike right? Had this been more about her than Ruby? Was she making excuses for something that she should be dealing with? Responsibility rolled over her shoulders and her eyes closed as she slid back under the water, letting it roll across her face. Who should she believe? What if she got this wrong? How could she know?

When Sara came back downstairs, she stood at the lounge door for a few moments, steeling herself for round two. But when she pushed it open, she found peace and quiet.

Ruby was sitting on the floor with her blocks in a line. Barbara was there too, passing the blocks to her one by one and singing softly. 'Twinkle, twinkle, little star. How I wonder what you are.'

For many families, this was an ordinary scene: grandmother and grandchild playing together. It was the ordinariness that pierced Sara. Barbara's patience, her calm, her gentleness; somehow it had brought peace to the room.

As Barbara sang, Ruby nodded along. 'Twinkle. Twinkle,' she said. 'Twinkle. Twinkle.'

Barbara looked up. 'Ah, here's Mummy. All better after her bath. Ruby's been a very good girl, Mummy.'

Sara swallowed. Barbara seemed to have succeeded with Ruby where she had failed. Maybe it was 'Mummy' who was the problem, after all.

CHAPTER TWENTY-SEVEN

The following Saturday, Sara heard the murmurings of conversation as soon as she walked back in the front door. Bending down to lift Ruby from her buggy, she kissed her warm cheek before setting her down on her feet in the hallway. Ruby made a beeline for the kitchen, stood in front of the fridge and patted the door. Milk.

The last few days had been calm. Sara had sent Mike a text:

All okay at the doctor's. Just need to keep an eye on her.

To which Mike had replied three hours later:

Good.

Barbara had looked after Ruby on Wednesday night so that Sara could pick up another evening shift, and on Thursday it had rained so they had spent the day indoors drawing. When Barbara had popped next door for a bit, Sara had tried singing 'Twinkle, Twinkle' with Ruby again, but she hadn't joined in. It was hard not to take it personally.

The sun had come out that Saturday morning, so Sara and Ruby had been out for a walk. If she'd known that Barbara had a guest, she might have stayed out longer. Filling Ruby's Nemo beaker with milk, she strained her ears to try to place the second voice. Just as she realised who it was, the lounge door opened.

'Sara! Perfect timing. We were just talking about you.' Barbara had two of her precious Cath Kidston mugs in her hand; she was out to impress. Giving Sara a customary glance up and down –whether or not she was impressed was anybody's guess – she held the door open with her elbow. 'Go on through. Would you like a tea or a coffee?'

'Actually, I need to go upstairs and get Ruby sorted out. She's had a long morning.' They both looked over at Ruby who was sitting contentedly on the kitchen floor, drinking from her beaker. Of course she was. *Thanks for the help, Rubes.*

'She looks happy enough to me. Come through and talk to Lisa. I was just about to put the kettle on again. I'll keep an eye on Ruby.'

There was no way out of it. Lisa could hear every word of their exchange and if Sara gave another excuse, it would be obvious that she didn't want to join them. *Bugger.*

Glancing back at Ruby, almost willing her to find something wrong with her milk and throw it across the kitchen, Sara painted on a smile and walked into the lounge. 'Hi.'

Lisa turned in her seat and did the same up and down of the eyes that Barbara had done. Surely Sara didn't look that bad? Lisa herself looked slightly incongruous, perched on Barbara's sofa in her crisp white shirt and navy capri trousers, flawless make-up more appropriate for a business brunch than a cup of Earl Grey with her neighbour. No wonder Barbara was so judgemental of Sara's appearance if she thought this was what a modern mother should look like.

But Lisa was friendly enough. 'Did you and Ruby have a nice walk?'

Actually, they had. Ruby had been up excruciatingly early that morning, which had the upside of her conking out in her buggy. This meant Sara could tune out a little and enjoy her surroundings. The flowers in the local park had started to bloom in the early

April sunshine and the colours were striking yet fragile. She'd been able to use the watercolour pencils that Leonard insisted she take, and the hour she and Ruby spent outside felt like a holiday.

'We just went to the park.'

'That's nice.'

They lapsed into silence. What could Sara talk to Lisa about? They had nothing whatsoever in common and female small talk wasn't Sara's strong point. Where was Barbara with the tea? *Think of something.* 'Do your two like the park?'

Lisa wrinkled her nose. 'Grant isn't keen on me taking them there. Sometimes the older kids from the Park Estate are hanging around. That's why we have the swings and slide at the bottom of the garden. They can play there.'

Of course. Why would you need to fraternise with riff-raff at the park if you have your own private playground at home? Sara glanced at the lounge door. What was Barbara doing? Harvesting the bloody tea leaves?

The clock on the mantel ticked loudly. Lisa smoothed an invisible thread from her trousers. Sara was no expert on couture, but they looked expensive. As did the navy-and-white-striped pumps and the diamond tennis bracelet. If these were Lisa's everyday clothes, what did she wear for special occasions? It was difficult not to be jealous; the bracelet alone would probably pay the rent on a small house for three months. At least.

'Well, your two have each other to play with. Ruby is an only child, so I like to take her places where she might meet other children.' Sara wouldn't have been surprised to see her own nose grow three inches. Even if Ruby did venture to the play area at the park, she had no interest at all in playing with the other children.

Lisa gave a small nod. 'Yes, socialising is very important at this age, isn't it? Barbara tells me you've started her at the preschool near the High Street?'

What else had Barbara been saying about Ruby? 'Yes. She seems to really like it there.' Another lie. 'Did yours go there?'

Lisa shook her head. 'No. We decided to go Montessori.'

Sara had absolutely no idea what that meant. 'That's nice.'

Another thirty seconds of silence stretched between them. Barbara was pushing her luck now. It was like being set up on a blind date with her worst nightmare.

Lisa cleared her throat. 'Speaking of socialising, the MD's wife at Grant's firm has decided we need a social club for the wives and partners, and Grant nominated me to organise the first meeting.'

Sara pictured middle-class women in Louboutins on the roundabout at the local park with the 'Park Estate kids'. She stifled a smile. How was she expected to respond? 'Um, that's nice?'

Lisa pulled a face. 'Not really, but there it is. I'm trying to find a venue with a function suite. Barbara suggested I speak to you because you work in the pub on the corner.'

A laugh escaped from Sara's mouth; she coughed to disguise it. Function suite? The Forester's? They just about had working toilets. Sara could really imagine Lisa and her cronies rubbing shoulders with Sid and drinking half a stout. 'I'm not sure it would be the right kind of venue for that.'

Lisa snorted. 'Of course not! I mean, I've never been in, but you can tell from the outside, can't you? No, I just thought you might know of somewhere, you know, being in the trade?'

Sara winced. Lisa sounded like the lady of the house who had come down to the kitchens to ask a favour from one of the chambermaids. 'Sorry, no. I don't know the area that well yet. Can't you find a hotel or somewhere? Or is that too expensive?'

Lisa laughed again. 'Oh, money is no object. Grant is more than happy to throw money at this to make sure we impress. I suppose a hotel might work. I was just hoping for something a little more… surprising or… interesting.'

Sara's brain went back to Louboutins in the park, but she didn't laugh this time. The 'money is no object' comment made her want to poke Lisa in the eye.

Barbara bustled in bearing a tray with the hot drinks and a plate of biscuits. 'Sorry for the delay. Ruby wanted her blocks and it took me a while to find where I'd put them.'

Sara glanced around; all of Ruby's toys had been removed from the lounge. Heaven forbid Lisa could actually detect that there was a child living here.

'Maybe I'll go and check on her.' At last. Escape.

But Barbara held up a hand. 'No need. She's very happy in the kitchen lining them all up.' She passed a floral mug to Lisa. 'Did you ask Sara about a venue?'

Lisa took the mug and shook her head at the proffered biscuits. 'Yes, Sara has suggested a hotel and I guess I'll have to look into that. It's just that some of the people coming will know all the local hotels. I just wanted something a bit different. Grant is keen that we make our mark.'

Sara had a sudden thought. Surprising? Interesting? Different? 'How many people is it for? Because I might actually know somewhere.'

'Oh, good! I hoped you would be able to help.' Barbara beamed with a relief akin to a parent whose child had played nicely with a new friend.

Lisa looked more doubtful as she sipped at her tea. 'Where were you thinking?'

Pause for effect. 'How about an art gallery?'

Lisa raised her eyebrows. 'Sounds interesting. Where?'

Sara took a biscuit. 'On the High Street. Above the toyshop.'

'I'm not sure I know where you mean.' Lisa put her mug down on a coaster and placed her hands back onto her knees.

Barbara frowned. 'No, neither do I. How do you get above the toyshop?'

It was no wonder Leonard's sales weren't great if two people living three streets away didn't even know there *was* a gallery on the High Street.

'It relocated there about a year ago. Ruby and I visit sometimes. It's lovely. A big open space.'

Lisa shuffled forwards on her seat. 'Sounds interesting. And they hire themselves out as a venue?'

This was a bit stickier. 'Not exactly, but I've got to know the owner and I'm sure he'd welcome the opportunity to make some extra money.' Whether or not he'd want a hundred wine-wielding executives and their wives click-clacking around his paintings was another matter, but she'd broach that later.

Lisa shuffled back again. 'I'm not sure. I can't have somewhere amateur.'

Was there no pleasing this woman? But now that Sara had come up with a way to repay Leonard for his kindness, she didn't want to let it go. 'But you said you wanted somewhere different. And it's definitely interesting – the art on the walls is fantastic. Plus, I could ask Kevin at the Forester's to source the drink and run a bar. And then all you'd need to do is find a caterer.'

Lisa shuffled forwards again. 'You make it all sound so easy.'

Did she? Probably because she was making it all up on the spot. 'It will be. Come and look at the gallery, see what you think. I'll meet you there and we can come up with a plan.'

Lisa smiled. 'Okay. That would be great. Thank you. How about Monday?'

Monday? She needed time to run this past Leonard. And rope in Kevin. 'I'm at work on Monday. How about Tuesday morning?'

CHAPTER TWENTY-EIGHT

Monday afternoon, Sara was a little late collecting Ruby from preschool, which is why there were so many other parents there before her. At first she thought that was why they looked unusual. It took her a while to realise it wasn't that there were so many of them. It was that they were all carrying gift bags and presents. Sara's heart sank. What had she forgotten?

Trying not to look like a crazy person, Sara surreptitiously scanned every parent that was waiting. They all seemed to have something. Most of the wrapping was pink and covered with My Little Ponies, Disney princesses or cartoon flowers. The gifts varied in size from a book-shaped box to something large and squishy and teddy-shaped. Sara wracked her brains. Surely she hadn't missed a letter? Were they supposed to bring something for a raffle or something?

When they got inside, the children were sitting on the carpet and a blonde little girl, around the same size as Ruby, scrambled to her feet and ran to her mother. 'Party time! Party time!'

Her mother laughed. 'Yes, poppet, party time at last. Now let's get going so that we can be there to welcome everybody.' She guided her daughter back out the door, nodding at parents as she passed them. 'See you in a minute! I'll have the coffee ready! Bring your ear plugs.' The other parents were also hurrying their children along.

Ruby wasn't on the carpet again. Sara better ready herself for another visit to the sensory room and an update on the goings-on of the day. But Ellie was waving at her from the corner of the main room, where Ruby was playing with a balloon.

Ellie smiled at Sara. 'I had some balloons in the cupboard from Christmas and I thought she might like to take one home.'

'That's nice of you. Did she not want to sit on the carpet with the others again?'

Ellie wrinkled her nose. 'They were all a bit hyper and noisy today and Ruby didn't seem comfortable, so I brought her over here. We thought we'd get a bit of peace and quiet, didn't we Ruby?'

Ruby didn't answer. She was transfixed by the balloon, patting it up and down onto the floor. Sara glanced back over to the carpet where parents were hurrying their children into coats or getting them changed into party clothes. 'Is there something going on?'

Ellie scratched her ear and blushed. 'Uh, I think there's a party for one of the little girls at the hall up the road. Some of them have been invited.'

Some of them? From where Sara was standing, Ruby was the only child not going. Her face began to heat up. It was probably just because Ruby hadn't been there long, that was all. *Don't show that you care.*

'I actually kind of need to update you on the doctor's appointment. Can we go to the office?'

'Of course. I'll see if Sharon is free too.'

It didn't take long for Sara to tell Ellie and Sharon about her conversation with the doctor, mainly because there wasn't much to tell. The two exchanged a glance when she told them the doctor had suggested she wait a while.

Sharon leaned forwards. 'Did you give him the letter I'd written?

Sara nodded. 'Of course. He seemed to think she was very young for us to start talking about autism.'

Sharon raised an eyebrow. 'I wonder if he'd have been so reluctant if she was a boy.'

Sara felt uncomfortable. Had she been too much of a pushover? At the time, with Ruby getting so upset, she'd just wanted to get the hell out of that surgery. 'Should I have demanded he do something?'

'Demanded is probably too strong. Doctors don't respond too well to demands.' Sharon paused. 'But you may need to be more forceful. Getting a diagnosis can be a bit of a fight, I'm afraid.'

Sara swallowed. 'So, you think she has definitely got autism?'

Sharon shook her head. 'I'm not qualified to officially diagnose. But I don't think that your GP is any more qualified than I am to make that call. Ruby needs to see an educational psychologist. Or at least a paediatrician.'

Psychologist? Why a psychologist? 'So, what do I do now?'

It was impossible to keep the wobble from her voice. Ruby was still playing with her balloon, batting it backwards and forwards between her hands. Her beautiful brown eyes watched it go back and forth. She was just a little girl, playing with a balloon. Happy and content.

Sharon sighed. 'You need to go back to the doctor. Tell him that you want a referral to an educational psychologist. With the report I wrote, he can't refuse you that.'

The thought of going back to that surgery filled Sara with fear. The doctor had seemed so confident that she didn't need to do anything yet. Who was right? Maybe it was just that Ruby was taking a while to settle in at preschool? Maybe a couple of weeks would make a big difference?

Sharon was standing up and shuffling some papers. 'I'm sorry to rush you out, but I need to leave – my son is playing rugby after school and I promised I would make this match.'

'Of course. Come on, Ruby. Bring your balloon.' She would take her home and they would have a damn party of their own.

One big upside of her meeting with Sharon was that the party guests and their parents had all disappeared by the time Sara came out. But when she got as far as the road, she met Jo – the come-for-a-coffee mother – walking the other way. She wouldn't be able to avoid speaking to her. *Dammit.*

Jo stopped in front of the buggy. 'Hi. How's it going?'

'Yeah, great.' Sara lied. 'You?'

'All good. I've just dropped Eddie off at the party and my eldest is with my mum, so I'm a free woman for an hour or so. Do you fancy going to get a coffee in the café around the corner?' Jo pointed down the road that Sara was about to walk down.

How was she going to get out of it when she was just about to travel in the same direction? 'Thanks, but I really should get home.' Sara motioned towards Ruby who was sitting in her buggy with her balloon, the picture of calm.

'Oh, please come. It isn't worth me going home before I have to go back to get Eddie and I'd really like some company.' She scrutinised Sara's face. 'And you look like you could really sink a bucket of latte right now.'

Sara opened her mouth to disagree before changing her mind. If she went home, it would only be her and Barbara avoiding each other. It might be nice to sit in a café and talk to someone her own age, especially as Ruby seemed very happy in her buggy. 'Okay, but I can't stay for long.'

Jo grinned. 'Great! Let's go!'

The café was small but bright and there were a couple of free tables when they got there. Jo insisted on queuing for the coffees, so Sara chose a table in the corner where the buggy could be poked out of the way of customer traffic.

Ruby was still playing with her balloon. It was amazing how long it had held her attention. 'Do you like that balloon, Ruby?'

Ruby didn't look up, but she did speak. 'Like that balloon.'

Sara drew in a breath. Was she answering or merely repeating? It was hard to know for sure. Was this progress?

Jo slid two coffee cups onto the table. 'I know these are huge, but it's not worth me going home and coming back, so I'm trying to keep you here as long as I can.'

Sara stirred her coffee slowly. 'Thanks. I'm flattered that you want to keep me here. You seem to know everyone at the preschool. Your son even gets invited to the parties.' She'd meant that as a joke but it just sounded bitter.

Jo grimaced. 'I'm sorry about that. I suppose they can't invite everyone.'

But Sara had seen how many were invited. It had looked suspiciously close to 'everyone' to her. Everyone except Ruby. She bit her lip hard.

'Anyway,' Jo continued hurriedly, 'I guess I just thought you looked like you could do with a friend. You're new to the area, aren't you?'

Sara picked up the birdbath of coffee; she needed both hands. 'Yes, we moved here a few weeks ago.'

Jo stirred her own drink and nodded. 'Yes, I knew that. You're Mike's wife, aren't you? Mike Lucas?'

The hairs rose on the back of Sara's neck. She put her drink down. 'Yes, I am.'

Jo nodded again. 'This is a surprisingly small town. I used to know Mike; we went to school together. Actually, we even dated for a while.'

Sara hadn't expected that. This just got weirder. 'And that's why you wanted to have a coffee with me?'

Jo laughed. 'No, no. That was all a lifetime ago. Couple of lifetimes ago. No, it was because you were having a tough time at drop-off. My son – the older one – was exactly the same. He's autistic so he struggles with any kind of change.'

The coffee was scalding. Sara replaced it on the saucer.

Jo kept talking. 'James used to start crying the moment we got to the top of the path. It was awful. I had to keep telling myself that it was for his own good. I felt like a monster.'

Was this woman suggesting that Ruby was the same? It was one thing having the preschool raise concerns, it was quite another to have a complete stranger give an amateur diagnosis.

'Anyway… I just remembered how it felt and when I saw how upset you were, my heart went out to you. Most kids do get used to it after a while, honestly.'

So she wasn't suggesting anything. Sara's defensive walls could go down a little. It would be good to have someone with experience to talk to. Could she trust Jo? Sara stared down at her coffee and turned the cup around in its saucer.

'Actually, I've been to see a doctor about Ruby. The preschool suggested it. But he seems to think she is too young to tell if…' She didn't actually know how to finish that sentence.

Jo nodded slowly. 'Ah, I see. I didn't know that. Well, you are doing completely the right thing. If you're concerned, you should definitely pursue it. If it would help to talk to someone who has gone through a similar process – even if the outcome is different – I'm happy to talk about it?'

Sara picked up the complimentary biscuit on her saucer and unwrapped it. For the first time in the last thirty minutes, Ruby's attention left the balloon and looked at her. Sara smiled. Her daughter might tune her out when she didn't want to talk, but her biscuit radar never failed. She passed the biscuit into Ruby's outstretched palm. Maybe she *would* talk to Jo about it some time. But not here.

'So, you used to date Mike?'

Jo laughed. 'Yes, many moons ago. It wasn't a particularly successful relationship. I don't think he was that into me – apparently there were a few other girls he found more interesting.' She laughed. 'Obviously he has grown up and settled down now. But he was a bit of a ladies' man back in the day.'

Sara shuffled a little in her seat, not about to enlighten Jo as to their current situation. 'Really?'

'Yep. And his mother – oh my word. She used to cover for him. Do you get on well with Barbara?'

How should she answer that question? Barbara had driven her crazy in the early days, but since Mike left, she'd been very sweet with Ruby. 'Can I pass on commenting on that one? We're living with her at the moment.'

Jo's eyes widened. 'I hadn't realised that, sorry! Actually, my mum used to know Barbara really well when they were young. She reckons that Barbara used to be a lot of fun. Y'know, before Lisa.'

Before Lisa? Why would the woman next door have such an effect on Barbara? Just as she opened her mouth to ask, Jo's phone rang.

'Hello?... What happened?... No, I'm just... of course. I'll be right there.'

Jo got up from the table and pulled on her coat. 'Really sorry. I have to shoot off. Eddie has bumped heads with another boy and he's upset. Why don't you find me on Facebook – it's Joanne Kelleher – or I'll give you my number when I see you next? It was really great to chat to you.' She waved as she darted out the café door.

Ruby was holding out her hand, flexing her fingers for another biscuit, so she gave her the one Jo had left on her saucer. She seemed nice. Maybe she would meet up with her to ask about this psychologist referral business. Maybe she might also be able to tell her what the connection was between Barbara and her perfect next-door neighbour?

CHAPTER TWENTY-NINE

Sara got to the gallery a couple of hours before Lisa on Tuesday. Leonard had now asked more than once about seeing some of Sara's paintings and she'd got up the courage to show him. She'd dug out some of the older pre-Ruby work and had also brought some of her more recent sketches.

As usual, Leonard made sure that Ruby was happy first. He always seemed to have something for her: coloured paper, a set of pastels, a new brush. Ruby would accept the gift without changing her expression – like a monarch who expected nothing less from her subject.

Watching this exchange felt like breathing out. This was the one place where Sara could just be. No judgement, no blame. 'Thank you, Leonard. You're so kind to her. To both of us.'

As usual, he waved it away. 'When she makes her fortune in the art world, she'll be my claim to fame. Speaking of which, is that your portfolio?'

Sara slid her art case onto the desk. 'I'm not sure it's professional enough to call it that, but you said you wanted to see it.'

There is something very intimate about sharing your work. Like opening a window into your mind, your heart, your soul. There's a vulnerability, a nakedness. It was why Sara didn't often show her paintings to others. Leonard looked at each piece in turn, taking an age over each one. It was unbearable. Agonising.

Ruby was content, humming to herself as she dragged pastels around a page. Sara didn't know where to put herself while she awaited Leonard's verdict. 'Shall I make some coffee?'

He nodded but still didn't speak.

Whilst the kettle was boiling, Sara tried to distract herself from Leonard's appraisal of her art by planning how she was going to sell the gallery as a venue to Lisa. She could imagine Lisa's face when she saw the dilapidated front door that needed a full body slam to open it. But hopefully she could be persuaded to think of it as quirky rather than crappy. Leonard himself had expressed concern when she called him to tout the idea, but had begrudgingly admitted the cash would help with luxuries like rent and heat. All they both needed was a bit of vision; it would be the perfect place for a posh party. Plus, who knows, Lisa's rich friends might be in the market for a bit of original art for their walls? Leonard had given her and Ruby a happy place to be these last few weeks; it would be great to give him something in return.

The ancient kettle finally boiled. She took two mugs of coffee and some water for Ruby back into the gallery. Leonard had only got through two more pictures. Did he know how desperate Sara was for him to like them? Maybe this had been a bad idea. She wasn't strong enough right now to have her dream punctured. However remote it was.

Might as well get it over with. 'So, what do you think?'

Leonard looked up and took his mug from her. 'Thanks.' He returned to her work. He'd just started on the sketches.

This was unbearable. 'Leonard. What do you think? Are they awful? Amateur?'

'Your mother is an impatient woman, Ruby.' He looked up at Sara and smiled. 'I really like them. You have talent.'

'Really?' Sara couldn't restrain the smile that bubbled to the surface. 'You're not just being nice?'

'No, Sara, I'm not just being nice. In fact, I'd be honoured if you'd let me hang some of these in the gallery. I think they're very commercial – if I can get some customers through the door, that is.'

He liked them! She didn't know about them being commercial, but she might be able to help with the customers. As if on cue, there was a knock on the door.

The look on Lisa's face was pretty much as Sara predicted: confused, unsure, a little disgusted. Before Lisa had a chance to comment on the insalubrious entrance, Sara took her to the other end of the gallery where the large sash window let in the late morning light.

'It's not quite what I was expecting.'

'Exactly!' Sara beamed. She wasn't a natural saleswoman, but she wanted to do this for Leonard, so she had worked out her pitch as she lay in bed the night before. 'And your guests won't be expecting it either.'

Lisa frowned. 'Okay. And that's a good thing because…?'

Sara took a deep breath. Now that she saw Lisa in her designer wrap dress, her perfectly smooth dark hair in direct contrast with the white uneven walls, she wondered if this was going to be too big a sell. 'Look, these people have been to hundreds of events in posh hotels, you said it yourself. This place would have much more impact.'

Lisa smiled awkwardly. 'Yes. But I'm not sure… I really need to impress them. I'm sorry.'

She couldn't have lost already? Sara looked at Leonard. He looked at the floor.

'No, wait. Just picture it for a moment. Think New York! Those awesome gallery scenes in *Sex and the City*. We can have a champagne bar set up over there, caterers with interesting and artistic canapés. We could even make little goody bags for the guests with arty items.' Sara gently guided Lisa towards the 'gift shop' area and then guided her away when she realised the items were all practical rather than aesthetically pleasing. 'You know, like a mini canvas, a pen that looks like a paintbrush.'

Lisa fiddled with her bracelet and looked confused. 'A pen that looks like a paintbrush?'

My God, she was hard work. *Eyes on the prize, Sara.* 'I know it sounds tacky, but it'll be fun. Fun and quirky and classy.' When she didn't get a reaction, Sara threw her last card in. 'What are your other options?'

Lisa sighed and put her hand to her head. 'I don't really have any. I'm just so worried that the whole thing is going to be a disaster. It's all I can think about and yet I've done nothing. I'm practically paralysed by the stress of it all.'

If they had still been standing by the window, Sara couldn't swear she wouldn't have propelled Lisa out of it. Paralysed by the stress? Of a party for a bunch of corporate wives? This woman didn't know she was born. 'Well, if you make a decision today, we can get organising and you can stop stressing.'

Lisa looked relieved at the prospect of that. 'How much is it going to cost?'

Sara tried to sound nonchalant. 'Five hundred pounds? Plus bar and catering, obviously.'

Behind Lisa, Leonard's eyes nearly popped out of his head. Even Lisa looked a little surprised. 'Five hundred pounds just for the venue hire?'

It was going to be four hundred pounds before the stress comment; Lisa only had herself to blame. Sara crossed her fingers behind her back. 'We have to charge that amount because of the insurance of the artwork.'

Lisa nodded as if she understood. More money than sense, Sara's grandmother would have said. Just then, Sara's phone rang. She didn't recognise the number. 'Why don't you have a wander around, get a feel for the place? I'll just take this.'

Sara picked up the call as she walked to the other end of the room. 'Hello?'

'Hi! Sara, it's Jo.'

Sara's stomach did a little flip. She had given Jo her number in a rush at drop off that morning. She hadn't expected her to call so soon. 'Hi. How are you?'

'All good, apart from an episode with a whole pot of chocolate spread and a fresh duvet cover, which I won't bore you with. Look, I'm meeting up with some other SEN mums at a play centre on Thursday at 10.00 a.m. It's a special session for SEN kids – music is lower, no flashing lights, no Judgy Judies. Why don't you come with Ruby? I know you said she hadn't been diagnosed or anything, but I still think she'd enjoy it. And we have to finish that coffee, right?'

Thursday was one of Sara's days off. There was no reason she couldn't make it.

'Er… yeah, that would be great. Where is it?'

'Fab. I'll text you the details. I'll look out for you, introduce you to the others. They're a lovely bunch, really supportive.'

'Thanks. That would be great. See you Thursday.'

Sara hung up and looked over at Lisa. First it was time to get her to agree to hold her party at the gallery, then Sara could begin to panic about walking into a play centre with Ruby to meet up with a whole bunch of women she'd never met before. And their 'SEN kids'. Whatever that meant.

CHAPTER THIRTY

The next day, Sara had barely got in the door of the pub when Kevin started bouncing around like an excited puppy.

'I want to show you something.'

Sara put her bag down on the counter. 'It's not a digitally remastered Bowie with an artistic cover is it? I've told you that I'm strictly a one-hit wonders girl.'

Kevin was already walking away. 'No, it's upstairs. Follow me.'

In the four weeks she'd worked there, Sara had never been to the apartment above the pub where Kevin lived. The stairs were very steep, but Kevin was bounding up them like a small child. Whatever it was, he was happy about it. At the top was a narrow corridor with doors leading from it. Kevin reached for one of the handles and threw the door open.

'Ta-da!'

Blue walls, a small bed, a desk with a blue lamp. If you looked up 'boy's bedroom' on Google Images, this would be it.

'Is it for Callum by any chance?'

'Yes!' he beamed. 'Go in. Go in. What do you think?'

Sara stepped into the room and stood on a rug covered in racing cars. The quilt on the bed also had cars on it, and there were stickers on the wall of, yep, cars. 'It's a good job he loves cars.'

Kevin wrinkled his nose. 'Too much?'

She laughed. 'Not at all. I bet he's going to love it. This is really great, Kevin. Does this mean Kelly has agreed to him staying over?'

'Not yet, but I want to show I am serious. Hold on, you haven't seen the best bit.' He reached into a plastic holster by the side of the bed and pulled out a walkie-talkie. 'I've got us one each. Cool aren't they?' He pressed the button and a crackling sound came out. 'Breaker, breaker. Daddy to Callum. Over.'

Sara didn't want to dent his enthusiasm, but… 'I'm not sure they're the *best* idea. He's only six. If you show those to Kelly she's going to assume you're planning to leave him up here alone while you work downstairs all night. Not really the message you're trying to get across.'

Kevin's face fell. 'That is definitely *not* the plan. Good point. Oh well, we'll leave those for a bit. What about the rest of it? I've been painting it in the mornings and I put up most of the furniture yesterday. What do you think of the desk?'

'It's great. It's all really great, Kevin. Any boy would love a room like this.' She placed a hand on the walls. She couldn't wait until she had the opportunity to paint a bedroom for Ruby. It didn't have to be pink. Yellow. That was a happy, bright colour.

'Now I just need to persuade Kelly to let him stay. I've been sorting out the rest of the place, so that she can come and see that it's a proper home. Do you want a look round?'

The apartment was bigger than she'd imagined: three bedrooms, a bathroom and a small kitchen. Kevin's room had a double bed and fitted wardrobe along one wall. Pine, like the cupboards in the pub kitchen. She only poked her head in and straight out again – there was something strangely intimate about standing in a man's bedroom.

The last room was empty, apart from a couple of boxes. 'This is the guest suite,' Kevin grinned, 'always available to women and children who need to escape from their mother-in-law.'

It was a decent-sized room with a second door on the far side. Kevin strode in and pushed it open. There was a step down into an adjoining room.

'I was going to have this room myself and turn that bit into an office. But I wanted a room at the front so I could keep an eye on the entrance if there was any noise at night.'

It would also make a fabulous dressing room. Or nursery. It would be perfect for someone on their own with a small child: your own rooms, but easy access in the middle of the night or first thing in the morning. Not that she was considering moving in. It was just surprising, how big it was up here.

Back out on the landing, there was an external door. 'Where does that go?'

Kevin followed her eyes. 'Oh, there's a staircase down to a little garden. It's a bit overgrown and too small to be much use as a beer garden, so I haven't tackled it yet. Do you want a look?'

A garden? She hadn't expected that either. 'Okay. If we have time.'

Kevin rummaged in his pocket for a bunch of keys and then opened the door. A metal staircase led down to a patch of ground. He was right. It looked like a forest. And it was pocket-sized. But it would be big enough for a child or two. Maybe even a swing.

'Might be worth sorting this out too. I'm sure Callum would like to play outside.'

Kevin nodded slowly. 'Good idea. How green are your fingers?'

Sara laughed. 'Not very. But I can pull up some weeds and mow grass.'

'Why don't you give me a hand one day and maybe you could bring your little one over for Callum to play with?'

The thought of Ruby in a pub garden sent a shiver of memory down her back. 'Maybe. Come on, I need to start work on those table tops.'

As Kevin locked the door again, she had another look around the hall and through the door into the 'guest suite'. He'd done really well up here. It really did look like a comfortable home.

Back downstairs, Sara made coffee for them both and told Kevin her plan for the party at the gallery, including the part she had hoped he could play in it, crossing her fingers as she spoke.

'Sounds pretty straightforward. If they want anything special in the booze department, I might have to stipulate a "no returns" policy, though. I can't imagine Sid sipping champers on a Friday lunchtime.' Kevin opened a new packet of chocolate biscuits and offered her one.

Sara took a biscuit and grinned. 'I'm sure that will be fine. I don't think money is an issue.'

Kevin had brought his laptop down with him. He opened it on one of the tables and fired it up. 'How come you got involved in this? I didn't think you were hugely keen on the perfect neighbour?'

'I'm not. I want to do something nice for Leonard, really. He has been good to us.'

'Us?'

'Me and Ruby. She loves the gallery. I suppose it's the quiet and the calm. Leonard just lets her be.' Actually, he did the same for Sara. When she was in the gallery, no one expected anything of her. There was no judgement, either. 'We've grown very fond of him.'

Kevin raised an eyebrow. 'So Leonard's allowed to meet your daughter, but Callum and I aren't?'

Sara knew he was joking, but he had a point. Why was she being so secretive with him? What was she afraid of? 'The thing is, Ruby is, well, she's… she might be…' For heaven's sake, why couldn't she finish a damn sentence?

Kevin held up his third biscuit. 'I'm only teasing. You don't have to explain yourself to me.'

'It's fine. I want to. The thing is,' she took a deep breath, 'I've been to see a doctor because the preschool thinks Ruby might be autistic.' There. She'd said it.

Kevin dunked his biscuit. 'I did wonder if it was something like that, when you said about the not speaking. My cousin's son has Asperger's. If you ever wanted someone to talk to, she's really great.'

Sara felt a rush of gratitude. He hadn't offered sympathy. He hadn't been shocked. He hadn't made it a big deal. 'We don't know anything for sure yet. The doctor I saw said we should wait and see. It's all a bit new to me to be honest.'

Kevin picked up the biscuits and offered her another one. 'Tell me to bog off if this is really interfering, but does Ruby's dad know about this? Have you called him?'

'I'm not sure he's that bothered right now. He has his precious play to worry about.' And maybe something – or someone – else. She snapped another chocolate biscuit in half.

'Again, I know this is none of my business, but sometimes people step up when something like this is going on.'

Sara knew Kevin was talking about himself. But she had tried to talk to Mike about the doctor's appointment and he hadn't been interested. Was that just because he didn't think there was anything wrong, though? Was Kevin right? Would Mike actually step up if there was something actually diagnosed?

'I sent him a text about the doctor and I will keep him up to date if anything happens. I can't really do more than that. At the moment, I have to just think about Ruby.' It was now two and a half weeks since Mike had left. His play opened this week, not that Sara knew where. She didn't want to know. He knew where they were.

Kevin smiled at her. 'Well, if there is anything I can do to help you out. Just ask. Honestly.'

'Thanks. I appreciate it.' She did, but there was nothing that he could do to help. What she needed was someone to tell her what to do next if the preschool thought Ruby was autistic and the doctor said she wasn't. Much as she was nervous about meeting Jo and her friends the next day, she was hoping they might give her an idea of what the heck she was supposed to do.

CHAPTER THIRTY-ONE

Sara held Ruby's hand tightly with her right hand as she pushed the door to the play centre with her left. They were in.

Inside, the place was just as she had imagined. She'd been to one of these soft-play places with Ruby before, back when they lived at the flat in London. It had been hellish. Ruby hadn't liked the noise or the atmosphere at all, and they had left pretty soon after they'd arrived. This one seemed exactly the same: loud, bright, frantic. Was this a big mistake?

From across the room, Jo was waving at her, sat around a table with five or so other mums. Sara's stomach tightened; her experience of other mums hadn't been tremendously positive so far. She plastered on a smile and waved back. 'Come on, Ruby. We can do this.'

When she got to the table, all five women turned and looked at her.

Jo smiled. 'So glad you could make it.' She looked down at Ruby. 'Hi, Ruby! Nice to see you.'

Ruby just stared at her shoes, but Jo didn't press her. She turned and introduced the other mothers. She gave their names and they smiled or did a little wave, but Sara was much too stressed to take anything in. Ruby was pulling at her hand to go towards the soft play area, which surprised Sara until she saw what there was: coloured bricks.

The only problem was, it was in the area for under-twos. Here we go.

'No, Ruby. We can't go in that bit. It's for little ones. You're a big girl now, sweetheart.'

Jo put a hand on Sara's arm. 'It's fine, Sara. This is an SEN session. Rules are off.' She grinned and waved her two hands as if she was suggesting they were about to strip naked and run around the room. Sara had googled SEN – Special Educational Needs – after their telephone conversation, so at least she knew what it stood for now. But where did Ruby fit in to that?

Sara let Ruby pull her over to the area with the blocks. It was only a matter of moments before Ruby was so focused on lining them up that Sara could back away a little and stand a few feet away with the other mothers.

'Lyndsey's at the bar. What do you want?' Jo motioned with her head towards an attractive, dark-haired lady standing at the refreshments counter.

Lyndsey turned around, looked at Sara and mouthed, 'Tea or coffee?'

'Oh, I'll have a coffee, please. I'll just find my…' she rooted around in her bag for her purse. It was in there somewhere.

Jo put a hand on her arm. 'Don't worry about money. We get freebies. Heather's sister owns the place.' She nodded at a slim, blonde woman who smiled and gave Sara a thumbs up.

'Let the woman sit down, Jo.' A red-haired woman with a butterfly tattoo pulled out a chair and patted the seat. 'If your day's been anything like mine, I'm sure you could do with taking the weight off your feet. I'm Caroline, Seth's mum.' She pointed at a little boy, slightly older than Ruby who was sitting in the ball pit with a huge grin on his face. There was something in his smile that made Sara smile too.

'Thanks.' Sara sat down. From this angle she could still keep an eye on Ruby, who had built herself a long line of bricks and seemed happy. *Breathe.*

Lyndsey arrived with the drinks and put a white mug down on the table in front of Sara. 'There you go, lovely. The coffee isn't Starbucks, but it's hot and free.'

'Bit like you, Lynds.' Caroline winked and leaned forwards to take her mug from the tray.

'You've met my comedienne friend, I take it.' Lyndsey raised an eyebrow at Sara. 'Jo said you've got a little girl.'

Sara nodded and glanced over at Ruby. All was still okay. 'Yes, Ruby. She's the one over there making a line of blocks.'

Lyndsey nodded. 'My Sam used to do that with cars. It looked like the M25 on a bad day through my lounge, didn't it, Jo?'

Sara leaned forwards eagerly. 'How did you stop it?'

Lyndsey laughed. 'I didn't. Now he does it with LEGO instead. And those buggers really hurt when you're padding about in bare feet.'

'Is your son here? How old is he?'

'He's seven.' Lyndsey pointed at a dark-haired boy who had just reached the bottom of the slide. Sara watched as he laughed, got up and climbed back up to the top before sliding straight back down again. Then back up to the top. 'And he loves a slide, does my Sammy.'

Sara's mouth was full of questions. 'Special Educational Needs' could mean anything, couldn't it? Were any of their boys autistic? How had they found out? What did it mean? Did they go to school? Could she ask them all these things?

Jo hadn't sat down. She was scanning the play equipment. Had she lost her son?

Sara checked on Ruby again. There was a little boy edging towards her. He shuffled closer. Sara hoped he wouldn't interrupt her playing; it would be so nice to stay and talk to these mums. She willed him not to move the blocks. *Please don't touch them. Please don't touch them.*

He darted in and took a block.

Ruby was on her feet. 'No!' she shouted. 'No!' She stuck a hand out at him. It was the playground all over again. And it had all started so well.

Sara was out of her seat, but Jo put a hand on her arm. 'I'll go. It's my slot. You sit tight and I'll call you if I need you!'

Sara frowned. What did Jo mean by 'her slot'?

'We take it in turns.' Lyndsey opened a packet of crisps and tore along the side so everyone could share. 'If we're here for two hours, we do twenty minutes each. In your twenty minutes you have to watch where all six kids are and go to them if they need a hand. It's a full-on twenty minutes, but it means we each get an hour and forty of chat and coffee.'

'It doesn't always work out.' Caroline helped herself to a crisp. 'Sometimes we can't settle them and they only want their mum, but it means we only need one of us to be watching. It gives us a bit of a break. That's why it's ideal here. It's small and you can see where they all are.'

Sara couldn't help but be impressed. 'Wow. You guys have really got it all together.'

Lyndsey and Caroline both burst out laughing.

'This is us on a good day. You should see me when Sam has asked the same question forty-seven times and I want to pull my actual ears off.' Lyndsey held out her ears as a visual aid.

Caroline wiped her eyes. 'Or when Seth has had an absolute meltdown in the aisle at Tesco because there's none of his letter spaghetti and I've had to endure judgemental looks from about ten people who think he's too old to be having a tantrum and I'm clearly a terrible mother.'

Heather leaned forwards. 'Oh, can I join in this one? Jed got into the fridge yesterday while I was in the shower and ate three packets of ham. I only had that much because I was expecting Shane's parents for lunch. And you know what that's like.' She rolled her eyes.

Lyndsey leaned towards Sara. 'Heather's in-laws don't think he's autistic.'

'They don't exactly say that. They just keep suggesting that he'd behave better if I fed him a better diet. Not three packets of ham, obviously. Or if I got him to play a sport.' Heather pulled a funny face.

Caroline giggled. 'You're too nice. I would have told them to bog off by now. How those two could have had a son as lovely as your Shane, I do not know.'

'Ah, Shane. We all love Shane.' Lyndsey held her hands together and batted her eyelashes.

'Shane is a saint.' Caroline agreed. 'He looked after our two along with his own kids so that we could take Heather on a spa day.'

Sara thought of Mike. How she could barely even get him to look after Ruby on his own. And that was before he decided to do a disappearing act. More importantly, the mums had mentioned 'The A-word'. Did that mean she could?

She picked up her coffee and took a sip. 'So, are your boys all autistic?'

Lyndsey nodded. 'Yes. That's how we all met. There used to be a brilliant support group at the Children's Centre.'

That sounded ideal. They would be able to help with all Sara's questions. 'Used to be?'

Lyndsey and Caroline answered in unison and Heather made a scissors motion with her fingers. 'Funding cuts.'

Sara checked on Ruby again. Jo had restored calm by giving the little boy his own set of blocks. She was standing next to them and scanning the room to check on the others. It was like working in the security services.

Caroline pushed the crisps towards Sara. 'Jo said you hadn't had much luck with your doctor.'

Sara had been going back and forth about this for the last week. 'He suggested we wait and see, but the preschool seems to think I should try again.'

Heather smiled. 'Not easy, is it? If you want anyone to do anything you have to be really firm. Keep pushing until someone listens to you.'

Sara's chest tightened. 'I'm going to make another appointment, but I don't really know what to say that is any different from what I've already said.'

'I kept a diary for a couple of weeks,' Lyndsey offered. 'It's difficult to remember everything you need to say when you're in there. It really helps to have stuff written down that you can refer to.'

'Yes,' agreed Heather. 'I actually recorded Jed on my iPhone. I felt bad, but I wanted evidence because every time we went to an appointment, he would be absolutely calm and I would look like I was making it up.'

Sara nodded slowly to show she was taking it all in. 'Do you know anyone who has been told that their child isn't autistic? That there's something else? That it's because of… something else and… they could just… Maybe that it's them that…' For goodness' sake, why couldn't she articulate what she wanted to say? Was it a fear of saying something that would be insulting to the others and their children? Or because she was afraid of their judgement?

'What, like you're just a really bad parent and you need some lessons?' Lyndsey laughed, but she wasn't a world away from Sara's thinking.

Caroline patted Sara's hand. 'We all think that all the time. Have I done something? Was it something I ate when I was pregnant? Am I just really crap at this parenting lark?'

'And that bloody doctor with his MMR rubbish didn't help matters.' Heather rolled her eyes. 'No one knows where autism comes from, lovely. And I'm not sure it would make any difference if they did. Our kids are who they are.'

Sara tried to take this calmly and keep the conversation on a nonspecific footing, but no amount of lip-biting would keep the tears from falling down her cheeks. 'It's just; I had this picture of how it was going to be. Having a daughter was going to be wonderful. We were going to do everything together, like best friends. Ruby and me.' She glanced over to her beautiful girl. Jo was crouched down next to Ruby and chatting, but Ruby wasn't looking up. 'And now…'

Lyndsey put an arm round Sara. 'She can still be your best friend, sweetie. All you need to do is paint yourself a different picture.'

CHAPTER THIRTY-TWO

Despite needing the extra cash, Sara was so drained she wished she'd turned down the offer of an extra Friday evening shift. At least Ruby was sleepy after her day at preschool, so she was able to get her bathed and ready for bed with a minimum of fuss. As she left, Barbara was trying to read a book to her. 'Trying' because she only got as far as the fourth word on each page before Ruby turned to the next one. Barbara had nearly lost a finger trying to point out a rabbit.

On the way to the pub, Sara turned over the things the other mums had told her yesterday. She hadn't been able to stop thinking about them. They were good people and she knew they were trying to make her feel better, but it had been overwhelming. She had wanted so much for her daughter to have a 'normal' life – the life Sara had never had. And now Ruby had an absent father and might have a condition that would make her life so hard. A condition no amount of toddler training books had prepared Sara for.

When she got there, Sid was propping up the bar as usual, but this time there was a woman next to him. She still had her coat on. 'Hello, love. This is the wife.'

Ah, the birthday girl from the other day. 'Hello. Nice to meet you.'

Sid's wife wasn't one for wasting time with niceties. 'I liked the picture you drew of Sid. It was good.'

Sara glanced sideways at Sid and he shrugged his shoulders at her. 'Oh. Er, thanks.'

'I'd like one of me. To put with it. I'm going to put them in a frame on the mantelpiece.'

Sara was flattered, but there was no way she had time to fit in a sitting for a portrait around everything else she was doing. 'That's so kind, but my weeks are a bit full at the moment. I just don't have the time.'

This didn't concern Mrs Sid. 'You could do it now.'

Now? 'But I'm at work.'

Mrs Sid looked around the bar. There were fifteen people, all of whom had a full drink. 'Sid said it didn't take long.'

Sara was not in the mood for drawing anything, but Sid's wife didn't look like she was one for compromise and Sara didn't have the energy for a fight. It was true; there was nothing for her to do while the bar was quiet. Maybe it would do her good to focus on something different for a few minutes.

When you're focused on a portrait, it's impossible to think of anything else. Sara lost herself in the folds and shadows on the woman's face. The curve of her nose, the lines from her eyes. For a few minutes Sara wasn't the mother of a possibly autistic child. She was an artist.

When she was done, she tore the sheet from the pad and handed it to Sid's wife.

Mrs Sid nodded. 'It's good.' She nudged her husband. 'Buy the girl a drink.'

Sara held up her hand. 'No, it's fine I…' The look on Mrs Sid's face made Sara shut her mouth. 'Coke, please.'

Mrs Sid looked like she'd swallowed the pencil. 'You will *not* have coke.' She turned to her husband. 'Get her a proper drink. What does she drink?'

From out the back, Kevin shouted, 'Red wine!' Traitor.

Mrs Sid got off her stool. 'Red wine it is. And you can pay the lady for my portrait, Sidney. I'm just going to the Ladies' and then I'll be off.'

Sara opened her mouth to argue and then shut it. A glass of wine would actually be welcome right now. As she poured herself a glass, one of the other regulars came up to get some nuts and noticed the sketch of Sid's wife on the counter.

'Hey, that's good. Did you do that, Sid?'

Sid blew out through his teeth. All four of them. 'Course I bloody didn't. That was Sara here.'

'That's really good! Can you do me?' Hands on hips, he pouted at Sara.

Kevin came out to the bar. 'What do you think, Sara? Good way to earn some extra cash for the deposit fund? I don't mind taking over here and you can set yourself up over there if you like?'

Sara started to object, but it was actually really nice to have something else to focus on, and she could definitely do with the extra cash. The pub stayed quiet for the evening and she was on her third portrait – and glass of wine – when Kevin called time and started to turf everyone out.

Once the last customer had left and Sara had run a cloth up the bar, she turned to see Kevin sitting at the table that had been her makeshift studio, flicking through the first attempts she had discarded during her session. 'I had no idea you were so talented. Those drawings you did tonight were really good.'

They had only been basic sketches, really. But it was nice to have them admired. The wine made Sara more confident than she'd normally be. She pulled her phone out of her pocket and scrolled back through to photos she'd taken of some of her portraits of Ruby. She passed it to Kevin.

'Wow. These are amazing. And your little girl is beautiful.'

'Thanks. And, yes. She is.'

They were quiet again as he continued to look at the pictures. She sat down to wait opposite him, watching his eyes as they flicked around them. He had such a kind and open face. She wanted his approval.

He passed the phone back to her. 'How come you're not doing an artistic job then? You're really talented. Didn't you want to be an artist?'

She smiled. He made it sound so simple. 'Of course. That was my dream. Still is, I guess. But, as my wonderful mother liked to tell me, "Pretty pictures won't pay the bills."'

'But there are other arty jobs. Designers. Advertising.'

'Yes, but it was far more attractive in my twenties to work part-time jobs and be a starving artist, dreaming of making a living.'

'And now?'

She looked down at her phone, at the last picture in the photo library. Ruby asleep in her buggy. 'Now I have Ruby. And my dream is different.'

Kevin sat up straight in his chair. 'My turn.'

She laughed. 'You're joking, right?'

'No. I think you owe it to me after you've slacked off tonight' He poured her another glass of wine and placed it, with the bottle, on the table beside her. Then he reached into his wallet for some notes and placed them on the small pile she already had. 'I'm not expecting a freebie.'

Barbara had sent Sara a message a while before to say that Ruby was asleep. Things had been a bit better between them lately. Less confrontational. They'd got themselves into a rhythm that was working, even if it was temporary. No real rush to get home, then. 'Okay, but I'm a bit fuzzy around the edges. Don't expect much.'

'That's okay. So is my face.' Kevin winked.

Drawing people's portraits means staring at them for long periods. A quietness settled on them both as Sara started to sketch out the shape of Kevin. The sweep of his brow, the angle of his jaw. Kevin's face was strong; these tentative strokes were not enough. She made the lines bolder, firmer, deeper.

His hair, short and dark. A kink in the fringe she hadn't noticed before. And his eyes. The lids heavy with fatigue, fine lines at the corners, but clear and honest and focused on her. She felt their weight and it made it difficult to breathe… Another swig of wine. A bigger one.

Concentrate, Sara. Look lower.

His cheeks were flushed. The heat? The wine? The line of his nose was straight; she focused there for a while.

Breathe. Just breathe.

And then his lips. The curve of the upper, the smooth sweep of the lower. Warm, soft, the shadow of a smile playing at the corners. He was actually quite good-looking. She'd not really paid attention to that before.

No.

It was the wine and the warmth and the drawing. Sara took a deep breath, put her pencil down and tore the sketch from her pad.

Kevin took it from her and smiled. 'I love it. You're incredible.'

It had been a long time since anyone called her that. They were sitting close together and Sara could feel something that felt a tiny bit like heat between them. Her head was fuzzy and he was looking at her and…

'I need to get home.'

'Of course. Look, it's gone midnight. Let me walk you back.'

She tried to argue, but he wasn't listening. When the night air hit her, she was glad that he'd persisted; she was drunker than she thought.

They walked home and kept to safer topics. The local area, the children. Sid and Mrs Sid.

When she got to the front door and put her key in the lock, it wouldn't open. She tried again. The key turned and clicked, but the door wouldn't move. Was there a bolt on the door? 'I can't get in.'

Kevin laughed. 'Uh-oh. You must have been locked out. You are *so* in trouble with your mum.'

She started to giggle and picked up the joke. 'OMG. I'm going to be *so dead*.'

Then he put his hand on her arm gently and looked at her. They stopped laughing. He was looking into her eyes, she was looking into his.

Just as Barbara opened the front door.

CHAPTER THIRTY-THREE

Dear Lisa,

Tonight I had the most dreadful conversation with Sara. She came home from the pub clearly a bit drunk and with a man in tow. She said he was just walking her home, but I could tell by the way he was looking at her that there was more to it than that. He made a sharp exit, of course, but not before he checked that she was okay.

I was well within my rights to ask her what she was doing with a man on my doorstep. This is my home. She's married to my son. Apparently, he is her boss at the pub – that awful pub around the corner – but to me he is a strange man and I'm not having it. What would people think if they saw the two of them together at my house?

Maybe I went on a little bit because she started to get cross with me. Started talking about moving out to 'give me my space back' – even suggested she move into the flat above the pub! Well, if that doesn't tell me everything I need to know about her relationship with the landlord, what does? And what kind of mother would take their daughter from a lovely home like this to live above a public house?

Before I could stop myself, the words were out of my mouth. It was panic. I said that if she tried to leave the house and take Ruby away from me and Michael, I would call Social Services. Well, she went white when I said that. Had to sit down. For a moment I was glad. Glad that I'd had an effect on her. But then

I felt bad. She kind of clutched her stomach and looked like she might be sick.

I am right though, aren't I? I have no idea if I could get custody of Ruby when Michael isn't here but I almost feel that it's my duty to take control. That little girl needs some stability. Some protection. It's Ruby I need to think of. I'm not saying that Sara doesn't love her, of course she does. But she didn't have a very good upbringing herself. And maybe she just doesn't know what Ruby needs. And she doesn't know what the consequences might be if she doesn't keep Ruby safe.

Like the preschool. How does she know that they will be watching Ruby all the time? All those other children rushing about. Someone like Ruby could easily hide, slip away, get lost. I would never forgive myself if it happened. Never.

CHAPTER THIRTY-FOUR

Sara peeled her eyes open and then shut them again. That light was bright. Had she opened those curtains? Memories of the night before crept back into her consciousness, each one felt heavier than the last. Why had she let herself drink so much?

The door opened and she clutched the quilt closer to her. Was Barbara coming in to start round two? But the footfall was light and quick: Ruby.

Sara turned on her side and held her arms out. 'Good morning, baby girl. Did Granny get you up?'

She frowned. Ruby was carrying something and holding it out to her. It looked like a folder of some kind. It was cream leather and it had a pretty little rose stitched in the bottom corner. When Sara opened it, there were pouches inside for envelopes and stamps and a notepad. 'Did Granny give you this, Rubes? Are you supposed to have it?'

It wasn't like Ruby to just take something, so Sara assumed she'd been given it to play with, to draw in maybe? She was about to close it when she saw the letter that had been started on the notepad.

Dear Lisa…

What was Barbara doing writing to the woman next door?

It was wrong to read someone else's correspondence, of course it was. But it took a lot of self-control not to. And, judging by last night, self-control was not one of Sara's top virtues currently. If the note was just about the placement of Lisa's bins, Barbara wouldn't have wasted such lovely notepaper, surely? And there was an envelope with Lisa's name on poking out of the left-hand pouch. This must be something more serious. Sara read it.

It took only two sentences before Sara sat up in bed, hang-over momentarily forgotten. It was about her! And Ruby! And Mike! How dare Barbara write to the woman next door about them! The more she read, the angrier Sara became. She had been under no illusions that she was Barbara's favourite person, hell, she probably wouldn't even make her top twenty, but she thought they had reached some kind of truce. Until last night. And now this.

The letter detailed all the events of the night before. Barbara was also questioning whether Sara is in a fit state to look after her daughter, and whether she should try to get custody of Ruby! Not only that, but she was asking Lisa for advice!

Lisa! Sara had just begun to warm to her too, thinking that she wasn't so bad after all. Had Lisa just been nice to her so that she could get more gossip from Sara directly? Was she reporting back to Barbara so they could both laugh at Sara behind her back? Worse than that – *plot* behind her back?

Ruby was holding out her hands for the folder, so Sara gave it back to her. Sara's hands were trembling as she picked up her jeans from the bedroom floor and began to pull them on. She picked Ruby up and marched downstairs. Ready for a fight.

But when she got downstairs, Barbara wasn't there.

Sara flung open the back door. Maybe she was in the garden or maybe chatting to her best bloody friend over the fence. The back garden was empty, but Lisa's wasn't.

Sara marched down the garden path. She'd neglected to put on shoes, so the path was cold and sharp beneath her feat. It merely added to her mood. 'Lisa!'

Lisa turned from where she had been pegging out washing. How many women did their hair and make-up before starting their housework? She smiled at Sara. 'Morning! How are you today?'

How was Sara? Did she already know about the drinking last night? Had Barbara abandoned the letter so that she could deliver the news in person as to what a terrible person Sara was?

'How long has this been going on?' Sara waved the sheet, which she had torn from Barbara's pad.

Lisa frowned. 'Sorry, I don't know what you mean.'

Sara trod on a stray stone and swore. She waved the sheet again. 'This!' She held the sheet in front of her and read. '*I almost feel like it's my duty to take control. That little girl needs some stability. Some protection.*' Reading it for a second time didn't make it any the less painful. 'How dare you! What gives you two the right to sit in judgement on whether or not I can look after my daughter?!'

Lisa glanced back at the house and then came over. She put a perfectly manicured hand on the top of the fence and lowered her voice. 'Seriously, Sara. I don't know what that is, but it has nothing to do with me.'

But Sara was too far gone to listen. 'Oh, I'm sorry. You haven't actually read this one yet. I have intercepted it halfway through. Forgive me. I'm sure it will make its way to you in due course. Just keep checking that bloody letterbox of yours. It'll be there by the end of the day, I'm sure.'

Lisa blanched when Sara mentioned the letterbox. 'My letterbox? What has my letterbox got to do with this?'

Sara heard the front door open and close. Barbara was home. Not even bothering to finish her conversation with Lisa, she turned and walked back to the house. She could deal with Lisa later. Barbara was the one she was most angry with.

Barbara was in the kitchen, taking a milk carton from a bag. She turned when she heard Sara come in. 'Oh, there you are. I just popped out to get some milk for Ruby's breakfast. She was up really early this morning, so when she dropped off to sleep again, I popped her back into her bed and…' she trailed off as she saw Sara's face.

'Well, she managed to open her bedroom door and came to find me. Not before a visit to your room, it seems.' Sara could feel the anger build for a third time that morning.

Barbara put a hand on Ruby's back. 'Oh no, I hope she didn't hurt herself?'

Sara whisked Ruby away from Barbara's touch. She was getting heavy and had started to squirm, so she put her down and let her walk into the lounge. 'Ruby is fine. But she brought a little gift with her when she arrived in my room this morning.'

Sara waved the correspondence folder. When Barbara saw what she was holding, it was her turn to whiten. She put a hand on the back of a kitchen chair and looked wobbly. Sara enjoyed her discomfort. She deserved to feel bad for being such an absolute cow.

'That's mine.'

Sara laughed. 'You think? That much I had worked out for myself. What I can't work out is why you feel the need to be so horribly nasty as to write letters about me to someone I barely know. And also, why you feel the need to write letters to Lisa at all when she lives next door! You could have just talked about me over the garden fence like other gossips and harpies throughout history. I mean, why waste your precious paper?'

Sara's heart was beating so hard and fast; she could feel it in her chest. She had so much she wanted to say, but her breath was almost gone. Looking at Barbara, she seemed to be the same.

Barbara was frowning and shaking her head as if Sara was speaking a foreign language. 'What do you mean, the garden fence?'

Clearly, she was going to pretend to be as confused as Lisa had been. Not really the best line of defence, especially as Sara was waving the evidence under her nose. 'This letter. The one about me and my terrible parenting. The one you wrote to Lisa next door.'

Comprehension came onto Barbara's face. Her shoulders sagged and she slipped onto the seat she had been holding. She took a deep breath and then looked up at Sara. Her face looked old and tired and sad. She shook her head again.

'Those letters weren't written to Lisa next door. They were written to *my* Lisa. My daughter.'

Sara froze. Barbara's *daughter*? But that would mean that Mike had a sister and he'd never mentioned her. The woman sitting in front of her suddenly looked different from the one who had just been bustling about with a shopping bag. Smaller, somehow. Weaker. Broken. Sara opened her mouth to speak. Closed it again. Opened it. 'I don't understand. You have a daughter?'

Barbara closed her eyes and opened them again. They were shiny but tired. 'Had. I had a daughter. Lisa.'

CHAPTER THIRTY-FIVE

Ruby was content to play with Barbara's notepad and a blue crayon in the lounge. Leaving the door open, Sara made tea for her and Barbara. They sat at the kitchen table, opposite each other.

Barbara turned her mug around on the coaster, staring into the beige liquid. It had taken Sara many attempts to learn exactly how Barbara liked her tea. She didn't look as if she cared this time. 'We tried for over a year to have Lisa and I was so happy when she was born. All I'd ever wanted was a baby. I know that sounds old-fashioned now, but it's the truth. And she was such a beautiful baby, some days I would just sit and stare at her. I couldn't believe she was mine.'

This was how Sara had felt too. She'd been blown away by her feelings for Ruby. How was it possible to feel such intense love for someone you'd just met? But she had.

'Michael's father wasn't the most affectionate of husbands. But it didn't bother me so much once I had Lisa. I would cuddle her for hours. My mother used to tell me off. "You'll spoil that baby," she used to say. But I didn't care. She was my baby and I wanted to be with her all the time.'

Barbara paused and reached down for her handbag. Sara thought she was trying to find a tissue in there, but she brought out a small leather wallet, which she opened, smiled at, then pushed across the table to Sara.

Inside was a little girl of around four with dark brown hair and big brown eyes. Sara almost gasped. 'She looks…'

Barbara smiled and nodded. 'I know. Exactly like Ruby. When you arrived with her a few weeks ago and I saw how much she'd grown like Lisa well… it took my breath away.'

Sara remembered how she'd read Barbara's reaction as disapproval or disinterest. She felt a pang of guilt. 'I can imagine.'

'And Lisa was like Ruby in other ways. Strong willed? Is that the best way to say it?' She smiled to show she was joking.

Sara smiled back. 'I think that's one word for it.'

Barbara took the photograph back and gazed at it. 'I absolutely loved being a mother. Walks with the pram, dressing her up in pretty outfits, chatting to strangers who stopped to tell me what a beautiful baby I had. Several friends had babies at the same time and we used to take it in turns to meet in each other's houses. For a while it was perfect. But then, as the children got older, they started to walk and talk and Lisa was always a bit behind. I started to worry about it, but everyone told me I was being silly. Except Trevor. He said it was my fault for picking her up too much.'

Barbara paused and took a sip of her tea, but Sara didn't speak.

'Anyway, the older she got, the more difficult it became. She wouldn't play near the other children. She would throw the most horrendous tantrums. I couldn't get her to do anything that she didn't want to do. My friends' children would sit on a blanket together, eating little jam sandwiches and playing with their toys. Lisa would just run around. Round and round the room. Sometimes she would hum, sometimes not, but she would not sit still.'

Barbara laid the photo down on the table and traced a finger down the little girl's cheek. 'The awful truth is that I was embarrassed. Ashamed of my own daughter. Just saying that out loud makes me feel wretched, but that's the truth. I stopped meeting up with the other mothers; I couldn't take it. Couldn't handle what they might be thinking of me and Lisa. Couldn't handle seeing their children growing up in a way that was so different to mine. We stayed home more often. The only time I would go out was to buy food and even that was a quick dash to the supermarket and then home again. Our world got smaller and smaller.'

Again, Sara could empathise. She could have made it to more baby groups with Ruby if she'd tried. But it was too painful. 'That must have been so hard.'

Barbara shook her head. 'It *was* lonely, but it was actually easier. Easier than continually making excuses about her being tired or teething or anything else that would stop people judging me, judging her.'

Barbara looked so sad that Sara wanted to put her arms around her, or somehow make her feel better. 'Maybe it was nicer for her to be at home too.'

Barbara stared into her cup, words rolling out as if they had been caged and had seen their chance for release. 'She never spoke. We lived in a silent world together. Some days I would just sit on the sofa and watch her run about. I would sing and sometimes she would hum. Trevor couldn't bear it. He said I was making her worse. That it was weird. But it was the only way I could play with her. She wasn't really interested in toys, but she was obsessed with the washing machine. *Obsessed.* When I put on a load, she would lean against it and then cry when it stopped. Eventually I realised it was the vibration that she liked so, next time I sang to her, I took her fingers and put them at the base of my throat. Her face, Sara. Her face just… lifted. She looked at me – *really* looked at me – and she smiled.'

Barbara swallowed; her eyes were full. 'That smile was the most beautiful thing I have ever seen or will ever see. For the rest of that week, she would come and sit with me and put her hand on my throat and I would sing or hum or do anything I could with my voice. Trevor got irritated with it in the end, told me how terrible my voice was. But Lisa didn't care. I would lay beside her in bed and sing until she fell asleep, then I would slide her fingers off my neck, kiss their tips and slip them under her covers.'

Barbara's voice wobbled, and a single tear spilled over. Watching her wipe it away, Sara's own eyes filled. What had happened to Lisa?

Once Barbara had composed herself, she continued. 'Michael wasn't planned. We wanted him, of course, but his conception was almost a miracle. Trevor and I were hardly in the same bed in those days because Lisa was such a bad sleeper. Still, Michael came along and I was overjoyed. But everything got even more difficult. Looking after two of them on my own was hard, especially if I had to get the shopping or take Michael to the clinic. My mum wasn't near to us and no one else wanted to look after Lisa for me because she was so... unpredictable.'

Sara knew how that felt. But she only had one child. 'What about Mike's dad? Didn't he help?'

Barbara snorted. 'Trevor? He was at work most of the time. Kept telling me he had a *lot of overtime.* Not that I ever saw any extra money. No, I was on my own with the two children. Well, until...' She pressed her lips together again.

Sara needed to know what had happened. 'Until?'

Barbara put her mug down again and looked at Sara. The expression on her face had changed. Her eyes round, almost begging for approval. 'I had only left her for a few moments. Michael needed a new nappy and I'd just popped upstairs to get one. She was sitting on the rug, she'd just started to become interested in some toy animals and was playing with them – the same ones I've given to Ruby – and seemed lost in a game. I thought she'd be okay.' She looked at Sara with haunted eyes. 'I had no idea she knew how to open the front door.'

Sara felt sick. She'd had no idea that Ruby could open her bedroom door until this morning. How did you ever know your child could do something until they did it for the first time? First crawl, first steps, first time they reached something from the kitchen worktop. Every parent was caught unawares by a new skill the first time it happened. There but for the grace of God...

'I was halfway down the stairs with the nappy when I heard it. A screech of brakes. A thud. Someone screamed. I almost fell through the front door onto the street.' Now Barbara was gazing past Sara's head. Staring at the wall as if the scene was playing out in front of her. 'Michael was still on his rug; he was only a few weeks old, he wasn't going anywhere. I didn't know that she could open the door. I ran it over and over in my head afterwards, trying to remember if I closed it properly when I got the milk from the step earlier that day. But I always checked it. I *always* did.' She looked at Sara again now, her eyes pleaded for understanding. Or forgiveness.

Sara reached forwards and put her hand over Barbara's. 'I'm sure you had shut it. It's impossible to be everywhere. It's not your fault.'

Barbara slumped back in her chair. 'That's not how it felt. Feels. She was such hard work and I didn't know what to do. And there were times,' Barbara's lip wobbled, 'there were times that I was so exasperated with her that I just wished… I wished…'

'That she was a different child?'

Barbara looked up through wet eyelashes. 'Yes. That she was a different child. Isn't that an awful thing for a mother to think? It's unnatural.'

Sara shook her head. 'It's not unnatural. It doesn't mean you didn't love her. Just that it was hard.'

'The ambulance man said she would have been killed instantly. She had a huge beetroot-sized lump on her head, even days later when I said a final goodbye at the funeral home.' Barbara's voice wavered and she produced a crumpled tissue from her pocket and blew her nose. 'A lot of that time is a blur in my mind. I must have been on autopilot. I would dream about her. Dream that she was with me. And then I would wake up and the loss would almost knock me over.'

Sara reached over and placed her hand over Barbara's. 'I am so, so sorry. I can't imagine what that must have been like for you.'

'It's a huge void that you can never fill. Oh, you try. Loving Michael helped, but you can't replace the love of one child with the love of another. Each one occupies a separate section of your heart. Maybe the section of my heart that belonged to Michael grew bigger than it would have done, taking some of the space of Lisa's section. But he could never take it over completely. And the guilt. The blame. Some days it weighed so heavy I couldn't move. It crushed me. If I hadn't had to feed Michael and change his nappy and rock him to sleep… I don't know if I would still be here. He saved me.'

That was the other part that Sara didn't understand. 'It's really strange that Mike has never mentioned her to me. He never said that he'd had a sister.'

Barbara sat up and rolled her shoulders back. 'We didn't talk about her, really. I didn't think it was a good idea. I was worried it might frighten him. After I lost Lisa, my biggest concern was keeping Michael safe.'

That didn't sound particularly helpful to Sara. 'Then who did you talk to? Did you get any counselling at the hospital?'

Barbara shook her head. 'I'm not even sure if it was available in those days. Anyway, Trevor said we were better off not to keep talking about it. We needed to move on. I didn't realise that he meant he would be moving on physically as well.'

Sara had no idea that this was why Mike's parents had separated. 'Your daughter had just died and he left you?' Even Mike's selfish departure wasn't as bad as that.

Barbara shook her head again. 'Not right away. The first few weeks we just stumbled around in the dark. I looked after Mike and Trevor was either at work or in the pub or in bed. Then he wanted to just act like it hadn't happened. He wanted to get rid of her toys and clothes and… I couldn't do that, so I hid them in the loft when he was at work, told him that I'd given them away. That's where I got the pink bedding for Ruby's cot.'

Another chill down Sara's spine. Poor Barbara. 'It must have been so hard for you. Looking after a young baby is hard enough, but while you were grieving too.'

There was whimper in the other room and Sara left the table to check on Ruby, grateful for a few moments to collect her thoughts. Ruby had worn her blue crayon down to its stub and was frustrated because she couldn't get it to work. Thankfully, there was another of the exact same colour and Sara was able to change it over with a minimum of fuss.

Sara sat back on her haunches for a moment and looked at her daughter. The thought of losing her was too awful to contemplate. It was hard staying on top of everything Ruby needed, anticipating what might happen and how problems could be averted, but she wouldn't be without her for anything in the world. She leaned forwards and wrapped her arms around her, breathing her in. 'I love you so much, baby girl.'

'I love you, Nemo.'

Sara smiled and stroked Ruby's face. If that was all Ruby could give, she would take it. *Paint a different picture.*

When she got back to the kitchen, Barbara was at the sink, washing the cups. She turned around. 'Everything okay?'

Sara nodded. 'Just averted a crayon crisis.'

Barbara smiled. 'It's non-stop, isn't it?'

'Sure is.'

Barbara wiped at her eyes with her crumbling tissue. 'That's what Trevor couldn't understand. He didn't know why I had to spend so much time with Michael. He was a baby. He needed me. And he was such a good baby, so easy to look after. Of course, Trevor said that was because I gave him everything he wanted, but what else could I do? He was all I had.' Her voice faltered again. 'And when he became a toddler, well, I wouldn't take my eyes off him for a second.'

'I'm sure anyone would understand that after what you'd been through.'

'Trevor didn't. When Michael was two, he met someone else. He said he needed someone who would love him. That I only had room for one man in my life and that was Michael. But was it wrong that I had to prioritise him?'

Sara shook her head. 'Of course not.'

'And that's when I started the letters. To Lisa. I know it's stupid. But I missed her. I missed her so much. When I first lost her, someone gave me a book about grieving. Different stages, anger, depression and so on. I could get through all five stages in a day and back again.' She put a hand on Sara's arm. 'People will tell you that time heals. But when it's your child, that's just not true. You never heal.'

'So, then it was just you and Mike at home?'

'Yes. And there was no one to tell when he did something new or clever. No one to talk to about it. So, I talked to her. To Lisa. To start with, I actually spoke out loud. "Look at him, Lisa," I would say when Michael did something funny. "Look what your brother is doing now." One night I was writing to an old friend and I wanted to write about how I was feeling, but couldn't. So, I wrote it to Lisa instead. Over the years I've written to her about everything. I mean, she'd be an adult now. I'd be calling her up or emailing her, wouldn't I? And that's the thing about losing your child. You don't just lose her once. You lose her in lots of little ways as the years go by. When your friends' children start school. When they leave school. When they get married and have children. Every birthday you wonder what you might have bought her, where you might have gone, what she would look like and sound like. Writing to her feels… well, it feels like I can pretend that I still have her with me. There's something soothing about writing it all down. Like Lisa next door; she writes to her mum every week.'

Lisa! Sara's face burned at the memory of her attack on Lisa. Once she'd finished talking to Barbara she would need to go over and apologise. She owed Barbara an apology too. 'I'm sorry for shouting at you. I feel absolutely terrible. I'm so sorry.'

Barbara waved a hand. 'It's me that should apologise to you. You must have thought I was a horrible grandmother. I tried to keep Ruby at arm's length at first. I didn't want to feel for her. I can't explain it to you, but it felt like a betrayal. And I was scared. I was scared that I would love her and then lose her. I'm not sure I would recover a second time. That day you gave me the portrait? It hit me like a punch in the chest. Michael looks so much like his father. It could so easily have been a picture of Lisa and Trevor. For the briefest of moments, I thought you had discovered a picture. I thought you knew my secret.'

'Why did you keep it a secret?'

'Shame? Guilt? Fear?' Barbara looked up at Sara. Her eyes brimming again. 'She was autistic, wasn't she? My Lisa was autistic.'

Sara could barely speak. 'I don't know. I don't know enough… but… maybe… it does sound as if…'

Barbara nodded. 'It's on the TV so much now; I have wondered for a while. But when you said about Ruby… I couldn't bear it. I couldn't bear the thought that it might be happening all over again. I couldn't face up to it.'

Sara took her hand. 'I haven't been able to face up to it, either. Not really.'

Barbara brought her other hand up from under the table and placed it over Sara's. 'We need to though, don't we?'

Sara swallowed. And nodded. 'Yes. I think we do.'

CHAPTER THIRTY-SIX

Lisa's door knocker was so shiny that Sara didn't want to touch it. Plus touching it would mean that Lisa would come to the door and she would have to face her. *Just knock, you coward.*

While she waited, Sara rehearsed her apology in her head. *Sorry, bad day. I didn't mean to take it out on you.* A bit flippant? *Sorry, must be the time of the month.* Too personal? *Sorry, got you confused with Barbara's dead daughter.*

The door opened and Lisa stood there with a bright smile, which froze when she saw Sara. 'Oh. Hello.'

'Hi. Can I talk to you? I owe you an apology.'

'Of course.' Lisa stood back so Sara could walk in.

Sara had never been in Lisa's hall, but it was exactly as she would have pictured it. Wooden floorboards, original art on the walls, a striped stair runner that looked as expensive as it was beautiful. Understated wealth and good taste. Sara tried not to hate her.

The sitting room was even nicer. Soft leather couches, an artistic rug, framed black-and-white prints of the children on beaches, in the forest, on a ski slope. Sara swallowed her envy and turned to Lisa. 'This morning, over the fence, I need to explain. And apologise.'

Lisa perched on the edge of a chair and indicated for Sara to sit down. 'Well, I was a bit confused.'

'Yeah, well that was my fault. I was confused too. You see, I found this letter.'

Barbara had agreed that Sara could tell Lisa about her namesake. As Sara retold the story, Lisa's eyes got wider and wider and her hand fluttered to her mouth. 'Oh, poor Barbara.'

Sara nodded. 'Poor Barbara indeed. You can imagine how bad I feel.'

'Of course, but you weren't to know. I can't believe she's kept this hidden all this time. She's been such a fantastic neighbour, really helped me out with the children. I wish she'd told me.'

'It seems she barely speaks about her even to her own son,' and he hadn't thought it important enough to ever mention to Sara. 'But when she was talking to me about Lisa, it was as if it happened yesterday. I want to suggest she tries some bereavement counselling. Maybe you could, seeing as you're closer to her than I am.'

Lisa nodded. 'That's a really good idea. I'm surprised you thought she was writing to me about you and Ruby, though? When I'm only next door.'

Rationally, Sara would have known that. She'd been an idiot. 'Your name comes up in our house quite a lot.'

Lisa eyes got even wider. 'Really? Why?'

'Because… well, you're so perfect! Perfect house, perfect marriage, perfect children. You're an icon next door. It feels like Barbara is only one step away from building you a shrine.'

Sara was trying to make light of the situation, but Lisa didn't laugh. 'Seriously? Surely you know that's not true.'

Sara had been horrible to this woman unnecessarily this morning, she might as well tell her the truth as penance. 'Look Lisa, I'll be brutally honest. I am just a bit jealous of you. That's probably why I was so quick to believe the letters were to you. You have everything. The husband, the kids, the house. Designer clothes, perfect hair and make-up every day. You've even got a picture-perfect postbox at the front of your lawn. You're like a Hallmark Card Mother.'

Lisa looked back at her. Saying nothing. Did she not have a sense of humour? Was she angry? Sara had been trying to pay her a compliment. Had she made things worse? Why was she still staring?

Sara couldn't bear the silence. 'I mean, it's great, obviously. I'm not mocking you. I would love what you have. I mean, look at me. Husband has done a runner, I'm living with my mother-in-law and I'm struggling to work and be a good mum. You have everything, Lisa. And that's great. I don't begrudge you, it's just...'

Sara tailed off; Lisa had raised her hand to make her stop. She'd been rambling and Lisa's shocked face might be about to give her a piece of her mind.

Lisa's eyebrows had risen a few millimetres with each of Sara's comments. 'Me? You want to be like me? But I'm a complete mess.'

Sara sighed. 'Thanks but you're not. Look at this place.' She swept a hand around the immaculate living room.

Shaking her head slowly, Lisa gave a short, dry laugh. 'You have no idea. You might think my life is enviable, but you wouldn't want it, Sara. Believe me. The postbox? I use it to send and receive letters with my family and friends back home in Yorkshire.'

Sara frowned. 'Yorkshire? But you don't have an accent.'

'No. I managed to lose that at university, snob that I was at eighteen. It still comes back when I go home. Not that I get home that often.' Lisa paused again, looked intently at Sara, and seemed to make a decision. She continued, 'I've had to invent this whole ritual of getting up early to collect the post and put it in a rack with Grant's morning coffee so that he doesn't get to the postbox first. And I can't have them text or email me because Grant checks all my emails and texts and they might write something that will send him off on a big rant about them not liking him. Because heaven forbid there is someone in the world who doesn't worship the ground he walks on.'

Now it was Sara's eyebrows that were rising higher and higher. 'But...'

Lisa held up a hand again. Now she had started, there was no stopping. 'The designer clothes you mentioned – which I hate by the way because I love vintage clothes – are ordered by Grant online and the hair and make-up are perfect because I never know when he might drop by from the office and he wants me to look good. On that note, he also makes me weigh myself every week and checks what I eat.' As Lisa finished, she let out a long, wobbly breath, as if she'd purged herself of something and needed to recover. Then she sat back. 'Wow. I've never actually said all that out loud.' She put a hand to her chest. 'My heart is thumping.'

Sara's brain couldn't take this all in after the shock of Barbara's revelations. 'I don't understand. He seems…'

Lisa raised a perfect eyebrow. 'Loving? Attentive? Thoughtful? Of course he does. That's the image he wants to project to the world. And in some ways, in his own way, he is. Don't get me wrong; I'm not looking for sympathy. He doesn't hit me or hurt me or anything like that. He loves the kids.'

Sara lowered her voice. 'But it's still not okay.'

How had she got it so wrong about them? She thought of Grant, always joining Lisa at the fence with a protective hand on her shoulder. Suddenly, there was different slant on what had seemed romantic and loving. 'What do your friends and family say about it? Surely they don't think you should put up with this.'

'My close friends don't live around here so we don't see each other often. They think I have a wonderful life of luxury and I can't bring myself to tell them the truth. My parents are old, and far away. I don't want to worry them.'

'What about your local friends? The women you are arranging the gallery party for?'

Lisa laughed. 'They're not my friends. They are the wives and partners of Grant's colleagues. All privately educated. All from wealthy backgrounds. I'm just a comprehensive girl from Leeds. I live in fear of them. That's why I've been so deranged about this party at the gallery. I can just imagine what they'll say about me if it goes wrong. And that won't go down well with Grant.'

Sara opened her mouth and closed it again. When she thought about it, she'd never seen anyone on Lisa's path except Lisa. And occasionally Grant. And lots of deliveries from expensive shops. *Guilt gifts.*

'Why do you put up with it?'

Lisa shrugged. 'Because what is my other option? If I left, I know that he would go for full custody of the children. He's made that clear. I don't work. I rely on him for money and the house and everything else.'

Sara shook her head. 'He's lying to you. Why would he get full custody? And he has a ton of money so he could pay a whack in child support and you wouldn't have to put up with him.'

'Sometimes I think that. Sometimes I imagine just packing our bags and going to live with my sister. I know she'd have us. But I would be making the children's lives so difficult. If I can just last until they leave home…'

Sara moved so that she was sitting on the sofa next to Lisa. She reached out and placed a hand on her arm. 'The children will be fine as long as they are with you. They wouldn't want their mum to be unhappy.'

Lisa placed a hand over Sara's. 'I'm not unhappy all the time. I've got used to the way he is. It's just… well, seeing the way you are has made me think. Your confidence and the way you make things happen. I can't imagine you letting anyone make decisions for you the way I do. Actually, I need to apologise to you too. The first morning I met you, *I* was jealous of *you*. You and Mike looked like such a good team.' She blushed. 'I even pictured myself in your position for a few moments.'

Seemed. Looked like. Imagined. Sara wasn't the only one with a skewed picture of someone else's life.

'And I envied your attitude. You're brave and independent and even though Mike has… gone, you're still out there working and fighting. Ruby is lucky to have you as her mum.'

A large lump rose in Sara's throat and almost choked her. Brave? That was the last thing she felt. 'I'm not independent by choice and I have no idea what I'm doing with Ruby. Has Barbara told you that she may have autism? How do I deal with that? I'm not sure I can do it on my own.'

Lisa reached out and patted Sara's hand again. 'But you're not on your own. You haven't been on your own since you came here. Barbara loves your little girl. You just need to accept her help.'

CHAPTER THIRTY-SEVEN

Dear Lisa,

I should have told her the truth. I should have told her what I've done. When I first saw she had your letters, I was angry. How dare she touch my things. But then I was ashamed, embarrassed that she would think I was a stupid old woman. But she wasn't, Lisa. She was lovely.

Sometimes I see mothers and daughters out together. Shopping for shoes or stopping for coffee and cake. Then I imagine it. I imagine you and me. In my mind you have long, dark hair, probably in a ponytail. We sit in a café – you have coffee, I have tea and we share a piece of cake because we're supposed to be doing a diet together. Not that we ever stick to it. We laugh a lot. I don't get to laugh very often in my real life, but when I imagine you, it's with your head thrown back and laughing. I never took the dream as far as grandchildren. I never thought I'd get one of those. But now I have Ruby.

I tried to keep my distance at the start. It seems stupid now. Was it superstition? Fear? I don't know. I just wanted to tell them to keep her safe, to watch her. It didn't last, though, the 'keeping my distance' thing. She's not one for cuddles and kisses, Ruby. But that's okay. I'm not used to those, anyway. Just being with her is wonderful. Watching her concentration as she lays her bricks in a line. Her little tongue peeps out of her mouth, just like yours used to. Makes my heart hurt.

Well, that's why I did it. I asked Michael if we could meet up one time when Sara was at work and I had Ruby. It sounds so wrong when I write it down. But what else could I do? I didn't want Ruby to miss out on seeing her daddy and it was only once. I haven't met him since. Should I have told Sara about it, though? I nearly did this morning, but it was so nice, talking together like that. I didn't want to risk it. Didn't want to spoil the fact we were getting along.

Maybe I could help to bring them back together? She's organised a party for the couple next door. Maybe I could persuade Michael to go? He'll see Sara and they'll spend some time together away from Ruby. Surely that's all they need?

CHAPTER THIRTY-EIGHT

It took another two weeks to get an appointment with the doctor and now Sara's heart was in her mouth as she sat in the waiting room, rehearsing her speech over and over in her mind.

The night before, she'd spoken to Jo on the phone for ages, getting advice on what to say, what to request and Jo even suggested she ask to see a different doctor at the medical centre. Apparently the one Sara spoke to last time was rather 'old-school'.

'Don't take no for an answer. GPs are not experts in special needs. You need to get a referral.' It sounded like Sara was going into battle; Jo's pep talk was worthy of Henry V. Sat in the waiting room, tapping her fingers on the arm of her chair, she hoped she could live up to Jo's belief in her.

'You've got this, Sara. Go fight for your girl.'

Barbara had offered to look after Ruby so that Sara wouldn't be distracted. Jo had agreed that it was pointless taking Ruby anyway – it wasn't as if the GP would be able to hear autism with a stethoscope. Sara had laughed and then felt guilty. It wasn't a joking matter.

In the corner of the waiting room was a pile of toys: a plastic telephone, a shape sorter and a couple of other primary-coloured plastic items. Two little girls were playing together with the shape sorter, taking turns to slot them in, naming the shapes as they clicked into place: circle, square, rectangle. They played so nicely, Sara assumed they were sisters, until one of the mothers retrieved one girl for her appointment.

Once her playmate had left, the second little girl bored of the shapes and turned instead to the telephone. 'Hello, Mummy!'

Her mother shifted forwards in her seat and put her fist up to the side of her own face, thumb in her ear and little finger towards her lips like a mouthpiece. 'Hello, Anna.'

The little girl tilted her head to one side and continued to talk into the play phone. 'How you today?'

'I'm very well, thank you. How are you?' The mother looked at Sara and rolled her eyes. Although she was only joking, Sara wanted to cry. She didn't know how lucky she was to hear her daughter call her Mummy.

Her name appeared on the screen and called her back to the present. *Mrs Lucas to Room Four.*

Time to step up.

Room Four was painted in a warm yellow and there were bright prints on the walls, pictures of apples and oranges and pitchers of wine. Sara recognised a Cézanne still life directly behind the desk. The desk itself was clear apart from a computer, a pot of pens shaped like zoo animals and two framed photographs of smiling teenagers. Dr Davis was also smiling and she looked a lot younger than the doctor Sara had seen last time. Would she help? *Don't take no for an answer.*

The smile stayed in place as Sara blurted through the whole of her prepared speech. The doctor listened and asked questions and didn't type on her keyboard once. Once Sara was done, the doctor nodded. 'At your last appointment, did you go through an M-CHAT?'

Sara had no clue what she was talking about. 'What's that?'

'Sorry, medical jargon.' Dr Davis made mock speech marks in the air with her fingers. '"Modified Checklist for Autism in Toddlers". It's a checklist that can be used on preschool children to ascertain whether they should be referred for further diagnosis. It's not perfect, but it can give a good indication. We can go through it now?'

Sara swallowed. Then nodded. Her heart began to thud.

Dr Davis smiled reassuringly. 'It's nothing to worry about – I won't be grading your answers.' She winked and turned to her computer, fingers flying confidently over the keyboard to find the test.

Sara twisted her wedding ring around on her finger. She should have asked Jo to come with her. Or Barbara, even. What if she answered anything wrong? Could she change her answers later if she realised?

Dr Davis was facing Sara again. 'Right then: when you point at something across the room – a stuffed toy, a picture or photograph on the wall, that kind of thing – does Ruby look at the thing you're pointing at?'

Sara's mind went absolutely blank. She couldn't think of one single time when she had pointed something out to Ruby. She must have done, surely? My God, had she never pointed something out to her? Was it her fault? She hadn't actually ever pointed something out to her daughter? She gripped the sides of the chair, her shoulders hunched up towards her ears, she couldn't breathe. She couldn't breathe.

Breathe.

Dr Davis must have seen her panic. 'It's okay. We can come back to that one. Have you ever wondered whether she might be deaf?'

Sara felt sick. Barbara had asked Mike that on the first night they arrived. She had spotted it within minutes of playing with her. Was that it? Was Ruby deaf? All this time and they hadn't realised?

Dr Davis was looking at Sara for an answer. 'Y… yes. Sometimes she doesn't respond when we ask her things. Especially if we are behind her, or across the room.' But she *had* responded to her cot mobile as a baby. 'But she used to. She definitely used to look up when we spoke to her.'

Dr Davis nodded and pressed her touch pad. 'Okay. Next one. Does Ruby play make believe? Feeding a baby doll, talking into a toy telephone, that kind of thing?'

The little girl in the waiting room, talking to her mummy on the toy telephone. The children at the preschool, dressed up as superheroes and saving each other. No. Ruby had never done that. Never. A lump rose in Sara's throat. She could barely get the word out. 'No.'

Sara looked down at her lap, her vision blurring. Tears began to spill down to the tip of her nose. She had known there was something not right for a while, wanted someone to listen to her and tell her what it was, what she could do. Only now she realised how much she had been hoping that she was wrong.

Dr Davis passed her a box of tissues. 'This is hard, I know. But you really are doing the best thing for Ruby. If we can get a diagnosis, there will be support, access to services, educational help. Let's get through the rest of this as quickly as we can.'

There must have been about twenty questions in all. Variations on a theme. Did Ruby make eye contact? Was she interested in other children? Did she point at pictures in books? With each successive question, Sara felt as if she was falling deeper and deeper into a big hole.

Eventually, Dr Davis pushed her chair back from the keyboard and swivelled to face Sara again. 'Well, that's the last one, Mrs Lucas. It should be pretty straightforward to get you a referral on the basis of what you've told me and the letter from the preschool.'

Surely it wasn't going to be that easy? Jo had made it sound as if she would have to wrestle the doctor into submission. 'Thank you. I was so worried that nothing would happen. That you wouldn't believe me.' She had videos on her phone of Ruby and her blocks, Ruby having a meltdown, Ruby ignoring her. Just taking them had been upsetting enough – it had felt like she was judging her own child – but Jo said she might need to show the doctor what was going on.

Dr Davis smiled again. 'Don't get your hopes up yet. There is a really long waiting list to get a referral date and, even then, it can take a very long time and many different appointments to get a formal diagnosis.'

Jo had already warned her about this. Even if it would take a long time, at least she had started the process. 'I'll do whatever I need to do.'

'Good. Because you have got a bit of a fight on your hands, I'm afraid. The process has always been slow, but it's got worse in recent years. I won't bore you with the politics, though. In the meantime, I can give you some websites to look at and it might be worth visiting a special needs school with a preschool. They could give you some strategies to help Ruby while you're waiting for the system to catch up.'

Jo's son had started school. Sara would ask if she could visit there. Thank God she'd met her. She would have been completely lost if she had to do this on her own. Maybe this is why the other mothers she'd seen moved in packs all the time – strength in numbers.

Walking home, Sara called Mike. Whatever was going on with the two of them, she owed it to Ruby to keep him informed. Maybe the doctor's referral would shake him up a bit, make him realise that Ruby needed him, that he had responsibilities. If Sara was honest, she could do with the support too. Barbara had been much easier to live with since the discovery of her letters, but she wasn't going to put her arms around Sara and let her have a good cry. There was no one else in her life who could provide that.

Mike's mobile rang several times before connecting to his voicemail. She didn't want to leave a message, so she clicked off and rang again. And again. And a fourth time. *Just pick up your sodding phone.*

The fifth time – on the eighth ring – it was picked up. By a woman.

Her voice was furry and irritated. 'Mike's phone. What's the emergency?'

Sara stiffened. 'Hello. Is Mike there?'

The voice yawned. It was 10.30 a.m., surely Sara hadn't woken her? 'He's just gone out to pick up some hangover breakfast.' She laughed huskily. 'It was a bit of a late one last night.'

Who the hell was this? As if she needed to ask. And she certainly didn't want a name to roll around her brain and torture herself with. She was stumbling under the weight of so much responsibility and worry while he was out living the life of a footloose single man. *Fool me once, shame on you. Fool me twice, shame on me.*

And Sara wasn't about to get into the details with this nameless woman. 'Can you tell him his wife called and he needs to call me. It's about Ruby. And her appointment with the doctor.'

The voice sounded confused and slightly horrified. 'His wife? Ruby?'

Sara gritted her teeth. 'Yes, Ruby. His three-year-old daughter. And yes, his wife. Didn't he tell you he was married? I suppose he wouldn't. Look, just tell him I need to speak to him.' She clicked to end the call. If she could have afforded a new mobile, she would have thrown hers to the ground and stamped on it. *Bastard.*

CHAPTER THIRTY-NINE

After hammering on the door for almost ten minutes, Sara resorted to calling Kevin on his mobile to let her into the pub.

He was red in the face and a little out of breath. 'Sorry, I couldn't hear you. I was carting this lot into the back room.' He pointed at a huge stack of boxes with the distinctive Veuve Clicquot name on the side. 'It's for your friend Lisa's party.'

Sara opened her mouth to say that Lisa wasn't her friend and then shut it again. Maybe she was. 'What can I do?'

Kevin sighed and leaned on the top of a three-box stack with his elbow. 'Make me a cup of tea? This is killing me.'

The galley kitchen was small and shabby with a microwave and a toaster. Kevin had been focusing his attentions on the bar area since he took over; behind the scenes hadn't been a priority. It was clean, but the cupboards had antique pine doors from the 1980s and the brickwork wallpaper was curling up where it met the counter top. Sara took out the tea and helped herself to a packet of chocolate biscuits. They were the least she deserved right now.

So, that was that then. Mike was seeing someone else. Or had at least spent the night with someone else. That had to be the case, didn't it? She might have explained it away in her mind the first time, but the tone of that woman's throaty laugh was unmistakable. That was a post-sex laugh. Not to mention the shock in her voice when Sara had said 'wife'.

After taking the milk from the fridge, Sara slammed the door shut with more force than was strictly necessary. How could he do this to them? How could he just leave them behind without a backwards glance and walk into a brand new life where he laid in bed until ten thirty and then went shopping for a 'hangover' breakfast? Not a care or a thought in his head apart from his own self-important, self-centred, self-serving, selfish, selfish, selfish… Her hand wobbled and the milk sploshed over the side of the mug and onto the counter top.

'Shit.'

The damp jay cloth hanging over the mixer tap cleared the milk in one wipe, but Sara kept rubbing at the counter top. God, she hated Mike right now, but how was she going to go through the journey to Ruby's diagnosis and beyond without him? What had the doctor said? Prepare for a fight? Right now, she had about as much fight as this damp rag, wiping tears as they dripped onto the counter top.

Once the tea was made, she had a quick visit to the Ladies' to wipe her face, then to the bar as Kevin reappeared from clearing the last box. He wiped his forehead with the back of his arm and took his tea from her. 'You're a pal. Thank you. Everything go okay at the doctor's?'

Sara sighed and leaned back against the bar. 'The doctor has referred her. She seems to think that autism is likely.'

Kevin nodded slowly. 'Okay. And how do you feel about that?'

How did she feel? Sat in the doctor's surgery she had felt relief; at last someone was listening to her. At last something was being done. Then she had gone straight into the phone conversation with Mike's breakfast buddy and anger had transcended everything else. And now? 'I don't know. I don't actually know what I feel.'

'It must be a shock.'

A shock? Was it? She'd spent the last few days thinking of nothing else but to have it confirmed… but yes, it was still a shock. 'I know she needs some help, but autism is so… serious. I mean, it's not like she can have some sessions with a therapist and everything is going to be okay.' She heard her voice wobble.

Time to change the subject or she might lose it altogether. 'So the champagne has arrived. Have you got everything else Lisa wanted?'

Kevin took a big gulp of tea. 'Yep. Champagne, craft beers and posh cider. Fancy sampling some of it?'

Sara could really go for a large gulp of free alcohol right now, but if she started, she might not stop. 'Thanks, but no. I need all my faculties for dealing with your punters.'

Kevin took a chocolate biscuit. 'Fair enough. It would have been easier to have it delivered straight to the gallery, but when I spoke to Leonard, he seemed a little nervous that someone might break in to get at it.'

Sara coughed on her biscuit. 'Bless Leonard. He's such a nice man.' The thought of Leonard and his kindness made her chest tighten. She swallowed. *Push it down.*

Kevin dunked his biscuit into his tea and then ate it in two big bites. 'He seems it. He spoke very highly of you and Ruby on the phone. I felt quite left out.' He winked at her.

'It's not that I don't want to introduce you to Ruby. It's just, being here, it's a break for me. That sounds really bad, doesn't it?' Her lipped wobbled and she pressed her fingers to her mouth to hide it.

Kevin put down his mug and placed a hand on her shoulder. 'Hey, hey. I was teasing. Of course you don't have to bring her here. I didn't mean to upset you.'

Tears came to her eyes again and she gulped them back, again. Today had been such an emotional day. Fear and sadness and disappointment were just below the surface. 'I know, I know. I just…' She needed to tell someone. She looked up into Kevin's face. 'I think Mike is seeing someone else.'

His eyes widened. 'Shit. I know how *that* feels. Are you sure?'

'I rang him and she answered his phone. Said he'd gone to get breakfast.'

Kevin took his hand from her shoulder and scratched the side of his head. 'Okay. But you don't know if…'

She shook her head to interrupt him. 'I know. I know *him*.' She took a deep breath. 'This is not the first time.'

Kevin raised both eyebrows. 'Oh.'

Sara looked down, spoke into her tea. 'There's a part of me that doesn't even care. Although logistics are a bit harder, emotionally it's actually easier not having to worry about someone else. Living with him has been like walking on eggshells for so long. Supporting everything he does. Not disagreeing with him. Not asking too much of him. Sucking it up when I want to scream or shout.' That traitorous lip started to wobble again. 'But this stuff with Ruby. I am so scared about going through everything on my own. I've already made so many mistakes, missed things that the doctor asked about. Not done the right thing.' A tear dropped from the end of her nose into her tea. She wiped her eye with the heel of her hand and looked up into Kevin's concerned eyes, reality descending upon her like a cold wind. The doctor. The preschool. They'd all seen what she hadn't. Her voice was just above a whisper. 'She's autistic, Kevin. My baby girl is autistic.'

Kevin held out his arms and slowly pulled her into him, her head under his chin as she sobbed. She felt his lips press softly on her hair. They stood for several moments and then he pulled her away gently and looked into her eyes.

'You are not alone.'

Somehow, they leaned forwards until their foreheads were touching. She closed her eyes. She could feel his breath on her face. It was comforting and warm and she felt herself sinking. Their lips touched and for a few moments it was wonderful. Soft and deep and warm and passionate in a way she hadn't felt in a long, long time. His hand moved from her shoulder to her back while he held her close. It was intoxicating. She didn't want to stop.

But they had to stop. As she pulled away, he looked at her, his eyes full of something she couldn't decipher. Lust? Longing? Love?

'I can't do this.' Sara picked up her bag and left the bar.

CHAPTER FORTY

The gallery was full of happy people with glasses of champagne in their hands. It was strange to see it so full and so loud. Sara scanned the crowd to check on Leonard. Hovering by the kitchen door, his face was mid-way between happiness and shock. He was okay. And hopefully the gallery would be too.

Sara hadn't spoken to Kevin more than a brief nod to questions about where to set up. She had texted to apologise about walking out and not doing her shift the day before, but this was the first time they had seen each other since the kiss.

The kiss.

Even thinking about it made her blush. She had been so naïve. Maybe her lack of friendships had given her a faulty radar for these things. She had enjoyed having someone to talk to about everything that was going on in her life. She hadn't wanted romance. Or a kiss.

But she hadn't exactly pushed him away, either.

Kevin had dressed up for Lisa's party. He wore an open-necked shirt, and dark grey trousers, which were a lot smarter than his pub attire, smiling and chatting with the guests as he poured their champagne or opened a craft beer. Sara caught herself smiling and then straightened her face.

'This is really great. Thanks, Sara.'

She turned towards Grant's voice and rearranged her expression so that it didn't give her away. It wasn't her place to tell Grant what she thought of him. Especially in public. 'My pleasure. I was happy to help Lisa out.'

Grant's smile would have seemed genuine last week, but now it looked faintly sinister. 'Yes. She gets a bit overwhelmed with this kind of thing, bless her. Good job you were able to help.'

Patronising arse. How the hell did Lisa put up with him? Well, Sara didn't have to. 'Sorry, Grant. Leonard needs me over in the kitchen. Enjoy your night.'

Leonard raised his glass of champagne at her as she approached. 'Do you want this? It's not really my kind of thing, but I didn't want to lower the tone with a mug of hot chocolate.'

Sara laughed. 'It's good of you to be here. I thought you might get some questions about the art.'

Leonard's eyes were bright. 'I've sold two pieces already. The brochures you made on Kevin's computer really helped, although I'm not sure how true most of the things you wrote were.'

Sara had knocked up a very basic Word document – using photos she'd taken on her phone and a bit of a blurb for each picture – during a quiet shift at the pub. Kevin had printed them for her.

She tapped her nose. 'It's called marketing. Hopefully they'll tell their rich friends about the place too.'

'That would be great. There's been some interest in those, you know.' He nodded at the corner where he had hung Sara's sketches. 'Someone asked if you did commissions.'

Sara turned to see a couple standing in front of her painting of Ruby. The man pointed something out to his companion and she nodded. In that second, Sara felt naked. Maybe she shouldn't have included the picture of Ruby in the three that Leonard had twisted her arm to display. It was too real. Too close. It wasn't just a picture to Sara. When she looked at the brush strokes, she could see her love, her fear, her hope for her daughter. She'd opened her heart and invited strangers to look inside.

Leonard read Sara's mind. He placed a gentle hand on her arm. 'You get used to it. Just don't watch.'

She smiled at him gratefully. 'I should go and find Lisa.'

Lisa was in the kitchen area, checking on the caterer. She also looked different to Sara than she had three days ago. She was still groomed and smart and pretty much perfect, but now Sara could see the anxiety below the surface. How had she not noticed before?

'All okay in here?'

Lisa nodded. 'It's great, Sara. Thanks so much for organising this. Everyone is chatting about the place. They've decided to find it "quirky", which seems to be a good thing. Such a relief.' She smiled.

Sara waited for the caterer to leave the kitchen with a tray of picture-perfect canapés. She lowered her voice. 'You don't need their approval, you know. Or his. You are good enough.'

Lisa glanced behind her at the open door before answering, 'Right back atcha, lady.' She leaned forwards and planted a light kiss on Sara's cheek. 'Better get back to the party.'

Sara watched through the open door as Lisa floated across the gallery, a smile here, a word there – the perfect hostess with the perfect life. The room was a sea of designer labels and manicures and perfect skin. A week ago, she would have been eaten up with jealousy for their easy lives. But not now. Now she saw the perfection for the veneer it was. Who knows what was going on below the surface out there? An arm around the waist – loving or apologetic? A glance across a room – romantic or obsessive? No one knew what was there unless they scratched the surface.

Before she could follow Lisa out of the kitchen, Kevin walked in with a tray of glasses. He stopped short when he saw her. 'Oh, hi. I needed to stretch my legs so the catering lady is watching the bar while I clear some glasses.'

Sara swallowed. 'Hi. Looks like you've been busy out there.'

'Yeah, they like their champagne. The bar should do well out of this.'

Sara thought about Grant footing the bill. 'Make sure you mark it up well.'

Kevin grinned. 'I will.' The champagne glasses clinked as he slid the tray onto the kitchen counter. He turned and leaned back against the fridge. 'Look, about the other night…'

Sara's heart knocked against her chest. She did *not* want to talk about this. 'It's fine, we've both had a stressful time of it lately and I was upset and…'

'No.' Kevin cut her off. 'It's true that I wanted to comfort you, but that's not why it happened. I've wanted to kiss you for a while.'

Now her heart was pounding right out of her chest. 'Kevin. Don't. I'm…'

He held up a hand. 'I know. That's why I wanted to apologise. I mean, I kind of got it into my head that you were separated and obviously that doesn't mean you're ready to… I mean, I should have…'

She needed to put him out of his misery. 'It's fine. It was a mistake. We can just pretend it never happened.'

'Please, Sara, let me just say this. I've been rehearsing it in my head. I don't want to jeopardise things, between us. I've enjoyed hanging out with you after work. Chatting and stuff. I don't want you to feel that we can't do that anymore. I'm not trying to seduce you or anything…' He put a hand to his head. 'I can't believe I just used the word seduce. I am getting this all wrong.'

Sara laughed. 'It's okay. Honestly, let's forget it.'

Kevin nodded and tried out a cautious smile. But as he left the kitchen he paused. Without turning around, he spoke. 'I also wanted to say that you mean a lot to me, Sara. If you need anything, anything at all, I'm here.'

After he'd gone, Sara closed the door to the kitchen to give herself a minute to collect her thoughts. She was pleased that Kevin had broken the ice between them. It wasn't as if she had a raft of friends and could afford to lose the ones she had. It was good that they had agreed that it was a mistake. She didn't know what the story was with her and Mike, but she definitely wasn't ready to move on yet. Her focus was Ruby: getting her the help she required, giving her the attention she needed. So then why did she feel disappointed? Time to shake that off and get back out to the party – to save Leonard if for no other reason.

She opened the door to the kitchen and ran straight into a smiling Grant. 'There you are! Someone's arrived to see you.' His smile was more than a little forced at the prospect of a gatecrasher at his fancy shmancy party. He stood to one side and pointed in the direction of Sara's paintings.

The middle painting of the three was the one Sara had painted of Ruby watching *Finding Nemo*. You couldn't see the television screen in the picture, just Ruby's captivated face, her wide eyes, slightly parted lips. Not knowing the context of the setting, an onlooker would assume she was reaching out for someone she loved. Her mother? Her father?

In front of the picture, with his back to Sara, was Mike.

CHAPTER FORTY-ONE

Wearing a fresh white shirt and dark jeans, Mike looked just as handsome as you'd expect an actor to look. As he turned and grinned, Sara's traitorous heart skipped a beat. Why did he still affect her like that? *Stay strong.*

He took a step towards her. 'You look good.'

She folded her arms, not about to fall for his charm. Anymore. 'What are you doing here?'

He moved as if about to kiss her cheek, then changed his mind. 'I came to the house and Mum said you were here, so I thought I'd surprise you.'

The cheek of him! He was acting as if he'd just got back from a business trip. 'Did your *girlfriend* tell you I called?'

Mike scratched behind his ear. 'She's not my girlfriend, Sarz. She's just… well, yeah… she said there was something wrong with Ruby, that you'd taken her to the doctor. So…' he held out his arms as if he was a magician appearing from behind a curtain, '… I'm here.'

He knew she'd been to the doctor and it had still taken him nearly forty-eight hours to make an appearance? How thoughtful.

'I don't want to have this conversation here.'

Sara glanced around the immediate vicinity to check if anyone was listening to them. Over by the bar, Kevin was looking at her. He raised a thumb and mouthed, 'Okay?'

She gave a tiny nod and turned back to Mike. Might as well get this over with. 'I'll get my coat. Wait here.'

She found Leonard over by the cow pictures chatting to a stocky man with no discernible chin in a dark blue blazer and chinos. Leonard looked different, his face a little flushed, his eyes brighter than usual. When she caught his eye, he excused himself and came over to speak to her.

'I think we're actually going to sell the cows! It's been amazing tonight, Sara. I must have sold at least five paintings and there has been interest in several others. I could have sold Jean's sketches three times over if I'd wanted. I wish she could have seen how much people like them. This is going to help pay the rent for sure. And it's all down to you.'

Sara was really pleased he was happy, although she was slightly sad to see the cows go; they were Ruby's favourite. 'Look, I need to leave. Will you be okay without me? I'll ask Kevin to sort the caterer out.'

Leonard glanced back at his prospective customers. 'Of course. I'll be fine. Is everything all right? It's not Ruby is it?'

At least someone thought of her daughter first. 'No, Ruby's fine. Just need to sort out some stuff. I'll pop in and see you in the week.'

Leonard smiled. 'Great. Bring Ruby. I've found some Nemo-esque orange pastels, which she'll love.'

On the way to ask Kevin about the caterer, Sara tapped Lisa's elbow to let her know she was going. Lisa glanced in the direction of Mike's back before turning. 'What is Mike doing here?'

Sara shrugged, 'Feigning concern? I'm going to go home with him and find out. I'll get Kevin to sort out the caterer and Leonard will lock up when you go. Do you need anything else from me?'

Lisa shook her head. 'No, it's all been great. Everyone is raving about what a "find" this little place is. Even Grant is happy, so that's good for me.' She pulled a face.

Sara was determined to help Lisa with the whole Grant situation, but right now she needed to focus on her own Mike-shaped problem. 'I'll talk to you tomorrow?'

'Yes.' Lisa leaned forwards and kissed her on the cheek. Sara was surprised by the lump that appeared in her throat at the contact. 'Thank you.'

Now she just needed to sort out Kevin.

Another backwards glance at Mike confirmed he was still in the same place, but was now chatting to two young women and had his back to Ruby's portrait. Kevin was handing two champagne flutes to the stocky man in a blazer, who was telling him that he was celebrating his first original art purchase. Good for Leonard.

Kevin turned, his deep blue eyes concerned. He walked around the bar and leaned towards her. 'You don't look happy. Are you okay? Is Ruby all right?'

Everyone seemed more concerned about Ruby than the one other person who should be. 'She's fine. Mike's here.' She motioned in the direction of the portraits.

Kevin looked Mike up and down and nodded. 'I did wonder if that was him. He hasn't upset you, has he?'

Sara couldn't help but smile. Where would she start with that question? 'I think he just wants to talk. Look, if I give you the cash for the caterer, can you make sure she has everything she needs and then pay her at the end of the night?'

Kevin placed a gentle hand on her shoulder, then took it off again quickly. 'Of course. Whatever you need. Are you leaving now?'

Sara nodded. 'Yeah, I think I need to get things sorted.'

'Of course. Well, you know where I am if you need anything. Anything at all. I mean it.'

She knew he meant it. But this was something she needed to sort out herself. 'Thanks.'

Away from the High Street, the pavements were empty as Sara and Mike made their way back to Barbara's house. The older terraced buildings gave way to the newer estate and row upon row of semi-detached family homes. Ashbridge's streets had become familiar to Sara through many tantrum-calming buggy walks with Ruby, so she found it weird to think that this was pretty much the first time she had walked them with Mike. The streets he grew up in now felt more like her territory.

'Why did you turn up at the gallery tonight?'

Mike coughed out a laugh. 'Whoa, straight to it, Sarz.'

She stopped dead in the street and looked at him. 'You leave without telling me, almost never answer your telephone and won't tell me where you're staying. I'm not in the mood to talk about what a warm evening it is and ask whether you've had your hair cut.'

Mike held up his hands in surrender. 'Okay, okay. When I got to the house to speak to you, Mum made it sound like you'd be pleased to see me.' He smiled the lopsided smile of someone who was used to using his charm to get his own way.

Not this time.

What was Barbara thinking, telling him to come to the gallery without warning her? She'd checked her phone every twenty minutes since she left home in case Ruby needed her, so she definitely hadn't missed a message. Anyway, that was beside the point.

'What I meant was, why have you come home *now*? Tonight? If you were worried about the doctor's appointment, you could have called me back immediately. After your *hangover breakfast*, obviously.'

'I wanted to see you. Look, let's get home so we can talk properly.' He tried to pick up the pace.

Sara slowed her step as the slow burn of realisation crawled up her back. 'She kicked you out, didn't she? I told her you had a wife and child and she kicked you out. Hold on. Shouldn't you be on stage right now? Don't they put you up in a hotel?'

Mike scowled. 'It wasn't like that. Look, just wait until we're home and we can talk face-to-face. I'll explain everything.'

Face-to-face he thought he had a better chance of making Sara see things his way. She knew how he worked. She'd had front rows seats for the penitent lover act before.

It didn't take long to walk the last few streets and, when they got home, Barbara greeted them with a hot drink before making herself scarce. Well, she was in the kitchen – quite possibly with her ear against the door.

Sara sat up straight, her arms folded. 'Well?'

'I've been an idiot, Sara. A real idiot. Everything just got too much for me and I needed some headspace.'

Sara could understand that. She'd had the urge to run many times over the last few weeks. The difference was, she hadn't. 'And?'

'And, I want to come home.'

Sara shrugged. 'It's your mother's house. It's more your home than it is mine. You don't need to ask my permission. Or are you planning on bringing your new girlfriend with you and you need me to move into Ruby's room?'

'Don't be like that, Sarz.' He put down his mug and leaned across to put his hand on her knee. 'The girl you spoke to isn't my girlfriend. She's just… well, like I said, I've been an absolute idiot and I want to make things right. When I got home and saw Ruby tonight, it made me realise what I was risking. It was fun, being out on the road, but it wasn't home.'

Sara stood up. She needed to get further away from him. Mike had some kind of aura that always dragged her in if she sat too close. She stood by the mantelpiece, in front of a grinning seven-year-old Mike with his front teeth missing. 'A bit like this place is for me, you mean? Not home?'

Mike sat back with a sigh, his legs splayed apart. 'Come on, it's nice round here. It's not like I left you in a slum. You and Ruby are comfortable and Mum said you've been getting on better.'

Barbara had made pretty fast work of giving him a status report before she sent him on his way to collect her from the gallery.

'Did she, indeed? What else did she have time to tell you?' She meant an update on Ruby and the fact that they were waiting for a referral from the doctor to a paediatrician, but it suddenly occurred to her that Barbara may have mentioned Kevin on the doorstep. Maybe that's why she'd sent Mike to the gallery. To make sure nothing happened between them. The guilt must have flashed across her face because Mike frowned.

'What do you mean?'

Barbara wouldn't have mentioned Kevin, surely? And if she had, Mike wouldn't have waited to mention it to Sara. It would have been the first thing he'd said. 'Ruby. I wondered if your mum had time to tell you more about the doctor's appointment and how Ruby is getting on? It's been six weeks since you've seen her.'

Mike frowned. 'But I saw her three weeks ago.'

Now it was Sara's turn to be confused. 'What do you mean?'

'Mum brought her when we met up.'

Sara's mouth was very dry all of a sudden. 'When you met up?'

'Yeah, we met for coffee three weeks ago and she brought Ruby. I assumed you knew?'

No, she didn't. When she'd gone to work and left Ruby with Barbara, she trusted that Barbara was looking after her at home. There were a couple of times when Barbara had mentioned that she'd taken Ruby out in her buggy to get her to take a nap, but there had been no mention of meeting up with Mike. She would definitely have remembered. What was going on?

Barbara chose that exact moment to come in with another cup of tea for each of them. A more suspicious person might have thought she had been listening at the door. 'I thought you'd be thirsty. I'll just take your cups out.' She smiled. 'It's so nice to all be at home together.'

Sara had no patience for niceties. 'Mike has just told me about your meetup. I was just wondering why you didn't tell me about it?'

Barbara's hand fluttered to her neck. 'We can talk about that later, let me just clear this all away and let you two talk some more.'

Sara swiped her empty mug from the table before Barbara could pick it up. 'I'll follow you out. I'm in the mood for some biscuits.'

As soon as the kitchen door was closed behind them, Sara hissed, 'Why the hell didn't you tell me you had seen him?'

Barbara sat down heavily in the kitchen chair. 'Because I thought you would say that I couldn't take Ruby.'

'Damn right I would say that. If he wanted to see his daughter, he could walk through that door any time he liked. Why the hell should she have to go and see him at his convenience? And when did you meet him? He's been away on tour.' To think Sara was beginning to trust her. To feel that they might be on the same team. 'You went behind my back, Barbara.'

'Sara, I know you're angry and I understand that. But in between tour dates he was back in the area and it seemed wrong that Ruby didn't get to see her dad. I was worried she would forget him. It was before we… before we talked.'

Barbara didn't say it out loud, but they both knew she was also worried that Mike would forget about Ruby. Since finding out about Barbara's daughter, Sara had had a lot more patience with her, but this was stretching it to the limit. 'Did he even *ask* to see her?'

Barbara started to straighten the tablecloth again. 'I knew that he wanted to.'

It was almost comical, if it hadn't been Sara's actual life. Without saying another word, she turned to go back to Mike.

He stood as she came in, moving towards her as if he was about to attempt an embrace, but she waved for him to sit back down. 'So, what's your plan? You want to move back in and we pretend like nothing has happened? Like last time?' She supposed it wasn't unbelievable for him to think that she would just roll over like a faithful hound. She'd done it the last time he left.

She might have had more sympathy with the tears in his eyes if she didn't know what a good actor he was. 'I've realised that I'm not happy when I'm not with you. You're my family, Sara.'

He hadn't asked about his daughter once. 'And Ruby?'

'And Ruby. Of course, Ruby.'

Sara shook her head. 'Family doesn't work like this. You can't just pick us up and drop us when you feel like it. Getting things sorted for Ruby, that's been hard. And it's going to get harder. I need someone who is going to work with me on this, not make my life more difficult.' Her words caught in her throat. It had been scary enough thinking about the future. Since that woman had answered Mike's phone, and she'd found out that Barbara was still lying to her, it felt impossible. She closed her eyes to stop the tears.

'Come and sit down.' He patted the sofa next to him. She shook her head, unable to trust herself. Mike sighed. 'Of course I'm going to work with you. If you think Ruby needs to see a doctor, we can do that. I got it wrong, Sara. I thought she was just a bit behind, but Mum explained it all and she said you've been amazing. I can't believe how much you've achieved.'

There was something very seductive about the thought of having someone to share the burden. Not that Ruby was a burden, but trying to find another job, look for a new home and navigate her way through the appointments was a daunting prospect.

'I had to do it. Who else was going to? You just skipped out when things got tough and now you expect to just walk back in and pretend like nothing has happened. Well, I'm sorry, but I can't do that. I need someone I can trust, someone who is going to be there for us.' She choked back a sob, livid with herself. She was so angry, and crying seemed so weak. *Stop bloody crying.*

Mike stood and put a hand on each of Sara's arms. 'Hey, hey. Come on, Sarz. Don't get upset. I'm here, aren't I? That's what I'm trying to say. I'm here to help out with stuff.'

Sara didn't want someone to 'help out'. She wanted someone who could take the lead. She was so tired of being the one who tried to drive them forwards. She needed to be the passenger for a while. She was so tired.

Barbara appeared at the hallway door, Ruby in her arms. 'Look who just woke up. She must have heard her Daddy's voice.'

Mike stood and took Ruby from his mother. 'Hey, Ruby. What are you doing up so late? Didn't want to miss out on the action, eh?'

Half of Sara wanted to wrench Ruby from Mike's arms. He didn't get to play daddy when she had been the one speaking to the preschool, visiting the doctor, meeting with other parents to find out what she could do to help her daughter. But the other half saw the Mike she had fallen in love with, who clearly loved his daughter.

He'd slept with another woman, she was sure of it. One night or an affair? Love or just sex? Either way, she didn't want to take him back. But what about Ruby? He was her father. And they were living in his mother's house. She had nowhere else to go except maybe the rooms above the pub, but – after that kiss – that wasn't really an option either.

Mike looked at her and, completely by accident, Ruby looked up at her too. 'Come on, Sara. Give me another chance. We can do this.'

'I'm too tired to think about this now. It's been a long day.' She held out her arms for Ruby.

'It's okay. I'll take her to bed in a little while.' He smiled at Sara. 'New me.'

Sara didn't believe the 'new me' act, but she was too tired to fight right now. She would think about it after a good sleep.

CHAPTER FORTY-TWO

Mike was being a model father. The day after the gallery party, he'd left Sara to have a lie in and taken Ruby to the park and then for a walk. They'd talked that afternoon and she agreed that he could stay on the sofa for the next few days until he left for Sheffield – his next venue. This was *his* mother's house, what else could she say?

Sunday had been remarkably calm and pleasant and, now that it was Monday, he accompanied Sara to drop Ruby at preschool and suggested they stop for a coffee at the café nearby.

Almost as soon as they sat down, Jo came in for a takeaway coffee. While she was waiting for the barista to create his masterpiece, she wandered over to say hello. 'Nice to see you in here, missus.' Jo turned to Mike. 'Hi, Mike. How are you?'

Mike frowned and then smiled as he recognised her. 'Jo? Wow. Long time, no see. How's life?'

'Good, thanks.' Jo turned to Sara. 'I just wanted to say, there's an SEN session at the play centre tomorrow if you and Ruby fancied coming? Same time as before. The others will be there again too.'

This time, the thought of going didn't fill Sara with fear. She'd already called Jo to give her a debrief on the doctor's appointment, but her head was an ants' nest of questions – it would be good to meet up with people who might be able to give her some answers. 'Yes, that would be great. Thank you.'

The barista waved at Jo and she gave him a thumbs up. 'Got to go. Coffee's ready. I'll see you tomorrow. Bye, Mike.'

Mike watched Jo go. 'Crikey. I haven't seen Jo for years. How do you know her?'

'Her son is at the same preschool as Ruby. Her older boy is autistic. She's introduced me to some other SEN mums.'

Mike shuffled in his seat and looked at his coffee. He'd looked like this every time Sara had brought up the subject of Ruby's referral. 'What's an SEN mum?'

'Special Educational Needs. The session at the play centre she mentioned is just for kids with special needs.'

He squirmed again. 'Oh.' He seemed to be thinking, considering his next comment. 'Do you think that's a good idea?'

'What do you mean?'

He twisted his cup. 'Taking Ruby to sessions where all the kids are… special. Wouldn't it be better to take her to somewhere with normal kids? She might learn more.'

Something twisted in Sara. 'It's not catching, Mike. And Ruby *is* one of those kids.'

Mike held up his hands. 'Don't get upset. I'm just asking. And, anyway, we don't know yet about Ruby, do we? She just has a referral.'

Another twist to her insides. 'It looks likely, though.'

He was back to turning his cup around. 'Yeah. Maybe. But, y'know.'

*

The next day was bright and warm. Sara spotted Jo and Heather at the same table as the last time. Ruby held Sara's hand as they walked towards the table, and then ran off to the area with the coloured blocks. This time, Sara knew it was safe to let her go.

'Hi, guys.'

'Hey, you're here!' Jo stood and gave her a hug.

'So nice to see you again.' Heather smiled. 'Glad we didn't scare you off.'

'Hello!' Lyndsey called out and waved from the ball pit; it was obviously her shift.

Sara looked around for the lady with the butterfly tattoo. 'Sorry I'm a bit late. Getting out of the house can be a bit challenging. Where's your friend with the red hair?'

'Caroline? Oh, she can't make it. She's had a bit of a shitty morning.'

'Literally, poor thing.' Heather screwed up her nose.

Sara was confused. 'What?'

Jo explained, 'When Seth gets stressed, he sometimes smears poo around.'

What? 'Oh my God. That's awful.'

Heather nodded. 'Yep. The school are working on it with him, but, you know, autism. The gift that keeps on giving.'

Sara's face must have given her away – *how were they being so matter-of-fact about something so hideous*? – because Jo put a hand on her arm. 'Don't listen to us. We've all had a rotten week. Something in the air. Tell us about your appointment with the doctor.'

Sara forced herself not to think about Caroline and Seth. 'Er, good, yeah. She was really nice. She's referred Ruby so hopefully we've got things going now.' She paused. 'I haven't really got my head around what happens next.'

Jo picked up her drink and settled herself. 'Well, that's where we can help. Basically, it depends on the diagnosis. If Ruby is diagnosed with autism or other special needs, you'll need to request an assessment for an EHCP: an Education, Health and Care Plan. It's a bit like a passport. It will list Ruby's needs and what provisions should be put in place for her at nursery, school and so on. It will stay with her up until she's twenty-five.'

'Twenty-five?' Sara couldn't imagine Ruby at twenty-five. She would be a woman.

Heather waved at Lyndsey that she was on her way to take over surveillance. 'I think the thing to remember is that you don't have to know everything from the beginning. Don't look too far ahead. Deal with what's in front of you right now. Looking too far ahead isn't good.'

Lyndsey arrived at the table as Heather finished speaking. She slapped palms with Heather who took up her position in the ball pit for optimum visual vantage. 'She's right. When I first got Sam's autism diagnosis, I tied myself in knots thinking about the future. What would happen when he left school? Would he ever be able to live alone? Would he have a relationship? A job? What happens if I die? Who will look after him?' She shuddered. 'It took me to a very dark place for a while. Like I was in a tunnel and I couldn't see the end.' Her usually animated face was serious.

Sara could definitely identify with that. 'What changed?'

'This lot.' Heather smiled and pointed a finger on each hand at the other two women. 'They pulled me out. Basically, our lives are frequently a shitstorm. But we get through it. And you will too. You're one of us now.'

That was so good to hear. 'Actually, I was going to ask a favour. I'd really like to look around a special needs school, get an idea of what I can do with Ruby to help her while we wait for the support to start. It was the doctor's idea.'

'I can help you with that.' Jo reached into her bag. 'I'm good friends with the Deputy at Charlie's school. Summer Hill. It's brilliant. I'm sure Tracey will show you around. Shall I text her now and ask her?'

'That would be great. Thank you.' These women were definitely the people to know. If Mike met them, and spoke to them, he'd understand why it was important to spend time with them. Important for Ruby *and* important for Sara.

Lyndsey stood and collected empty cups from the table. 'While you do that, I'm going to get a drink – anyone want anything?'

'Yes, please – a white coffee.'

Sara bent to get her purse from her bag, but Lyndsey shook her head and mouthed, 'Free.' Sara had forgotten that Heather's sister ran the place.

While Lyndsey was at the refreshment counter, Sara updated Jo on the situation with Mike. She skirted around the subject of the other woman and him leaving and then coming back. But she said enough that Jo knew that things hadn't been good between them. She told her that he was home at the moment and was being more supportive. As was Barbara, with her offer to look after Ruby whenever Sara wanted.

'Bloody hell, I'd bite her hand off.'

'I know. It sounds great, but I don't want to take advantage of her. Ruby's my responsibility.'

Lyndsey slid two mugs of coffee onto the table for her and Sara. 'What have I missed?'

'Sara's mother-in-law has offered to look after Ruby and she doesn't know whether she should accept her offer.'

'I'd bite her hand off.'

'That's literally what I said!' Jo chinked her mug on Lyndsey's. 'We've clearly been spending too much time together.' Jo turned to Sara. 'Look, I know you want to do everything yourself. We all felt like that at the beginning. But you just can't. You won't stay upright. You have to accept help.'

'Definitely.' Lyndsey nodded. 'You're fortunate that you live with her, to be honest. 'My parents are miles away and I'd do anything to have my mum around the corner.'

'I never expected to be living with her this long. It's not exactly what I'd planned.' As Sara said the words, she realised how stupid they sounded.

Lyndsey laughed. 'None of us have planned all this, lovely. But it's what we've got. And we have to make the best with what we have.'

Sara smiled. 'Paint a different picture, eh?'

'Yes!' Lyndsey nodded. 'That's a great way to put it!'

Sara nudged her. 'It was *you* who said it to *me* last time I was here.'

'Did I?' Lyndsey tapped her head. 'God, I'm clever.'

And they all laughed. It felt good.

CHAPTER FORTY-THREE

Summer Hill School was a vast, glass edifice. From the car park, without the aid of the large sign with the school name and motto, *Being our Best*, you could be forgiven for thinking you were about to enter the offices of a computer software company. Sitting behind the steering wheel and waiting for Mike, Sara tried not to feel intimidated. It was just a school. One was much the same as another. Wasn't it?

Sara hadn't been inside a school since her own school days and that was a while ago. It hadn't been a happy time for her. Not particularly academic, she'd avoided the attention of most of her teachers and hadn't made any close friends. Most of her lunchtimes had been spent in the art block, headphones in her ears, painting and drawing. She could still smell the acrylics and the white spirit.

Jo had explained to the school that Ruby was waiting for a diagnosis, but that Sara wanted to see what her options might be for Ruby. Someday Sara would find a way to pay Jo back for everything she'd done. She really was a lifesaver.

9.50 a.m. Sara and Mike weren't due to meet the Deputy Head until quarter past ten, but Sara had wanted to get there in plenty of time. After dropping Ruby at the preschool, she'd gone back home to pick up Mike, but he had gone out. Sara had waited as long as she could, but then she'd got a text from him:

I'll meet you there.

Things had been a little better between them that week. Actually, a lot better. After he'd spent two nights on the sofa, she'd given the bed up to him and slept on a roll-up mattress in Ruby's room, but last night they had actually slept in the same bed. He had been patient with Ruby and had even come to drop her off at the preschool a couple more times. It had been nice to have him beside her when she spoke to Ellie about Ruby's day, sharing the responsibility.

Barbara was ecstatic to have him home. Who knew that he had that many favourite dinners? Or breakfasts? Now that Sara knew about Barbara's daughter, she had a different outlook on the way she was around Mike, though. It was less annoying. Maybe a little sad.

9.55 a.m. *Where is Mike?*

Barbara had also been talking about selling the house. She kept saying that it was too big for her now, that she was 'rattling around' in it. She'd even hinted that she might be able to help them out with a deposit for a house. An actual house of their own. Sara wasn't hugely comfortable with the thought of taking money from Barbara, but it was a tempting idea. She had even let herself dally in front of the estate agent window yesterday. It would be wonderful.

10.00 a.m. Maybe Mike didn't know where the school was? No, that couldn't be right because he'd been embarrassed when she told him the name of it. Said that it had been called other names when he was at school. Sara didn't ask what they were.

Sara knew that Mike was going to be coming and going for the next couple of months, but he was certain he'd be able to get something else in the West End with the reviews from *Cat on a Hot Tin Roof.* He said he'd do anything to make sure he was home full-time. Could she dare to hope that they really could make a go of it? She hadn't made him any promises so far, but she was definitely thawing out. For Ruby's sake.

Her phone rang. Barbara.

'Hi, Sara. It's me.'

Sara didn't bother to say that she'd guessed that from the caller display. 'Hi. Have you seen Mike? He's supposed to be meeting me here.'

There was a pause at the other end. A pause that spoke volumes. A pause that made Sara's stomach fall to her feet. A pause that she should have seen coming a mile off.

'He's asked me to give you a ring…'

Sara couldn't be bothered with the long explanation. 'He's not coming, is he?'

'Uh, he might get there later. He got a call from the director. He said there was a lunch, called it a "networking opportunity". He wants me to say he's really sorry and he'll get back as soon as he can.'

'Networking opportunity'? That meant a piss-up somewhere with his acting cronies; she wasn't stupid. Or maybe she had been. It wasn't just this meeting he wouldn't be turning up for. And Barbara was still sticking up for him. He probably didn't say he was 'really sorry'; she was just trying to cover for him.

'Did he not have the balls to make this phone call himself?'

'He… he was in a bit of a rush.'

I bet he was. Probably on his way up to the bar before he put the phone down.

'I have to go. I've got an appointment.'

Sara would be angry later. Later she would cry and throw something and fantasise about ways she might kill him. Right now she felt cold and she felt focused. This was about Ruby. She walked towards the front entrance of the school and pushed the square silver button to open the front door.

Ruby.

The reception area was a double-height atrium and the sun shone in to make it warm and welcoming. To the right of the reception desk was a display cabinet of trophies and certificates. To the left was a noticeboard with photographs of the teaching staff. They looked friendly enough.

'Good morning. Can I help?' The receptionist was a short, smiley woman with a neat red cardigan.

Sara took a deep breath. 'Hi. I'm here to see the Deputy Head so that I can have a look around the school. I'm Sara Lucas and my little girl is called Ruby. My friend Jo has arranged the appointment so I don't know if the Deputy Head will recognise my name.'

Why was she gabbling like a mad woman? Still, the smiley lady didn't seem to mind. She just pushed a signing-in book towards her. 'That's grand. Sign in here and I'll give her a buzz. Is your wee one hoping to come here?'

Sara signed her name, which was difficult with a trembling hand. 'We don't know yet. I mean we don't even know if she… we're waiting for…' She couldn't finish the sentence because she realised there was no 'we' there. It was just her. *She* didn't know. *She* was waiting. There was no one else waiting with her. 'I don't know yet.'

'Ah, that's fine. It's a lovely school. I'm sure Tracey will show you all around. Oh, here she is now. Tracey, this is Sara Lucas. She's come for one of your tours.'

Tracey held out a hand and Sara shook it. 'I thought we could have a little wander around and then we can go back to my office for a chat. You're in luck; it's a calm day today. Two of our middle school classes are out on a trip to Aldi, so it's all quiet on the western front, eh Julie?'

Julie chuckled. 'God Bless Aldi, that's what I say.'

Tracey leaned down to swipe her pass card on the door and they were in.

Sara's own primary school had had large, echoey corridors and had smelt of deep heat. Summer Hill was possibly the exact opposite of that. The hallway was carpeted in dark blue, there was a light smell of floral disinfectant and she could hear the faint sounds of classical music from one of the classrooms they passed.

Tracey walked briskly, so Sara had to almost skip to keep up. 'When you say they are on a trip to Aldi, do you mean the supermarket?'

'Yes, it's part of the life skills we teach here. Students have a shopping list and a budget to keep to and they have to buy the ingredients to make something when they come back to school.'

That sounded like a good idea. 'So, you are preparing them for an independent life then?'

Tracey paused with her hand on a classroom door and grinned at Sara from beneath a raised an eyebrow. 'Of course. We are teachers. Not babysitters.'

The classroom was bright and light and there were nine pupils inside who looked to be a couple of years older than Ruby. 'This is one of our reception classes. We have a maximum of ten pupils in each of our classes – including the college which is on another site down the road.'

Sara followed Tracey into the room. At first glance, it seemed like any other primary classroom: a display of spring flowers and rabbits on the wall, a reading corner with bean bags and bookshelves, a sink in the corner with plastic cups and plates. A teacher sat at the front of the class with a huge plasma screen beside her: they were learning numbers. Tracey gave the teacher a wave as they stood just inside the door and the teacher nodded hello whilst she continued to talk to the class.

Most of the children wore uniforms, a couple only had T-shirts and trousers and one little boy – who didn't seem able to sit still – was wearing shorts. The teacher was speaking to a girl who was wearing a pink coat over the top of her uniform and who had positioned her chair almost directly next to the teacher. 'What number is this, Poppy?'

Poppy screwed up her eyes and then gave the answer. 'Five!' Her voice was surprisingly loud and strong for such a little girl.

'Fantastic. What about this one, Freddie?'

A boy who Sara hadn't even noticed, lying on the beanbags in the book corner, called out, 'Seven.'

'Brilliant.'

The teacher was moving her hands as she spoke. 'Is she using sign language?' Sara whispered.

Tracey nodded. 'Makaton. Signs to help communication. It's particularly effective with some of our non-verbal children. Like Abby.' She nodded at a young girl sitting directly in front of them.

Sara swallowed. Non-verbal? Did that mean that she was still learning to speak or that she never would? Abby had a small folder on the desk in front of her, full of pictures.

Tracey noticed Sara looking at it. 'It's a strategy we use with some of our non-verbal students, Picture Exchange Communication System, or PECS. They can point at the picture to communicate what they want.'

Sara thought of Ruby patting the fridge when she wanted milk. She was finding her own ways to communicate. This was something they could try at home. Something Sara could actually do.

A little boy with big brown eyes turned around to look at them. When he saw the Deputy Head, he got out of his seat and came over to hug her. 'Miss Plane! How are you?'

Tracey bent down to hug him back. 'I'm great, Victor. How are you?'

The Deputy Head in Sara's old school definitely didn't hug the pupils.

Back out in the corridor, Tracey motioned with her left hand. 'My office is this way. Shall we sit and have a chat? I have about fifteen minutes and then I have a meeting with the Assistant Heads.'

Tracey's office was large but welcoming. Children's paintings and 'Best Work' lined the walls alongside wall calendars and school policies. Tracey placed a cup of coffee in front of Sara. 'So, was there anything you wanted to ask me?'

Sara took a deep breath. She had a thousand questions, but was frightened about phrasing them badly, causing offence. Where should she start? 'The sign language – Makaton was it? – that the teacher was using. Are there a lot of children who don't speak?'

'We have quite a few, yes.'

'Is it because, you know, parents didn't catch it early enough or…' she trailed off. This sounded judgemental already. She was making a hash of this.

Tracey put her cup down. 'The thing with autistic children is that, like all children, everyone is different. We tailor our teaching to what each child needs.'

'And what do you teach? I mean isn't it a…' She nearly said, *isn't it a waste of time?*, which wasn't what she meant.

Tracey smiled. 'Our focus here is on life skills. Whether our students go on to live independently or whether they need assisted living, we want them to have the best life they can. Isn't that what any parent wants, too?' She sat back in her chair. 'Please don't take this the wrong way, but you might have to go through a big period of adjustment. Your little one is very young. You can't know yet what she is going to achieve and what will be out of her reach. But a good school – and supportive parents – can ensure that she will have a good life, even if it is a life a little different from the one you thought she would have.'

Ten minutes later, Sara was still asking questions as Tracey walked her back to reception. Along the walls of the main corridor were photo canvases, very similar to the ones at Ruby's preschool, each one framing a smiling child. Some were in wheelchairs, some had Down's syndrome, some had soft helmets or wrists that looked a little twisted. But all of them had smiles on their faces. All of them were busy doing something: playing, moving, learning. *Paint a different picture.*

At the entrance, Tracey held out her hand and Sara grasped it. 'Thank you so much for letting me take up your time. I can't tell you how helpful it's been. This is a wonderful school.'

Tracey smiled. 'I'm glad. I just wish we had the space for every child that needed it. I hope that you can get the support your daughter needs. If you have any more questions, my email is on the school website.'

Outside the air felt fresher, the world brighter. Sara felt more in control than she had in a long while. She wanted to learn Makaton and make a photo book and do everything she could to help Ruby.

But what about Mike? He hadn't even made it here. So much for him wanting to support her and Ruby. Had that all been more words? How was he ever going to understand if he didn't come and see somewhere like this for himself?

For Ruby's sake, she would have to *make* him understand though. After today, she could at least give him concrete ideas of things that they could do. Together. She resolved she would talk to him as soon as he got back.

CHAPTER FORTY-FOUR

Sara got back to Barbara's with an hour to spare before she had to go to work. For the first time in the last two years, she could see some hope, a light at the end of the tunnel. If she could share that with Mike, maybe he would feel differently too. She was angry with him for flaking out on the school visit, but they could get through this. Then they could help Ruby to make the progress she was sure she could.

Barbara opened the kitchen door with a wobbly smile on her face. 'Oh, Sara. You're back. Come through to the lounge. I'll make some tea. Or would you prefer a coffee?'

From the look on Barbara's face, Sara would prefer a large glass of Shiraz. 'What's happened?'

Barbara wouldn't meet Sara's eye. 'Let me make us a drink and then we can sit down and…'

Sara's heart was beating out of her chest. 'Barbara. Just tell me. Is Ruby okay?'

Barbara seemed to sag in front of her eyes. 'He's gone again.'

Once Sara knew the distress wasn't something to do with Ruby, she let Barbara go and make them a drink. She sank onto the sofa. The room had been vacuumed and dusted within an inch of its life; a sure sign that Barbara was upset about something. The mantelpiece looked different. Some of the photographs of Mike had been removed from frames and had been replaced with photos of Ruby. It was so difficult to get Ruby to look at the camera. In most of them she was looking past the photographer at someone or something else. The best were the ones that had caught her in the middle of playing or drawing. The focus in her eyes. So beautiful. Whatever Mike felt about Sara, how could he leave that face?

'Here we are, then.' Barbara slid the tray onto the freshly polished coffee table. Cath Kidston mugs. This must be serious.

She waited for Barbara to pick up her mug and sit down. 'So?'

'How was the school?'

So, they were going to skirt around it first, were they? 'Actually, it was great. The pupils were lovely and they all seemed to really like being there.'

'Was there anyone… like Ruby?'

Sara was about to ask her what she meant by that, but stopped herself. If she was going to help Ruby, she needed to start being a realist. And that began with not taking offence if someone noticed she behaved differently. 'Yes, there was a little girl a couple of years older. She was doing really well.'

'Will you try and get her into that school?'

Sara shrugged. 'She doesn't even have a diagnosis yet. Every person I speak to keeps warning me what a long road it's going to be. And it also depends if we're still living around here. What's going on, Barbara. Where's Mike? What time did he say he'd be back?'

'He left half an hour ago. An audition in Manchester. He came back to pack up his things and then he… left.'

'Manchester?'

'I'm not really sure of the details. He's had a big row with the director. Apparently, there have been issues since the first performance three weeks ago. Mike says the director keeps threatening to use the guy that was his understudy or something. Either way, Mike's contract isn't likely to be extended after this current run, so he needs to have something else in the pipeline. Someone in the cast has a contact at a large theatre in Manchester. They're driving up together tonight to speak to the casting director because they have a couple of free days before their next performance.'

And finally the last piece of the puzzle slots into place. 'And this friend of his. A woman by any chance?'

'I don't know.'

Sara didn't move. After all the conversations they'd had that week. He'd said he was sick of being on the road, wanted stability, to be with his family. Promising over and over again to be there for Ruby and for her. Berating himself for being such a fool.

But no. *She* was the one who had been a fool. An absolute bloody idiot.

She reached for her mug, then put it down again. Her throat was too tight to drink. 'And that's it. He's planning to leave us and move to Manchester.'

'I don't think it's permanent. I mean, I can see why you're upset with him but…' Barbara trailed off.

Did she really and honestly believe what she was saying? Was she completely blind where Mike was concerned? 'If that were true, Barbara, why is it not Mike who is sitting here telling me this? Why has he got you to do his dirty work? And you can't tell me he couldn't spare one hour this morning to look at the school for Ruby?' She almost felt sorry for Barbara. The poor woman was clearly trying to make everything okay. But it wasn't. And Sara wanted to stop pretending that it was.

Barbara crumpled. 'I don't know what to say.'

'You don't have to say anything. It's not your problem, Barbara. It's not your fault.'

Barbara looked up with haunted eyes. 'But it is. It *is* my fault.'

She wasn't making sense. 'I don't understand. What do you mean?'

Barbara held a tissue, twisting it between her hands as she prepared herself to speak. 'I know Michael doesn't love me like I love him, Sara. I'm not stupid. I know that he came to visit because he needed somewhere to live and he has stayed this long because it suited him. That's the curse of being a mother, isn't it? There is no way your child can love you the way you love them. A mother's love is so big, so all-consuming; a mother would throw herself under a train to save her child.

'He loved me when he was a little boy. He would put his hands on either side of my face and tell me that he was going to marry me when he grew up. But it doesn't last. The older they get the more they grow away from you. First, they stop holding your hand. Then they spend more time in their room alone. Then there are friends, girlfriends, work colleagues, wives and then children of their own. It's the way it should be. They don't need you anymore; they have other people to care for.

'But a mother's love never changes, does it? You still worry, still think about them, still want the best. You're still proud and it doesn't matter how old your child gets – or how little they give you in return – you would still throw yourself under that train.'

Barbara's voice cracked and she brought the tissue to her nose, covering her trembling mouth. *Yes*, Sara thought, *I would do anything to help Ruby. Whether it was throw myself in front of a train. Or maybe just fight blindly to stay in a marriage even though it isn't working.*

Barbara continued to speak. 'I know that you understand what I'm saying. I've seen you with Ruby. When you lie next to her. And sing to her. And tell her how beautiful she is. Even when you get nothing in return, you just keep loving her.'

Sara's chest felt tight. It was hard to speak. 'But Ruby can't… she's… she can't…'

Barbara nodded. 'I know. But what if Michael can't either? Your daughter was born autistic, Sara. But what if I made Michael the way he is? What if it is my fault?'

Sara shook her head. Barbara was not to blame. 'He is a man. He makes his own decisions.'

Barbara smiled sadly. 'But every man was a little boy once. And he was *my* little boy. I know I spoiled him. I know I was overprotective.' She held up a hand to stop Sara from interrupting. 'You're going to say that it was understandable after losing Lisa. But I still did it. In everything I did I tried to make his life easy and safe. If he wanted something, I made it. If he needed something, I bought it. He only needed to ask and I would come running. I was his biggest supporter, his biggest fan. I told him over and over what a wonderful actor he was and how he was destined for great things. Maybe I spoiled him for ever enjoying an ordinary life.'

Sara swallowed, shuffled forwards in her seat and put her hand over Barbara's. 'There's a time limit on being able to blame your parents. Mike is a grown man. You are not responsible for the way he is behaving, Barbara.'

But Barbara wasn't really listening. 'And I was so unfair to you. It got all twisted up in my head. I was obsessed with Ruby being safe. I know you are angry with me about taking her to see Michael, but I really hoped that if he saw her it would make him realise what he was giving up. I needed you and Michael to stay together so that I didn't lose Ruby, but in doing that, I have pushed you away.' She paused and looked up. 'You're not going to stay with me, are you?'

How could Sara answer that question when she had absolutely no idea what she was going to do? 'I don't know. I don't know anything right now. I understand how you feel about Mike because I am going through this every day. Every day I wonder if I am doing the right thing for Ruby. Am I playing enough? Should I be firmer? Is the preschool the right place for her? It's like living with a beehive in your brain. A constant buzz of thoughts and worries and decisions that need to be made. What if I make the wrong one? What if I let her down?'

Now it was Sara's voice that was cracking and Barbara's turn to take *her* hand. 'You are a wonderful mother, Sara. Anyone can see that.'

Sara shook her head. 'If I was wonderful, I would have worked this out a long time ago. I knew there was something wrong, but I did nothing. I should have pushed harder for someone to listen. What if I've left it too late?'

Barbara squeezed her hand. 'There's nothing else you could have done. You're not an expert in all this. You're a mother.'

Could she open up and tell Barbara? 'Maybe I didn't push harder because I didn't want there to be anything wrong? Maybe I was ignoring all the signs because I couldn't face up to the fact that she was different? That doesn't make me a wonderful mother, does it? That makes me a… a… selfish, horrible—'

'Shh… that's not true. We all want our children's lives to be easy, surely? Wanting her to have a life that's free from struggles doesn't make you bad or selfish. Anyone can see how much you love that little girl. Watching you with Ruby, seeing everything you do for her, it's shown me so much. Made me realise that I didn't *make* Lisa the way she was any more than you have caused any of this with Ruby. If she'd been born now, maybe I would have understood better. Maybe I would have had more help. I don't know. But I do know that I can help you and Ruby. And I want to. I want to so much, Sara. If only you will let me?'

Sara couldn't speak. It was all too much. Mike leaving. Ruby's diagnosis. Kevin's kiss. Lisa's revelations. And now this. How was she to make sense of it all?

'Look, I found you this.' Barbara retrieved her handbag from the side of the sofa and rustled around in it. She brought out a piece of newspaper, a clipping, inside a plastic folder. She passed it to Sara, looking hopeful. 'It's a course, a graphic design course. The college is only thirty minutes away and it's once a week in the evening. I called them; they have spaces.' She paused. 'I thought I could pay for it for you. A late Christmas present. For the last five Christmases.' She gave Sara a weak smile.

No one had ever done something like this for Sara. No one had encouraged her in her art, or had made her think she could have a career from it. The lump in her throat got bigger. She stared at the clipping until her eyes stopped blurring. 'Barbara, I can't—'

'You *can*. If you stay here, I can look after Ruby for you. You'll need a babysitter while you go to college and also when you need to do all your homework.'

Sara smiled. 'Homework' made her feel about fifteen. At fifteen she didn't actually do much homework; her mother hadn't been the most encouraging of academic endeavour. *Pretty pictures don't pay the bills, Sara.*

'Look, it's really kind of you, but…'

Barbara held up her hand. 'Just think about it. If that course isn't right, there might be something else. Please, just think about it.'

Sara reached out and put her hand on Barbara's. 'Okay, I'll think about it. If you promise that you will stop thinking that any of this is your fault. And maybe think about bereavement counselling. You need to talk it through with someone professional. Someone who can help you. You're still grieving, Barbara. And it's been too long.'

Barbara placed her other hand on top of Sara's. 'Maybe you're right. Maybe I would benefit from some help, Sara. But so would you. I know that you can look after Ruby and do everything she needs. But just because you can, doesn't mean you have to. Please let me help.'

And then something incredible happened. Something that Sara would never have predicted. A mother opened her arms for a daughter, and a daughter leaned inside them.

CHAPTER FORTY-FIVE

Two Months Later

Artists learn to see differently from other people. That had been the opening statement from Sara's painting tutor at college. Artists don't see objects; they see the light and shade they create. There had been an awful lot of shade for Sara these last few months. Worry. Fear. Guilt.

*

Ruby had woken early again that morning. Peel-the-lids-from-your-eyes early. Now that summer was finally here, it was light enough to come to the park at 6.00 a.m. The very empty park. Sara could sketch, and Ruby could do her circuit of the slide – step, together, step, together – as many times as she liked with no one to get in her way.

Sara lowered her sketchpad and snapped a photo of the slide for their PECS communication book. This was Book Two. Sara had spent a whole weekend drawing beautiful pictures of a milk bottle, cereals, building blocks and tens of other everyday objects. What a disappointment when Ruby had rejected them all. Jo – or Saint Jo as she'd been newly christened – had advised trying real photographs. The first time Ruby pointed at a picture of Nemo to say she wanted her DVD, Sara had cried. So had Barbara.

The last time Sara had sketched the large tree reaching over the playground, the branches had been bare. Now leaves waved and whispered in the early morning breeze, casting a thousand tiny shadows across the ground.

When an artist looks at shade, she doesn't just see a block of grey. She looks closely and sees lilacs, mauves, blues, greens. Learning about autism, and specifically about Ruby and autism, was a lot like that. Looking closer, Sara could see the small signs that were helping her to understand what Ruby wanted. And she was beginning to see some light.

The last time she had sketched the playground tree, Sara had also had a picture in her head of what she thought their life should be. But Mike's leaving had changed all that: he wasn't coming back and they didn't have a home of their own.

But of course there was new light, too: Barbara was trying so hard to make it good for them at home; Lisa had invited Sara to come for coffee and she'd accepted; the mums at the SEN play session had welcomed her into the fold; Leonard had earned enough from Lisa's party to keep him afloat a while longer and Kevin…

'Hello! This one was already up when I got your text, so we thought we'd join you.' Kevin strolled towards the bench as Callum made a run for the swings. He remembered from last time not to bother Ruby on the slide.

Sara lifted her face for a kiss. 'How was he last night?'

'Better. He seems settled in his room now. Kelly even said he can stay for two nights on my next weekend, so we're making progress.' Kevin nodded at Sara's drawing. 'Don't let me stop you. I might just try and grab a ten-minute nap.' He stretched his arms along the bench, leaned back and shut his eyes.

Sara tore the page from her sketchpad and tucked it into her plastic art folder. Taking her pencil, she watched Ruby slide down for possibly the twenty-fifth time and began the preliminary drawings for her next piece.

It was time to paint a different picture.

EPILOGUE

Six Months Later

Dear Lisa,

This will be my last letter. I've been seeing a therapist and she thinks it might be time to stop my writing. These letters make me look back rather than forwards, she says. I need to say a proper goodbye.

Sara and Ruby are still living with me, for now. Sara has enrolled on a graphic design course and she absolutely loves it. Her tutor thinks she's a natural. It's a competitive industry, Sara says, she doesn't think she'll be able to get a job that easily, but I am crossing my fingers for her.

She's been painting more too. You should see the portraits she does of little Ruby. Absolutely beautiful. She's sold some of them in the local gallery and she's had commissions, too – some of Lisa next door's friends. Sara and she have got quite friendly, which is lovely. I think Lisa needed a good friend her age. I was never sure she was quite as happy as she pretended. But she seems stronger, more independent somehow, since Sara came into our lives.

Ruby continues to be our dear Ruby. She has a diagnosis of autism now, but otherwise not much has changed. She sees a speech and language therapist and she has a support person at the preschool, but the big focus for Sara is Summer Hill; I think she'd cut off her own arm to get Ruby in there.

Sara is still working some shifts at the pub around the corner, so I get time on my own with Ruby. She still doesn't say very much, but I chat away to her and she doesn't seem to mind. She still gets terribly upset about things when they don't work out the way she wants. It can be something as silly as a tower of blocks falling down. She's stopped watching Finding Nemo *on a loop, at least. It's some* Pets *film now; I could almost recite the whole script.*

Speaking of scripts, Mike didn't get a job in the West End or a role in the play in Manchester, but he hasn't come home, either. He did turn up here a few weeks ago, but I told him he couldn't stay. It was so hard. He's my son, my boy. But Ruby is so unsettled when he is here and it's not fair on Sara. I can't risk them moving out. I can't risk losing Sara and Ruby. Like I lost you.

My therapist says that I need to stop blaming myself, that what happened was an accident. I'm not sure that I'm quite there yet, but I'm making progress. Her words, not mine. And stopping these letters is the next stage of the process.

So, my beautiful girl, this is goodbye. I wish with every part of my heart that I had you here now. That I had known more about how to keep you safe. I wouldn't wish the pain of losing a child on anyone; it never goes away. I will miss you every day, my darling, and I will love you for the rest of my years. I won't write again, but I won't ever forget you.

I promise.

Love forever,
Mum. x

A LETTER FROM EMMA

I want to say a huge 'thank you' for choosing to read *My Silent Daughter*. If you enjoyed it, and want to be kept up to date with my future releases, just sign up at the following link. Your email address will never be shared and you can unsubscribe at any time.

www.bookouture.com/emma-robinson

After my first novel, *The Undercover Mother*, was published, I was thrilled to receive letters from other mums who identified with the character of Jenny, a first-time mother trying to navigate the first months of motherhood and work out how to juggle the demands of a baby with her career and friendships. In *My Silent Daughter*, I wanted to explore those same feelings of being lost in a foreign country, but this time it's because Sara's daughter had special needs that Sara has to understand and accept. I read the incredible essay 'Welcome to Holland' by Emily Perl Kingsley, which inspired the advice given to Sara by one of the SEN mums: you just need to paint a different picture.

My Silent Daughter is not a book about autism; it is a book about a mother. Every mother wants their child to live a full and happy life, but if your child has special needs, your role in making that happen gets tougher. Plus, like Sara, the rest of your life doesn't necessarily give you a break during the times your child needs your full focus. When I look around me at the friends and family who have children with autism or other special needs, I never cease to be amazed by how they keep going, even when life is really, really hard.

When I first wrote Sara's story, I worried about getting it 'right' with Ruby, feeling the responsibility to represent her autism accurately and honestly. A wise friend who has a son with autism reassured me that – just like children who don't have autism – every child is different. Sara and Ruby are just at the beginning of their journey, but I hope that I have done them justice and that you have enjoyed spending time with them.

If you have enjoyed *My Silent Daughter*, please help me to reach other readers by writing a quick review. I'd also love to hear what you thought of it, especially if you have experienced a similar journey to Sara's. Reviews make a huge difference in helping other people find my book and I am grateful for every single one.

I also love hearing from my readers. Come and join me on my Facebook page: *Motherhood for Slackers*. You can also find me on Twitter or my website below.

Stay in touch!
Emma.

motherhoodforslackers

@emmarobinsonuk

www.motherhoodforslackers.com

ACKNOWLEDGEMENTS

First thanks, as always, to my brilliant publisher, Isobel Akenhead, who has given me the confidence to 'go deeper' this time. I hope I have repaid your faith in me. Also to Kim Nash for her fabulous PR skills and to everyone at Bookouture who have helped bring this novel to market including copy-editor Grace Glendinning, proofreaders, cover designers and marketing masterminds. Retrospective thanks to Gabbie Chant for copy-editing my other books and for sending me the lovely message from a reader that made my day and a big kiss for Carrie Harvey for running her eagle eyes over the last proofs. I also wouldn't get through the rollercoaster of writing with my sanity intact if it weren't for the support of the other Bookouture authors, who are witty, talented and generous. You are all wonderful.

An absolutely heartfelt 'thank you' to the mums who generously shared their experiences of raising a child with autism. Particularly Lyndsay Robbins and Heather Hill. Your willingness to speak honestly and articulately were absolutely invaluable. Any mistakes are mine.

I spent a wonderful day at Columbus School and College in Chelmsford as part of my research and want to say a huge 'thank you' to Tracey Plane, Claire McClean and the fantastic students in Jaguar Class for letting me sit in on your maths lesson. I learned a lot!

For support during the writing process, thanks to Elizabeth Symonds, Martin Ross, Kate Machon and Marie Dentan for reading early chapters and for an inspiring weekend in Southampton; to Kirsty Ireland for accommodating me at Walton Hall again during edits (Room 6 will have a blue plaque one day); to Bareham Kennels in Orsett for looking after Aria so that I could actually get some work done; to the staff at Corringham café for a great breakfast on writing days and to the lovely people who run Corringham Library for giving me a nice, quiet place to write.

Again, my Coopers colleagues have saved me. For insight into art and artists (and for decent coffee at lunchtime!) a huge thank you to Paul Withyman and Gregor Claude. For answering a hundred questions about actors and theatre, often via late-night WhatsApps, thank you Brendan Ryan.

Shout out to my husband for dealing with a wife who is both writing a novel and perimenopausal. Love to my wonderful mum for taking the children for the weekend so that I could finish the first draft and they could eat proper dinners.

And lastly, to all the mums and dads out there who are raising children with special needs. It's a tough job and the system is often against you. You are warriors. We see you. We support you. We salute you. x

Printed in Great Britain
by Amazon

21706453R00161